Michael Kingston, aka William Saunders, aka Dirk Brandt. An English schoolboy turned very young soldier turned spy.

Tommy Hambledon, aka Hendrik Brandt. A schoolmaster and a British intelligence agent, who is Bill Saunders' mentor in both personas.

Max von Bodenheim. A German intelligence officer who is Bill's friend and worthy adversary.

Diane Causton. The niece of a vicar and the daughter of a colonel, who is very much in love with Bill..

Leutnant Kaspar Bluehm. A young German soldier who befriends Bill.

Marie Bluehm. His pretty younger sister.

Flug-Leutnant Anton Knirim. A German soldier who talks too much..

Elsa & Hedwige Schwiss. A singing sister act known as the Bavarian Nightingales. Elsa is very much smitten with Flug-Leutnant Knirim.

Professor Amtenbrink. An elderly scientist who is fond of his roses.

Reck. A science master, really a British agent who is a wireless operator.

Denton. Also a British agent.

Ludwig Wolff. Bill's lanky, good-natured assistant in the import trade.

Dixon Ogilvie. A school friend of Bill's with a talent for music, who becomes a soldier.

Mrs. Lomas. Bill's housekeeper in England.

Books by Manning Coles

The Tommy Hambledon Spy Novels
Drink to Yesterday, 1940
A Toast to Tomorrow (English title: *Pray Silence*), 1940
They Tell No Tales, 1941
Without Lawful Authority, 1943
Green Hazard, 1945
The Fifth Man, 1946
Let the Tiger Die, 1947
With Intent to Deceive (English title: *A Brother for Hugh*), 1947
Among Those Absent, 1948
Diamonds to Amsterdam, 1949
Not Negotiable, 1949
Dangerous by Nature, 1950
Now or Never, 1951
Alias Uncle Hugo (Reprint: *Operation Manhunt*), 1952
Night Train to Paris, 1952
A Knife for the Juggler (Reprint: *The Vengeance Man*), 1953
All that Glitters (English title: *Not for Export*;
Reprint: *The Mystery of the Stolen Plans*), 1954
The Man in the Green Hat, 1955
Basle Express, 1956
Birdwatcher's Quarry (English title: *The Three Beans*), 1956
Death of an Ambassador, 1957
No Entry, 1958
Concrete Crime (English title: *Crime in Concrete*), 1960
Search for a Sultan, 1961
The House at Pluck's Gutter, 1963

Ghost Books
Brief Candles, 1954
Happy Returns (English title: *A Family Matter*), 1955
The Far Traveller (non-series),1956
Come and Go, 1958

Non-Series
This Fortress, 1942
Duty Free, 1959

Short Story Collection
Nothing to Declare, 1960

Young Adult
Great Caesar's Ghost (English title: *The Emperor's Bracelet*), 1943

Drink to Yesterday

by Manning Coles

Introduction by Tom & Enid Schantz

Rue Morgue Press
Boulder / Lyons

ISBN: 978-1-60187-014-8

Rue Morgue Press
87 Lone Tree Lane
Lyons CO 80540

Printed by Johnson Printing
Boulder, Colorado

PRINTED IN THE UNITED STATES OF AMERICA

This book
is
dedicated
to an old gentleman
who loved
his roses

Manning Coles
The Truth of the Fiction

Manning Coles was the pseudonym of two Hampshire neighbors who collaborated on a long series of entertaining spy novels featuring Thomas Elphinstone Hambledon, a modern-language instructor turned British secret agent. But in *Drink to Yesterday*, their first collaboration, Tommy isn't really the central character at all. That role falls to young Bill Saunders, a teenage student of Tommy's, who lies about his age, enlists in the army during World War I, and is eventually recruited by Tommy, now a full-time agent himself, into the British secret service. That book, first published in Britain in 1940 and in the U.S. in 1941, was an immediate hit and the authors were implored to write a sequel.

For reasons that will become obvious once you've read a *Drink to Yesterday,* a sequel presented certain difficulties and it became necessary, through a very clever literary sleight of hand, to give top billing to Tommy in *A Toast to Tomorrow* (published as *Pray Silence* in Britain) and all subsequent books. While the first two books are often quite different in tone, they still constitute, as Anthony Boucher, the genre's most famous early critic, put it, "a single long and magnificent novel of drama, intrigue and humor." While admittedly most of the humor is in the sequel, Tommy's sardonic wit shines through in *Drink to Yesterday*, especially when he makes fun of popular notions of what a spy's life is like.

Its realistic portrayal of the real world of espionage is what makes *Drink to Yesterday* one of the most important books in the development of the spy novel, a fact that was immediately recognized not only by the critics but by the general reading population. Howard Haycraft, the genre's first historian, wrote in his seminal *Murder for Pleasure* that it fell first to Eric Ambler to give new life to the spy-and-intrigue story by bringing it close to a legitimate marriage with detection in such works as *Background to Danger* (1937) and *Coffin for Dimitrios* (1939). Gone from Ambler's works were the "stereotyped cliches and slinky females in black velvet" found in

the works of fanciful novelists such as William Lequeux, E. Phillips Oppen-
heim and H.C. McNeile ("Sapper"). Writing in 1941, the year the first two
Manning Coles books appeared in the United States, Haycraft commented
that "the mood of subtle understatement which [Ambler] established seems
already to have found an echo in such superior works as... *Drink to Yesterday* and *A Toast to Tomorrow*." He later added both books, with an assist
from Frederic Dannay (one half of the Ellery Queen team), to his list of
cornerstone books in the development of the genre.

The authors' American publisher was also quick to point out that these
books "were as different from the old spy stories as a Hitchcock movie is
from silent pictures in the days of Lon Chaney. We would like you to forget
any ideas you have about spy stories and approach this as a novel with
humor, three dimensional characters, realistic narration and breathtaking
suspense." The two books almost immediately went into large reprint edi-
tions. This was a most unusual circumstance during the early years of World
War II when anti-German sentiment was at its height, given that the books,
while denouncing Naziism, presented a balanced, sympathetic and often
appreciative portrait of the German people, whom the authors clearly felt
had been betrayed and deceived by all sides following World War I. Yet
there is never any question as to Hambledon's loyalties. "If a country is
worth living in," he said, "it is worth fighting for."

The books came to be written thanks to a fortuitous meeting. After Adelaide Frances Oke Manning (1891-1959), rented a flat from Cyril's father in
East Meon, Hampshire, she and Cyril became neighbors and friends. Educated at the High School for Girls in Tunbridge Wells, Kent, Adelaide, who
was eight years Cyril's senior, worked in a munitions factory and later at the
War Office during World War I. A birth defect had left her with a deformed
ankle, limiting her employment opportunities. A career as a writer seemed a
natural choice. In 1939 she published a solo novel, *Half-Valdez*, a fanciful
tale of a hunt for lost Spanish treasure hidden in the days of the Armada in
a remote outpost on the British coast. Burdened with pages of dialog told in
thick dialects, the book was a critical and financial failure. Yet there were
flashes of untamed literary talent in those pages. Cyril was also interested
in writing fiction. An indifferent student as a youth, he had excelled in school
in only two areas, modern languages and creative writing, in spite of being
dyslexic (as were his son, grandson and great granddaughters). Dyslexia,
while presenting certain obstacles to a writing career, can be overcome, as
has been demonstrated by many successful authors, including novelist and
television writer Stephen J. Cannell and mystery writer Deborah Crombie,

creator of a popular series featuring Scotland Yard detectives Duncan Kincaid and Gemma James. While having tea, Coles and Manning discovered their common interest in the literary life and hit upon the idea for a spy novel based on Cyril's own World War I adventures. The two settled into a comfortable working partnership made possible, in part, as Cyril pointed out in a note written when *Drink to Yesterday* was being rushed to the printers, by the fact that "the absence of physical attraction between them was more than compensated by their remarkable friendship." While Adelaide never married, Coles had married Dorothy Cordelia Smith in 1934. The Manning Coles collaboration, which lasted longer than many marriages, ended when Adelaide died of throat cancer in 1959. During those twenty years the two worked together almost daily, although Cyril's continuing activities with the Foreign Intelligence Branch, now known as the Secret Intelligence Service or, more commonly, MI6, often required that he be out of the country, especially during World War II.

What set their books apart, in particular *Drink to Yesterday*, was Cyril's intimate knowledge of real world of espionage. Cyril, in fact, abandoned an attempt at autobiography in his later years partly because so much of the story of his early years had already been told in that first collaboration, cloaked as fiction in part to avoid violating the Official Secrets Act. We'll never know for certain what was fact and what was fiction in *Drink to Yesterday*, as Coles asked his two sons, Michael and Peter, to destroy his private papers without reading them. But the many striking parallels between the lives of the fictional Bill Saunders and the very real Cyril Coles makes one wonder if any of the events in *Drink to Yesterday* are actually pure fiction.

Like Bill Saunders, Cyril was attending private school when war with Germany broke out in August 1914. Churchers College in Petersfield, Hampshire, was a school originally established for the sons of members of the East India Company. Young Cyril did not think much of the place, writing years later that it had the usual "spartan discipline and terrible food that may be questioned in a penitentiary of today." It was at Churchers that Cyril published his first short story. But it was his remarkable aptitude for languages, French and German in particular, that drew the attention of a teacher named John Radwell, who also was captain of the cadet corps at school. Radwell encouraged his student to drop classics and concentrate on modern languages. Cyril recalled that Radwell's teaching methods were modern and imaginative for the day. He often worked with Cyril on German conversation outside of class. Cyril later wrote that "Little did the boy realize that this teacher would one day help to make him famous as it was he on whom he based his universally known character of Tommy Hambledon." Hambledon, by the way, was the name of a small village just down the road from where Cyril lived. In the books, Cyril shaved thirty years off Radwell's age.

But even the special attentions of this teacher could not keep Cyril interested in school work once war broke out. He was completely caught up in the frenzy. It struck him as a grand adventure and he attempted to enlist at the age of fifteen. His parents thwarted that attempt, pulled him out of school in 1915 and apprenticed him at Thornycroft's Ship Building Yard in Southampton. Not long after Cyril arrived in Southhampton he found a familiar name in the casualty lists, an admired hero from his school days who had been a very promising musician (presumably allowed to live on in fiction as Dixon Ogilvie, a minor character in both *Drink to Yesterday* and *A Toast to Tomorrow*). Cyril hitched a ride to London, walked into the recruiting station and when asked his age, replied, without hesitation, "Eighteen." He was placed in the 2nd Hants Regiment as a private and soon found himself on the front lines in France. There is some evidence in Cyril's notes that he may well have reconnected with Radwell, now a major and second in command of the 6th Hants Regiment, at this point. Radwell also served in India and Mesopotamia. In any event, Cyril was overheard talking with German prisoners and was soon employed as a translator away from the front. Cyril ended up being conscripted into the Secret Service, becoming Britain's youngest intelligence officer. He went behind German lines working out of Cologne and did not return to England until 1920, two years after the war ended. Between the wars, Cyril ran an import export business in Cologne, much as Bill and Tommy do in *Drink to Yesterday*, and may have known Konrad Adenauer, who was mayor of Cologne from 1917 to 1933, at this time since he was on a first name basis after World War II with the future first chancellor of the West German Republic. It gave Cyril first hand information on what life was like in Germany between the wars, which would be invaluable in writing *A Toast to Tomorrow*.

Whether or not Cyril participated in the actual missions conducted by Bill Saunders is open to question. Certainly German scientists were working on biological and chemical weapons. Is the elderly German scientist Amtenbrink in *Drink to Yesterday* the same man to whom the book is dedicated— "an old gentleman who loved his roses?" If so, it's a chilling acknowledgment. Did Cyril, as Bill did, blow up a Zeppelin base? Probably not, but the incident in the book is obviously based on the January 5, 1918, explosion at

Ahlhorn, German's largest Zeppelin base, which destroyed five German airship bombers, thus effectively ending the role of Zeppelins in the war. It is usually attributed to an accidental hydrogen gas explosion, but more than one military expert has suggested that sabotage was a more likely explanation. Certainly the automatic along with its wooden box found in Bill's garage apartment is based on the weapon owned by Cyril Coles which Cyril's grandson, Steven, came across as a small child when his father, uncle and other grandfather were cleaning out his grandparents' house after Dorothy's death. It was, as Cyril always maintained it, fully loaded, with the safety on. Since it was not registered, the family turned it in to the government.

Bill's experiences as a spy in World War I may remind some readers of the recent movie *The Good Shepherd*, which was based on the life of an actual CIA agent who was recruited straight out of college. Both are understated but moving stories of lost innocence about young men whose life in the shadows makes it impossible for them to connect with people in the regular world. Unlike Bill, however, Cyril seems to have adjusted well to postwar life. After the war, he emigrated to Australia where he worked on the railway, as a garage manager (as Bill does in England), and as a columnist for a Melbourne newspaper before returning to England in 1928. When asked what periods he worked for British Intelligence, Coles replied somewhat cryptically by saying that you never really leave the service. He told his sons that his pay from Intelligence paid for the "extras."

Cyril was definitely back on active duty once World War II broke out in September 1939, operating for a time in Holland and Germany. Once, while in the field, he was picked up by plane and flown back to England. En route, the pilot and navigator were seriously wounded and Cyril was forced to take the controls and land the plane. As a result, he refused to fly after the war and only would travel by boat or various land transports.

Some of his wartime activities were closer to home. When he was six or seven, Cyril's son Michael recalls watching a German plane fly so low near their house on the outskirts of Southhampton that they could see the face of the pilot. His mother, fearing the plane would crash, pulled Michael and his twin brother Peter to safety. Years later Cyril told his son that the plane had indeed crashed and that he had interrogated the pilot. One of Cyril's more important tasks during the war involved transmitting false information to confuse the enemy during the D-Day landings. While writing took up most of his time, Cyril continued to work for British Intelligence until the late 1950s. That link helped provide the background for Tommy's Cold War adventures. After Adelaide's death in 1959, Cyril completed *Concrete Crime*

(1960) on his own. Two subsequent books, *Search for a Sultan* (1961) and *The House at Pluck's Corner* (1963) were written in collaboration with Tom Hammerton. While the series was at its best when Tommy and his cohorts were battling the Nazis, the Cold War era novels are not without charm and Tommy was still Tommy, an engaging hero who never quite forgot what it meant to be an Englishman. If realism sometimes took a back seat to comedy, the books were still filled with what Boucher described as "good-humored implausibility."

That same good humor—and a good deal more implausibility—is to be found in the collaborators' four ghost books, which began with *Brief Candles* in 1954 and included two other books featuring the ghostly Latimers, *Happy Returns* in 1955 (published in England as *A Family Matter*) and *Come and Go* in 1958. A fourth ghost book, *The Far Traveller*, which features a displaced, displeased and deceased German nobleman who finds a movie company employing people of the most common sort invading his castle, appeared in 1956. Although the books were quite popular and appeared in the U.S. under the Coles byline, they were published in England under yet another pseudonym, Francis Gaite. Boucher described this new venture "as felicitously foolish as a collaboration of (P.G.) Wodehouse and Thorne Smith." The ghost books ended with Manning's death, and one can only hope than the two collaborators are having as much fun in the next world as they gave readers in this one.

Tom & Enid Schantz
Lyons, Colorado
January 2008

The editors would like to thank Cyril Coles' sons, Michael and Peter, as well as Michael's son, Steven, for their tremendous help in compiling this short biography of an extraordinary man.

Drink to Yesterday

CHAPTER ONE
BROKEN GLASS

The coroner's inquest was opened at the Dragon Inn, Lime, in Hampshire, at 2:30 p.m. on Saturday, July 19, 1924, the first witness being Mrs. Lomas. She said that the deceased man employed her daily for domestic work in the bungalow attached to his garage. She always got there at about eight every morning, cleaned up the kitchen and sitting room, and got his breakfast. Sometimes he was astir before she arrived, but more usually she would knock on his door at about 8:30, and he would have his breakfast a quarter of an hour later. While he had it, she would tidy up his bedroom and the bathroom, then do any work, such as washing, which required doing, and go home to her cottage to do her own work and get the children's dinners ready by noon. She always came back to the garage soon after midday, cooked the meal which he had at one o'clock, washed up after it, and did any domestic shopping which was necessary. After that she had finished for the day, usually by about three o'clock, and did not return till eight next morning. He always got his own tea and supper.

"Yes," said the coroner. "So after about three o'clock every afternoon he was alone in the place?"

"In a manner of speaking," said Mrs. Lomas.

"What do you mean?"

"I mean there was no one else lived there, but judging by the glasses and sometimes plates that was to be washed up, he wasn't much alone."

"More glasses than plates, I imagine," said the Lime grocer, who was on the jury.

"Order, please," said the coroner. "I should have expected members of the jury to know their duties better than to cause unseemly interruptions in these grave and important proceedings by irrelevant interpolations. An opportunity will be given, at the end of each witness's evidence, for members of the jury to ask any such questions as may be proper—I said proper—to the elucidation of this unfortunate occurrence."

"Quite," said the squire's son, who was sitting in the front row. Mrs. Lomas smiled in a superior manner at the grocer, and somebody at the back of the packed room laughed.

"Order," said the coroner. "Will you tell us what happened on the morning of Thursday, July 17?"

"I got there a few minutes late," said Mrs. Lomas, "not that that made any difference to 'im, poor thing. But I knocked on the door at 'alf past eight as usual and didn't get no answer. So I knocked again, and bein' as I still didn't get no answer, I thought 'e might 'ave gone out early, so I opens the door and looks in. Well, the curtings was drawn and the lamp on the table still alight, so I sees the bed hadn't been slep' in, an' there was something on the floor between the windows looked like an 'eap of clothes. So I says to myself, innocent an' unsuspicious-like: 'Been 'avin' a night out,' I says, so I clicks off the light an' pulls back the curtings at the first window I comes to, but when I sees what the 'eap on the floor reely was, oh dear, oh, I thought I should ha' dropped. Seemed an age before I could fetch my breath, an' then I lets out a screech you could 'a' heard at the church, I'm sure, and bolts out of the place. Mrs. James opposite, she 'ears me and comes out, an' one or two others, and Jimmy Jackman, he runs for the policeman, and he come, and then—"

She stopped from emotion and lack of breath, and the coroner gave her a moment or two to recover herself.

"Then the police took over, did they?" he prompted.

"George Smith did," she said. "He is the constable, of course. He locked all the doors and drew the curtings again an' told no one to go near, not as anyone would want to, not anyone with decent feelings, but some there are as are born without any, so rightly shouldn't be blamed, seeing as they know no better," she added, allowing her glance to fall as if by accident on the grocer in the jury.

"Quite, quite," said the coroner hastily. "Is there anything more you can tell us which has a bearing upon this tragic occurrence?"

"The police called me in again," she said, "that would be about eleven, I suppose. There was a lot of policemen and other men about there then. They wanted to know if there was anything out of the way about the place, if you know what I mean."

"Anything unusual, presumably. Was there?"

"No, sir. 'E'd fried bacon for 'is supper, an' 'ad tea with it. The cup and plates was put out in the kitchen. Then there was two glasses on the table, a bottle of whisky with a little left in, an' a soda siphon. The winders was all open, bedroom likewise. He didn't generally leave the sittin' room winders open, but it was an 'ot night. No, nothing unusual, bar the broken glass."

"Broken glass?"

"There was a glass he set great store by, sort of wine-glass like, with some foreign words wrote on it. It was lying at the side of the fender, all in bits. Wine-stained it were, which I've never known him use it before. It were kep' in a glass cabinet, like, and many's the time he's said to me: 'Have a care of that glass, Mrs. Lomas,' he says, 'it being a memento like,' he says."

"I expect he dropped it," said the coroner, "poor man. Well, is there anything—"

"Which it wasn't dropped," said Mrs. Lomas firmly, "having been throwed against the side of the fireplace as anyone could see from the splash."

"Dear me," said the coroner. "Tell me, did he seem in his usual health and spirits lately, or did you—"

"Oh yes, sir. Very merry and bright 'e was, as the sayin' is. Why, only Sunday 'e was telling me what 'e'd like to do to them as don't pay their bills, made me laugh like anything."

Mrs. Lomas's mouth quivered; she pressed her handkerchief against it and stood silent.

"Does any member of the jury," said the coroner, "wish to ask this witness a question?"

The butcher got up and asked if the deceased had ever been known to threaten to commit suicide.

Mrs. Lomas shook her head. "Not but what he said if the Nursing Association didn't buy nurse a new car soon he'd blow his brains out. But—but I didn't th-think he meant it," she said piteously, and burst into tears.

"Thank you," said the coroner gently. "You may go and sit down now, Mrs. Lomas. Call Dr. Gibson."

Dr. Gibson said he had been summoned to the garage by the police at 8:45 a.m. on the morning of Thursday the 17th. He found the body of the deceased lying in a huddled heap between the two windows in the bedroom. In his opinion life had been extinct about six hours, so that death had probably taken place at about two a.m. Say between one and three o'clock.

Death was due to a bullet which entered the left temple, was slightly deflected upwards, and passed through the brain, leaving a large exit wound. Death was instantaneous.

"Have you any further comment you wish to make?"

"None," said the doctor.

The coroner looked towards the jury, and the butcher asked if the doctor had any idea how the deceased came to do it. The coroner said that that was rather a matter for the police witnesses; the doctor was merely there to certify the cause of death and to give such other medical evidence as might be required. This brought the grocer to his feet. He fixed his pale eyes on the doctor, and asked: "Was he, in your opinion, sober at the time of death?"

"I could not possibly say," said the doctor shortly. He had liked the garage proprietor.

"Did you not, then, examine the contents of the stomach?"

"Why do you ask?"

"He—he might have taken poison—"

"He was not poisoned. Nor strangled. He did not even cut his throat. He died from the effects of a bullet through the brain," snapped the doctor, and looked at the coroner.

The coroner stared coldly at the grocer till he sat down, then let his eyes pass along the two rows of the jury and asked: "Any more questions?"

"Has the doctor any idea how far away the weapon was when it was fired?" asked a farmer whose name was Morpeth.

"That again," said Dr. Gibson, "is more a matter for an expert police witness. There was no singeing round the entry wound, and I could not say how far the pistol was from the head. But I have had little experience of this sort—happily."

The police witnesses followed. Police-constable George Smith gave evidence of having been fetched to the garage at 8:35 a.m. on Thursday, July 17, of finding the deceased's body in the bedroom, of sending for the doctor and telephoning to the district superintendent at Mark. Formal evidence merely, and he was not questioned. He was followed by District Superintendent Harlow, who said that the deceased had met his death by a bullet from an automatic pistol which was lying by his side. It was fully loaded except for the one cartridge which had been fired. There were no fingerprints on the pistol other than those of the deceased. On a small table near the body were an electric reading lamp with a green shade, a tin box containing some empty clips and two boxes of ammunition, and on the table itself some soiled cleaning rags, a small bottle of oil, cleaning brush and rod, and two clips of ammunition. In the opinion of the police the shot was fired about fifteen inches from the head—perhaps a little more. Answering the coroner's questions, he said there seemed no evidence to suggest foul play. In fact, there was no evidence to suggest that there was anyone in the bedroom with the deceased man that night at all, though presumably he had had a visitor in the sitting room, since there were two used tumblers on the table. Yes, inquiries had been made as to the identity of the visitor, but so far without result. He understood that deceased was in the habit of having visitors in the evening, people who came and went in cars and were not known, except in some cases by sight, to the village people. It did not seem worth while making an exhaustive search for the visitor, though doubtless he—or she—could be found, because to his mind the case appeared to be clearly an accident. It might, of course, be suicide, but in the absence of any evidence he saw no reason to presume that.

The jury felt that this was all very well, but they understood that they had been summoned to inquire into the death of their neighbor and to decide how, in their opinion, it had come about; and they were perhaps a little nettled at being, as it were, told what to say by a man who, although superintendent of police for the whole Mark district, was yet only a policeman, and his manner was a trifle authoritative. So the questions began.

"Does anyone know," asked the same farmer who had put a previous question to the doctor, "if the deceased was in the habit of handling this sort of weapon—was he used to automatics?"

"I have no means of knowing."

"An automatic is not a usual weapon to possess in this country, is it?"

"No," said the superintendent.

"Do the police know how long he had held a license for this pistol?"

"No," said the superintendent.

"Did he 'old a license for it at all?" asked the grocer.

"No."

"Oh. Then what business had 'e with it at all?"

"In view of the fact," said the witness, "that the man is now dead and the pistol is in the hands of the police, the question hardly arises."

There was one woman on the jury, the widow of an auctioneer in Mark, and a kindly soul. She asked if it had not been possible to trace any of the poor man's relations.

"No, madam. We have found no clue among his papers to the existence of any near relatives. In fact, he had very few private letters at all, and those only of a recent date. The writers have been communicated with and can tell us nothing of his past."

"Then even the name he went by may not have been his own," suggested Mrs. Carter.

"It is possible, madam."

"Isn't it possible," said the grocer, "to find out where he got this automatic thing from?"

"Inquiries are being made," said the superintendent.

"Is it not a fact," asked Morpeth, "that automatics are forbidden in this country?"

"Except to certain members of His Majesty's forces."

"Was he a member of His Majesty's forces?"

"It does not appear so."

"I don't like this," said the grocer. "I feel there's something bein' hid up."

"You have had all your questions answered, sir," said the coroner in an Arctic voice.

"Yes, but we've had to fish for answers, as it were."

"I take it," said the butcher, "that there is definitely no question of murder in this case?"

"In my opinion, none," said the superintendent.

"Then it is a question of choosing between suicide and accident?"

"I shall advise the jury that that is so when I address them before they retire," said the coroner.

"Was there any finger marks on the second tumbler as was used?" asked the grocer.

"I take it you mean fingerprints," said the police witness. "None. Only smears."

"Do the police," asked the butcher, "attach any importance to the broken glass in the fireplace?"

"None."

"I can't help thinking," said Mrs. Carter, "that that should have a meaning if only we could see it. For why should he use a glass he never did use, and then deliberately smash it, or so it seems. Why break a glass he valued when he was just about to die?"

"If the police are correct in supposing the death to have been accidental, madam," said the superintendent, "he did not know he was about to die. As to why he broke the glass—if it was he who broke it and not the visitor— the police have no theory to offer."

"It takes the ladies," said the grocer, "to get a real answer out of this witness."

"I had occasion," said the coroner, with remarkable energy, "only a few minutes ago, to express my views on the subject of irrelevant interpolations made by a member of this jury. When these interruptions are not only irrelevant but offensive, I assure the jury that I know my duties and powers in such a case!"

He glared at the grocer, who merely looked straight in front of him.

"I am waiting for an apology, sir," said the coroner.

"Oh, are you?" asked the grocer in a surprised voice. "Sorry I spoke," he added cheerfully.

"Bumptious little beast," said the squire's son in a perfectly audible voice which the coroner pretended not to hear.

The farmer, Morpeth, rose again. "May I ask if the police have any views as to how he came to shoot himself in the left temple? I knew the deceased quite well, but I never noticed that he was left-handed."

The superintendent answered. "The police theory is that he was stooping over the table holding the pistol in his left hand with the barrel pointing upwards and was about to do something with his right hand—pick up a piece of rag, for example—when something caused him to turn his head to the right. Something slipping, perhaps, or a mouse in the wall, or some such slight interruption. Or possibly he was merely looking round for something. Anyway, we think that at that moment the pistol, being oily, turned in his hand and he inadvertently pressed the trigger."

"Thank you," said Morpeth, and sat down.

"Is it really credible, sir," said another juryman, the schoolmaster, "that a shot could be fired in a room with open windows in the middle of the village, and not a soul hear it?"

"Apparently, sir."

"Very strange."

The butcher asked if inquiries had been made as to whether anyone had seen a car standing at the garage that night.

"Yes, sir, but without result," said the superintendent. "That is, as regards material times. There were cars in and out in the course of the evening, but none were observed at the garage after midnight."

"What about his financial affairs?" asked the schoolmaster. "Was he being pressed for money?"

"Apparently not, there is no sign of it. The business, though small, was fairly prosperous, and the turnover increasing. There are some outstanding accounts, but more money was owed to him than he owed."

"Are there any more questions?" asked the coroner, and as no one answered, he dismissed the witness and addressed the jury.

"You are here to inquire into the untimely death of this man," he said, "and I ask you to dismiss from your minds matters which cannot be relevant to this inquiry. It is unfortunate that several such irrelevancies have arisen here. It cannot, for example, concern us whether the name by which he was known among you was his real name or not, since there is no question of murder here. For the same reason, the identity of his overnight visitor is not important, though, as the last person to see the deceased alive, this visitor might have been able to tell us something of his frame of mind that evening which would have been of use to us in deciding whether it were a case of suicide or of death by misadventure. For I would advise you that 'death by misadventure' is the proper verdict to bring in this instance if you should decide that it is not suicide. I would further suggest, without wishing to dictate to you, that there is absolutely no evidence to support the latter hypothesis. His finances appear to have been in a satisfactory condition, so far as is known he had no pressing anxieties, nor was he at all subject to periods of mental instability. Unless, therefore, there is any further point upon which my guidance would be of service to you, will you retire and consider your verdict?"

"'S'truth," said the squire's son, under his breath this time, and the jury went out of the room.

They sat round the table in another room and the foreman spoke.

"As you know, madam and gents," he said, "I am a man from Hammead and not one of the fortunate in'abitants of your peaceful vale; consequently I 'ad not your privilege—"

"Lumme," said the grocer, "he's caught it now."

"I was about to say I did not 'ave the honor of knowing the deceased man personally, as most of you did; consequently I am not going to put myself so far forward into your personal feelin's as to suggest any discussion unless it can't be 'elped. The dead man was a friend of most of you, and I expect you'd rather settle this up quick and decent, if I may so express it."

"I think that is very nicely put," said Mrs. Carter.

"Thank you, ma'am. I propose therefore to start with the lady at my right 'and 'ere, and go round the table askin' each in turn to say 'Misadventure' or 'Sooicide' accordin' each to his views. Madam?"

"Death by misadventure, poor dear," she said, and her voice trembled a little. The foreman made a note.

"Death by misadventure," said the schoolmaster.

"The same," said the butcher.

"Death by misadventure," said the next voice.

"Misadventure," said Morpeth shortly.

"Suicide," said the grocer.

Someone started to speak, but the foreman said: "One moment, please," and continued his round of the table till it appeared that Mr. Brown was the only dissentient from the general verdict.

"Now, sir," said the foreman, turning his face towards the grocer, "it seems that we are all agreed but you. Now, if you could but bring yourself to agree, wouldn't it be pleasanter all round, if I may say so? The poor gentleman is dead and nothing can bring him back. He hasn't been murdered, so there's no question of punishing anybody. What use is there, may I ask, in making unpleasantness over a thing that don't really make no odds to us one way or the other, and won't make no odds to the deceased either, not till the Last Judgment, when I suppose we shall all know the rights of it an' not before. Now, sir, won't you change your mind?"

"No," said the grocer.

"Why not?"

"Because in my 'umble opinion he shot himself in a fit of drunken depression and I don't 'old with all this smug hypocritical whitewashing—"

"*De mortuis*," said the schoolmaster, "*nil nisi bonum*."

"You are, I believe, a total abstainer, aren't you, Brown?" asked Morpeth.

"I am, and proud of it. Not a drop of alcoholic—"

"Yet I believe you 'ave an off-license," said the butcher and before Brown could answer, the farmer went on:

"If you had the sense and self-control to take drink in reasonable quantities, you'd know the effect of a little alcohol is cheering, not depressing."

"Little alcohol, you've said it!" said the grocer. "But that drinking repro—"

"Mr. Brown," said Mrs. Carter. Brown stopped in the middle of a word and she leaned across the table towards him. "Mr. Brown, if we were all perfect, which none of us are, we should still have no right to judge our fellow men. Mr. Brown, if that poor man drank more than we thought he should sometimes, perhaps there were reasons we know nothing of. Mr. Brown," she went on, tapping the table, "he did more kind actions every week than you do in a year. And finally, Mr. Brown, if you persist in your horrible, beastly remarks about our poor friend who is dead, not only will I never come inside your nasty poky little shop again, but I'll make this place too hot to hold you or my name's not Maria Carter," and she burst into tears.

"Hear, hear," said the farmer. "There, there, ma'am."

"Will you not agree with us now?" asked the foreman.

"Suppose I can't disoblige a lady," muttered Brown.

So they returned to the coroner with a unanimous verdict, and the big room cleared slowly as the talking people drifted away.

The coroner stood chatting to Superintendent Harlow for a few minutes, till they noticed a slim woman come quietly in against the crowd and look round as though for guidance.

"Can I help you, madam?" asked the superintendent.

Slowly she turned her eyes on him and said: "Is the inquest over?"

"Yes, madam."

"And the verdict?"

"Death by misadventure."

"So. Please can I have him now," she said, "all to myself at last?"

"Who are you, madam?"

"I am his wife," she said.

CHAPTER TWO
TIME OF OUR TRIBULATION

Michael was sent to Chappell's School at Weatherley in Hampshire, and though the life undoubtedly had its brighter moments, on the whole he loathed it like poison. For one thing, he had always been a rather solitary boy, who liked being by himself, and here there was no privacy and no solitude, he slept, bathed, dressed, worked, ate, and played in the almost unbroken companionship of numerous others, most of whom he might have liked if he had been able to seek their company voluntarily, but it was thrust upon him at all hours, and often he just ached to be alone and to be let alone. He discovered that languages were easy, and that mathematics were not. The head was a believer in discipline, and visits to his study were frequent and unpleasant; "Come to my study, Kingston," and you went. Sometimes you deserved it and sometimes you didn't, and very occasionally you deserved it and didn't get it, which atoned for a lot. Michael enjoyed cricket, the clean smack of the bat, which is unlike any other sound, and the smell of mown turf, and the sharp definition of white flannels against green, and the sting of a hard catch well held, and the taste of grass when you pull the stem out carefully so that it comes up white and sappy at the end and you nibble it, and the sun is hot on your back as you lie on the ground waiting to go in, and the other fellows are talking and arguing and you hear without listening in the days of thy youth when the evil days come not nor the years draw nigh—God! let me get out of this! Stop. Don't start that again.

The stuffy mixed smell of the lab on hot afternoons, and particularly that afternoon when he and Chator and Minster were mooning about looking for nothing in particular. Michael leaned negligently against the end of a form and said: "There's a pump."

"Ass," said Chator, "it's been there simply ages."

"And there's some rubber tubing," went on Michael.

"It might be quite a good wheeze to pump something somewhere," said Minster.

"And there's a gas-bracket," said Michael. "If you pump air into the gas-pipe, what happens?"

"It wouldn't go in," said Chator. "The pressure of the gas would keep it out."

"Not if the pressure of the pump was greater than the pressure of the gas," said Minster.

"Gas will compress, won't it? Air will."

"If you get up more pressure than the pipes will hold there'll be a bang somewhere, that's all."

"It will go back along the pipes to where it comes from at the gas place—"

"Not if there's some sort of non-return valve—"

"Let's try," said Michael; so they connected the pump to the gas-bracket, turned on the tap, and pumped. Whatever became of the gas, it put up no opposition, and for two solid hours they pumped, taking it in turns.

Later on, when they were all doing evening prep, the jets in the big chandelier were lit and threw the usual yellow glow on the usual dog-eared books and inky fingers and ragged blotting-paper and variously shaped heads bent over the long table—

"I say! it's a washout," whispered Chator.

"Wait," said Michael, and went on with Caesar having embarked wherever the winds should take him—

"Nothing's happening," said Minster in low tones.

"Wait," said Michael again. "Hang these ablative absolutes, they mean too many things."

At that moment the lights quivered and sank, rose again, as it were gibbered, and went out. At once all over the school arose sounds of indignation and inquiry and excitement, till the gas was turned off and candles brought and discipline supervened. Next morning the gas company was summoned, and said there was nothing amiss but a little air in the pipes. Michael could have told them that. No, there was no evidence as to how the air got in the pipes.

So they got away with it that time, and later on saw fit to try again, but with water instead of air. Again the lights quivered and sank, but this time little fountains rose and played from each darkened gas-jet, and fell gently upon the upturned faces beneath the great chandelier. This time the gas company protested. Air, they said in effect, was all very well, air in the pipes was a thing that might occasionally happen to the best-regulated supply, but water, no. Definitely not water. They would put it right, certainly, but they disclaimed responsibility, and it remained a mystery.

"That was rather decent," said Chator.

"Yes, quite decent," said Michael.

Tommy Hambledon took the Scripture lesson on one occasion. It was not really his job, because he taught modern languages, and his ideas of doing so were not stereotyped. He taught the boys how to talk effectively to taxi-drivers and how to ask for whatever they might happen to want, and not to be obviously British but to adopt the manners, customs, and modes of thought of whatever country they should be in. He always went abroad for his holidays, most often to Germany, and this was curious, for he was a parson's son with exiguous private means, his pay was small, and his tastes cheerful and expensive. Yet he could always go abroad in the holidays and one would really wonder where he got the money from unless one had an idea that perhaps he sometimes did something else besides teaching languages at Chappell's School. Of course no such idea occurred to Michael at the time, but afterwards he knew. Hambledon used to say that when he landed at Ostend he stood his stick upright in the sand, and in that direction in which it fell he went forward. Perhaps. Anyway, he was very good at languages, and a good bat, too, and he encouraged young Kingston.

The portion assigned for the lesson was the eleventh chapter of the second book of Samuel. He skated awkwardly but firmly over the highly informal relations between David and the wife of Uriah the Hittite, but when he came to the fighting he had both feet on familiar ground.

So Joab "assigned Uriah unto a place where he knew that valiant men were," and when the people of besieged Rabbah made a sortie Uriah was among the fallen, as is likely to be the case with valiant men. Others of his party also died from arrows shot from the walls, and from "stones and boiling water and molten lead thrown down from upper windows when it came to street fighting," said Tommy Hambledon, getting perhaps a little mixed in his periods, for after all it was not his subject. "Boiling oil was another good idea, too, it does tend to discourage people. You know, all down the ages men's ideas about war have got more and more ingenious and beastly. Better and brighter arrows, and bigger and noisier guns, first solid shot and then explosives. There will be another war soon," he went on, drawing squiggles on his blotting-paper, "quite soon, and it will be much beastlier than any war ever was before. There will be bombs dropped from aeroplanes, starting fires, and there will be gas. Gas to choke you and blind you and blister you, and high explosive shells, and shrapnel, which is very noticeably unpleasing. Yes, there'll be war quite soon," he went on, looking from one to another with an expression which Michael now recognized as pity, "and you boys will be in it. You will stand firm and take what comes," he said, "for if a country is worth living in, it is worth fighting for. Let us return to Second Samuel."

At the end of the lesson he came over to Michael, who was putting his books together.

"You must work really hard at your languages, Kingston. They may be useful."

"How, sir?"

"There are other ways of making yourself useful to your country besides fighting, boy."

"I don't think I understand, sir."

"Never mind. I can't do anything about it, but if you asked your people to let you give up classics and take up bookkeeping and modern languages, it might be a help to you some day. Think it over."

Accordingly, next term Michael found himself learning German as well as French, and sometimes sitting at a desk by himself working at languages instead of other things he should, officially, have been doing. He took to German as to something once loved and temporarily forgotten, and Tommy Hambledon looked on.

Michael joined the O.T.C. and learned to shoot on the miniature range till the day came when he was handed the regulation army long rifle, considerably taller than himself, and told to see what he could do at five hundred yards. Helpful seniors told him to hold the rifle well away from his shoulder as then it didn't kick so hard; he tried it once. He aimed at six o'clock on the target, shut his eyes, and pulled. After that, things went better, and the five shots went down.

Somebody shouted something, and someone nearer repeated it. "He's made a four-inch group."

"What's that?" thought Michael. "Wonder what I've done now."

But when Hambledon came up and gave him half a crown he gathered that a four-inch group was desirable, and shooting became a hobby of his.

In July 1914 the O.T.C. went to North Camp, Aldershot, Michael being just fifteen, and began for the first time to learn platoon drill instead of company drill. Hambledon was there of course; as well as running the O.T.C. at Chappell's he was a captain of Territorials. Rumors began to fly about, and were discussed and argued while the boys fished in the canal or bathed in the Mytchett Lake. On one occasion the Public Schools O.T.C. had a night attack and got lost in the darkness and all mixed up, so they gathered into groups of schools and yelled for the others. "Eeton, E-eton! Win-chester! Harrow, Harrow! Chappell's! Oundle!" till they sorted themselves out and marched in at one in the morning, to drink hot cocoa and munch biscuits and roll into bed feeling like men.

On another day some of them wandered into the artillery lines and watched men loading up ammunition wagons with live shell and thereafter departing for an unspecified destination. That was on Wednesday, July 29, and every day the tension increased.

One night they had a singsong, and shouted the choruses of "Roamin' in the Gloamin'," and "The moon shines bright on pretty Redwing," and "Anybody here seen Kelly?" and a tall captain sang "Just a wee dochandoris," which somehow gave one small boy a lump in his throat. Or perhaps Michael only imagined the small boy felt like that, for the man was killed a fortnight later. And every hour the tension increased.

There was a *Daily Mail* newspaper kiosk—just a wooden shed—at North Camp in those days, and on Sunday the 2nd of August it did not open, so no news was available. The angry troops turned it over, for every moment the tension increased.

On Monday, August the 3rd, quite early in the morning, the boys were paraded and told they had two hours in which to break camp, proceed to the station, and take themselves home. They were going home, of course, because it was holiday time, and they had to take themselves home because the O.T.C. officers, including Hambledon, had urgent business to attend to elsewhere. With one accord these men vanished from the places where they had been known, and most of them had done with the schools in which they had taught.

After a fruitless attempt to join, as a bugler boy, an army filled to capacity with bugler boys, Michael went back to school, but nothing was the same. Tommy Hambledon had apparently disappeared completely; no one seemed to know where he was or what he was doing. Seniors left untimely, and sometimes their names reappeared on a list which the head himself wrote out and himself pinned up on the notice board. Junior masters also left, and their places were taken by queer old gentlemen, some of whose names were a legend at Chappell's; it seemed impossible that old Quest, who gave Minster's father such a memorable tanning for blowing the big window bodily out of the lab when making gunpowder, could still be alive. The time went on, the war was not over by Christmas, and Michael was getting more restless every day.

Sometimes he worked furiously, and sometimes he did not work at all, and his marks varied in all subjects from V.G. to definitely Bad or even "X" which meant you had not done your prep, so you got a tanning. When the black moods were on him, music was the only thing that comforted him, and on these occasions there could be heard the sound of a piano played with many wrong notes, but with a real sense of rhythm and phrasing, by a small boy with a scowl on his face and an ache in his heart. On such a day Michael was trying to read something new to him, and tapping the time with his foot on the floor. In due course the door opened, and there entered a tall skinny boy, with untidy brown hair and the dreamer's absent look.

"For a kid," said he, pushing his hands into his trouser pockets and leaning against the doorpost, "you don't play too badly."

Michael blushed, and knocked the music off the stand with embarrassed pleasure, for even in his schooldays Dixon Ogilvie was, at music, definitely a swell.

"In fact, not to exaggerate, you are about the only kid in the place whose hideous attempts are not a torture to listen to. I heard you tapping on the floor—my room's just below—what's the matter, can't you get the hang of something?"

"I think I know how it ought to go," said Michael, "but when I try it doesn't seem to work."

"Perhaps I could show you," said Ogilvie, and played the piano transcription of "Softly awakes my heart." "You see, this bit is nearly syncopation."

"I thought syncopation meant ragtime."

"Not necessarily; there are syncopated bits in some of Beethoven's overtures. You know, nobody ought to try to play this thing on the piano. It's meant for voice, or violin. Though it's wonderful what you can make a piano do," said Ogilvie, and abandoned Delilah for other music Michael did not know. "You can make water drip and trickle"—he played on, passing from one thing to another and talking at intervals—"or the dawn break, and the stars fade and the sun come up—or the wind blow through the trees. Hear it? That's a thing called *Frühlingsrauschen*. I'll see if I can find you some things you might like to play," he said, and left the room as unexpectedly as he had entered it.

Next day he bought Michael a cake. Life at school never looked quite so black again that term, for whenever Michael got depressed, there was Dixon Ogilvie and the piano. There was a certain disturbance on one occasion, because Simpson said that Ogilvie was a bit dotty.

"He's not!" flared Michael. "He's—oh—"

"He moons about, leaving things behind," said Simpson.

"He's just thinking about something else."

"He strums the piano all day—"

"Strums—"

"And his hair looks scruffy."

Michael hit him in the eye, Simpson landed one on Michael's nose, and thereafter the battle became, as Hambledon had said, increasingly beastly, till a door opened and old Mr. Quest put his head in.

"Simpson!"

"Sir?"

"You will go to Dr. Williams's study. Kingston!"

"Sir?"

"You also."

And that was that.

Dixon Ogilvie left school at Easter 1915 to study at the Royal College of Music, and Michael missed him horribly. But in the summer holidays that year he arrived, with a motorcycle and sidecar containing a small tent and other camping equipment, at Weatherley Parva, and suggested that Michael might like to come camping with him for a few days. Michael's heart swelled with pride till it nearly choked him, but he managed to reply in a tone of assumed calm that it might be rather decent, and they went.

During those holidays Dr. Williams, headmaster of Chappell's, had an onset of militant patriotism. He composed a recruiting message, had a number of copies printed on postcards, and, returning to school, sent a copy to each of his old boys whom he did not definitely know to be serving in the forces. It ran something as follows:

> "Now is the time for all good men to serve the State."
> I cannot believe that any of you whom I have known will shirk your plain duty at a time when your Country's need of your services is so great.
> What are YOU doing?
> *"Dulce et decorum est pro patria mori."*

Dixon Ogilvie received his copy at Weatherley Parva one afternoon when they had come into the village for bacon and sausages, and took it back with him to their camp by the beechwood on War Down. After supper he picked it up and read it aloud.

"But I think war is just beastly, Kingston. To go out and kill people you don't even mildly dislike is just madness. I suppose you'll think me a freak for saying so."

Michael could not have thought Ogilvie a freak under any circumstances, but he said: "No," slowly, as though considering the point, and went on: "No, I don't think that. But if anybody attacks us—"

"Yes. I don't mean that I think England was wrong to get into this war, but that it never ought to have been started by anybody. I don't want to go to war at all, I want to stay in peace and make music. If I were killed and couldn't write music any more, what good would I be to the country? Suppose I lost my hands—"

Michael wriggled, and said: "Oh, I dare say you'd come through all right. Lots of chaps will."

"Possibly I'm just cowardly, but I don't really think it's that. I just feel it isn't my job. But—perhaps old Williams is right. 'Your Country's need of your services is so great.' Your Country," he repeated, and looked at the dreaming land below them, miles and miles of the most typical of all English scenery, the wide valleys among the South Downs. "O Peaceful England," he quoted.

"I don't see that it really matters much," said the practical Michael, "what we really think about war, does it? I mean, once you're in it. Still, I see what you mean. I don't think everybody is cut out to be a soldier."

"I should probably lose my rifle," said Dixon Ogilvie.

"Then you'd be crimed."

They talked far into the night till the moon rose high, a full moon, making all things visible but unreal. *"Che sarà, sarà,"* said Ogilvie. "What will be, will be. I suppose I must go for a soldier. Let's go and pick blackberries, I want to make jam."

So they picked blackberries and thereafter made jam on an oil stove, and it was not a great success because they had not quite enough sugar. It was runny but edible.

The holiday ended next day and Ogilvie returned to London, while Michael, left behind in Weatherley Parva, attacked his uncle on the subject of returning to school.

"It's so useless, Uncle John, to go on there sitting at a desk and plugging up math and history and chem when there's all this going on. It's driving me dotty."

"You're too young to join the army, Michael."

"I know, but I might get in. Besides, I've got my Certificate A from the O.T.C."

"What's that for, rifle-shooting?"

"Oh, heaps of things. Lots of chaps have got in the army at sixteen who don't know half as much about the job as I do."

"Besides, Michael, you are all your aunt has—"

"Lots of men are all somebody's got, and they've gone. Sorry," he added, feeling he had been a little callous, "but if anybody asked me why I didn't join up and I said I was all Aunt Dora had got—"

"No one will ask you why you don't join up when you are two whole years under age," said John Andrews testily. Michael did not appreciate that it was his uncle and not himself who had to put up with Aunt Dora's lamentations.

"But I look older," said Michael, which was a delusion, for in point of fact he looked absurdly young and innocent, particularly when he had been in mischief.

"I venture to differ," said his uncle, considerably amused. "But I do sympathize with what you feel," he went on. "Even an old crock like myself feels it. In fact, I have joined the Special Constables."

"Oh—splendid," said Michael awkwardly. "What do you do?"

"Put on an armlet and carry a truncheon—there it is—and spend three nights a week guarding the viaduct beyond Drake's Farm."

"Oh, good. Rather decent."

"But what precisely is supposed to happen to the viaduct if I don't guard it is not really clear to me. I gather somebody might possibly try to blow it up; after all, it is on the main line to Portsmouth."

"And if anybody tries it, you biff them with this, I suppose," said Michael, aiming blows at an imaginary Hun with the loaded stick.

"Presumably. Though I think if I ran as much like an antelope as is compatible with my figure and yelled blue murder, it would do more good."

"You should creep up on the chap from behind, leap on him, lay him out with your thingummy here, tie him up with your braces, and drag him off to the nearest lockup."

"Suppose I leaped on the explosives? Then the heavens would fall and justice would not be done," said Andrews, who belonged to a generation which liked to show that it had a classical education. "Besides, how do I keep my trousers up?"

"Oh, that's easy. You hold them up with your teeth. Or just let 'em go. Anything *pro patria* is decorum, isn't it?"

"That's a good one, Michael! I shall remember that and work it off as my own—on the vicar. But, seriously, if the cowardly brutes try anything like that, I shall do my best to—to—"

"Up and smite them. I suppose it was your mentioning the vicar made me think of that. But cowardly? I don't know so much, Uncle John. I don't think a man is much of a coward to go and live in an enemy country and do what he can for his own side, all by himself, and if he's caught he'll be shot at dawn, I suppose. I think that would need quite a lot of pluck."

"Spying is a cowardly business, Michael."

"Is it?" said Michael. "I wonder," and suddenly he thought of Tommy Hambledon, who had said there were other ways of being useful to your country besides fighting for it. Work hard at your languages, Kingston. I don't understand, sir …

"No, I don't think it's cowardly," said young Kingston.

"Well, we won't argue the point. Finish this term at school anyway, and I will see what can be done. This is the half-term; there's barely six weeks to go. I will think it over, I promise you that."

When Michael came home at the end of term he found he had been apprenticed to a famous shipbuilding firm and was to start work in three days' time. But if his uncle expected gratitude he was disappointed, for Michael howled his rage and grief to high heaven.

"But I shan't be able to get out!" he wailed. "I shall be stuck there in a soft job till the end of the war while all the other fellows—oh!"

"You will be serving your country, Michael."

"I want to go in the army."

"You can't, you're not old enough."

Michael stuck his lower lip out and did not answer.

"Besides, if you try hard and turn out good work, you will be just as useful there as in the army."

"Nice safe job," grumbled Michael. "Nice soft bed every night. And there's Dixon Ogilvie, he's in the K.O.S.B.'s—"

"Michael, stop it at once. Your aunt and I have made considerable sacrifices to pay your premium, you might have the common courtesy to appear grateful. Besides, the war won't last for ever and this will be a career for you."

Three days later he was walking through big open gates at six on a horribly cold morning, for this was Christmas 1915, in company with hundreds of other men and boys who looked at him entirely without interest, or did not even look. On his left as he entered was a wooden building with red crosses on it, and even as he walked forward two men came down the road from the works bearing a stretcher which was occupied, and the stretcher had red patches on it. Michael felt cold in the middle.

"I will not faint," he said to himself, for the thing of which he was most ashamed was his tendency to faint at the sight of blood, and he used to lie awake at night and worry about what would happen if he did that when he went to France. But he pulled himself together and went on, and presently found himself in a great workshop, with a driving-shaft running the whole length of it twenty feet up under the roof girders. The shaft had pulleys on it, and belting from these came down and turned lathes and grinding machines and milling machines and many others of whose uses he had no notion. When the machinery was started up there was a hum which grew to a drone and increased to a roar so that he could not hear himself speak, and when men started working on the lathes and grinding tools and filing, the noise increased tenfold till he felt that if he stayed here another two hours he would be deaf for life. Yet in three days' time he had got so accustomed to it that he could hear a whisper.

Michael's letters home from his Southampton lodgings afforded a sketchy running commentary upon affairs. He noticed with satisfaction that the Zeppelin L.15 was brought down in the Thames estuary, but that she broke up while being towed in, that he got thirty-eight miles an hour out of the two-stroke, which was pretty decent, but that he was always having trouble with his rear light blowing out, and that petrol had gone up again. April 26 was an eventful day—this was still 1916—for the Germans shelled Lowestoft from the sea, he heard of the surrender of Kut, and went to see Charlie Chaplin in an Essanay two-part comedy *Dough and Dynamite*. On the next day Casement was captured running arms into Ireland, street fighting was going on in Dublin, and martial law was proclaimed all over Ireland. It was easy that time to write his weekly letter home, no padding necessary at all. There was the Friday night when the buzz went round the yard that there had been a great battle in the North Sea; he remembered that it was a week or more before he knew that it was called the Battle of Jutland.

CHAPTER THREE
WILLIAM SAUNDERS

IN AUGUST 1916 Michael saw a name which he knew in the casualty lists: "Ogilvie, Dixon, Pte., K.O.S.B., missing, believed killed."

He thought this over for two days, then got up one morning and dressed in his blue overalls as usual, but instead of going to the works he walked off in the direction of London. Walked, because he did not want to run the risk of being seen at the station by anyone who knew him. On the road he had the luck to get a lift on a Foden steam wagon which took him as far as Guildford; from there he went by train to London and walked into a recruiting office off Conduit Street.

There he waited in a queue and stared at the little posters of German atrocities on the walls. One was a picture of some British fishermen captured by Germans and taken to Hamburg; the Germans had shaved half their faces vertically—they were hairy men—and they were being led through the streets of Hamburg to be jeered at by the crowds.

"That isn't an atrocity," thought Michael, "that's just a bad joke. I doubt if it's true."

Presently his turn came, and he passed into an inner room and stood before a desk at which were seated a sergeant, who asked questions, and a couple of orderlies who took notes.

"Name?"

"William Saunders," said Michael, who did not intend to be turned down this time.

"Age?"

"Eighteen."

The sergeant looked at his boyish face and round blue eyes, but did not query this.

"Address?"

"Weatherley Parva, Hampshire. P-A-R-V-A."

"Religion?"

"Church of England—why?"

"We puts it on your identification disk."

"What for?"

"Think it over. Nearest relatives?"

Michael told him. After all, his uncle and aunt would have to know some time, and he did not suppose the army authorities would communicate with them unless something happened to him and then it wouldn't matter.

"Medical examination, through that door. Next, please."

Michael, telling himself that he was no longer Michael but William Saunders and must get used to answering to the name of Bill, passed the doctor without difficulty and was sent to Kingston Barracks. There he, together with a number of other equally new recruits, were given uniforms and also a sheet of brown paper and a piece of string in which to pack up their civilian clothes if they wished to send them home. They changed, were marched out on the barrack square, lined up, and looked over.

Then the sergeant in charge of their destinies divided the line into approximate thirds with a chopping gesture of his hand and said: "You—for Ireland. You—for the North of England. And you—" to the group which included Michael, "to Gosport, for the Hampshires."

The new Bill Saunders gasped. This was awful, this was impossible. To get clean away, enlist in London, and then get sent back to Gosport of all places, which was on the doorstep of home—horrors, no. He stepped back, slipped quietly along behind the line, and touched a man on the arm.

"Hey, you for Ireland—change places with me for Hampshire?"

"Righto," said the lad, but instead of passing behind the line he strolled along in front and was, of course, immediately spotted.

"Hey, you! What you doin'? Get back there. You there! Come back 'ere."

So the attempt failed, and Michael traveled again the familiar line to Gosport.

New Barracks, Gosport, are of a rather curious design. Once upon a time, many years ago, the War Office commanded designs for two barracks to be submitted to them, one to be built in India and the other in England. Someone presumably put the designs in the wrong envelopes, for the Indian barracks were built in England and the English barracks in India. If anybody noticed there was something a little wrong, it was nobody's business to make a fuss. Theirs not to reason why. So Gosport Barracks have wide verandas, large and frequent windows, and fine airy rooms, just bearable to a fresh-air fiend in a hot August but Dante's Cold Circle all the rest of the year; while its Indian opposite number has nice small windows, careful admission of the maximum amount of sunlight, and fireplaces nearly every where. And nobody has done anything about it to this day.

So to this tribute to a far-flung Empire came Bill Saunders on a summer's evening, and the first thing he saw was an unconscious man being carted like a sack of potatoes out of a doorway and placed in the fresh air to recover. Bill and his fellow recruits stopped to observe this portent, and behold, in a few minutes another fainting man was carried out, and yet another, and they were all laid out in a row.

"God lumme," said one of the recruits in a tone of unmitigated horror, "what ever can be a-goin' on in there?"

"S'all right," said a man standing by. "S'only inoculations. When they sees the needle bein' stuck in the other chaps, an' knows their turn's comin', some of 'em just rolls over like rabbits. They're all right."

Bill Saunders was reminded of the morning when Michael Kingston first arrived at the engineering works. There always seemed to be some little tableau arranged specially for his encouragement. But he discovered that evening how lovely it was to be able to lie in bed and smoke; he had never smoked in bed before. If only the blankets didn't smell quite so frowsty. ...

Towards the end of his two months' training Bill Saunders got ten days' draft leave. He had, of course, made his peace with his uncle and aunt long before, and they, seeing that it was useless to try to keep him out of the army, had unwillingly agreed. He spent his leave at Weatherley Parva, walking the hills in the early October days or pottering about the garden with his uncle, singularly content to do nothing in particular till one day he received an invitation to tea at the vicarage.

"Oh Lord!" said Michael. He was Michael again here; Bill Saunders seemed—and was—a very different person.

"My dear," said his aunt.

"Better go, boy," said John Andrews.

"But what do I do if they talk about what was his name who was killed?"

"Antony? Oh, they never say much. Just make a few sympathetic noises," said his uncle. "Perhaps they won't mention him."

"I hope they won't. I'm sorry and all that, of course, but that sort of thing makes me feel all feet—large ones, in hobnailed boots."

"I know. Never mind, you can't very well refuse, but you needn't stay long."

So Michael went, and met the vicar in the garden, busy cutting down dead sunflowers. He greeted the soldier cheerfully and talked of this and that, and how he was plowing up the lawn and paddock to plant potatoes in the spring.

"Come in and have some tea," he said. "By the way, I have a niece staying with me—Diane Causton. A pleasant child."

"Oh gosh," thought Michael. "A pigtail with a huge black bow on the end, and a doll, I suppose. Or a windmill—"

Tea was laid on a table in the hall, and as they entered, a tall slim girl came down the stairs. She had plaits of hair, but they were wound over her ears, she had long, slender hands and fine ankles, and the darkest blue eyes Michael had ever seen. Her hair was dark and curling, she had curved eyebrows and long lashes, and poor Michael, who had been rehearsing sentences like "Do you go to school?" and "Do you like pantomimes?" took one look at her and metaphorically fell down flat.

"Diane, my dear, Mr. Kingston. My niece."

Michael had no recollection of moving, but he must have done so, because the next moment they were shaking hands at the foot of the stairs and all he could think of was what hideous knobby wrists he had and that his tunic sleeves were far too short.

"I am going to wash my hands," said the vicar. "Ring for tea, will you?"

He went out, and Diane rang the bell and stood before the fire with Michael beside her.

"My uncle tells me you are going to France," she said.

"Yes, on Thursday," said Michael, and found to his surprise that his voice was not quite steady.

"And today's Saturday," she said, and looked into the fire.

"Yes, today's Saturday, but I don't leave here till Tuesday afternoon. So we've got Sunday, Monday, and half Tuesday."

"We?"

"How is it," said Michael, "that I've never seen you before?"

"I only came yesterday, and I haven't often been here before. We almost always went abroad for the holidays," she said, "and I was at school in Switzerland for a whole year."

"I suppose you've left school now."

"Oh, ages ago. Last year, in fact; I'm nineteen now."

"That's odd, so did I, though I was only seventeen in June," said Bill, feeling years and years older than Diane by reason of eight months in a shipyard.

"Oh—but I thought they wouldn't have you in the army till you're eighteen. My brother only got in early this year."

"Oh, these things can be arranged," said he airily, and at that moment the maid came in with the teapot, followed by the vicar and his wife. Michael never remembered anything about that meal, but after it Diane said she would take the letters to the post, and Michael naturally went with her and escorted her back to the vicarage gate.

"When shall I see you again?"

"After church tomorrow?"

"Right," he said. "Do you like walking? Splendid. We might go for a stroll in the afternoon if you'd care to."

So they walked together all Sunday afternoon, and at evening church Michael sat two pews behind her and noticed how two little curls lay close to the nape of her neck.

On Monday morning he drove her to Weatherley for shopping in his uncle's pony-trap.

On Monday afternoon he took Diane up the downs to a point from which you could see the Solent and the Isle of Wight and, with field glasses (for the day was clear), ships going in and out from Portsmouth harbor. The sun shone and the larks sang and the air was filled with the scent of wild thyme where their feet had trodden it. She was just about to ask whether he would sail from Southampton, but checked the question. Already they had reached the point where a parting is to be endured if needs must, but not mentioned sooner than one can help. But he answered the unspoken question. "I don't know where we sail from," he said.

"Hush," she answered, and put her hand in his.

He took her home to tea at his uncle's house and later went to supper at the vicarage, after which they all played "Sevens" till ten thirty, when the vicar's wife rose.

"I hate to break up a happy party," she said, "but we are an early household and I expect yours is too."

So he had to go and there was absolutely no opportunity to kiss her goodnight although he lingered in the garden till midnight hoping she would slip out, and watching a window which he took to be hers, though in point of fact it was the cook's, but as he didn't know that, it served just as well. He wished then that he had kissed her during the day, but somehow the right moment never seemed to arrive, or if it did there were people about, so he had told himself he would wait till they said good-night, and pictured them together under the great cedar. And now this—

He went up next morning to say good-bye, and was treated with the most excruciating kindness by the vicar and his wife, who seemed to have no idea whatever how beautiful they would look walking away, though it is possible they had a very clear idea indeed. However, just when Michael was on the point of suggesting wildly that he and Diane should go and look for owls or something, providence intervened in the persons of Sir Egbert and Lady Somers, who came upon parish business.

Michael rose, took a polite but rapid farewell, and fled the room, and somehow Diane came too. They drifted into the garden, across the doomed lawn into the rosery, with a few late blooms still to be seen, where the gardener and the cook saw them coming hand in hand like children.

Cook cast one look at their faces, said: "Poor lambs!" and dragged the gardener away.

Diane said: "Look, I've got something for you." She tried to unclasp with one hand, the other being occupied, a fine gold chain she wore round her neck, but could not manage it, so Michael had to help with his spare hand and at last they undid it.

"I want you to have this," she said; it was a tiny crucifix. "Perhaps it will keep you safe. I hope it will," she said quite steadily, and the next second burst into tears.

"Please," said Michael chokily. "Please don't. I don't want ever to make you cry. Oh, Diane—"

She turned in his arms and looked up at him with the tears running down her face. "I love you," she said, "please come back, Michael, please. I love you—love you."

CHAPTER FOUR
FRONTAL ATTACK

Dover to Boulogne and thence to Rouen.

They left Rouen in an immensely long train with the last cars filled with Chinese laborers going to Étaples, and no sooner had they entered the tunnel on the long hill up from the station than the engine broke down and they had to wait there till another came out from Rouen and pushed them on.

They leaned out of the car windows and saw, in the rear of the train, dozens of Chinamen, each holding a two-inch stump of lighted candle, inspecting with solemn faces the slimy tunnel walls. After that they spent days traveling round France, passing, for some mysterious reason, Calais, then Étaples, where the station notices were also written in Chinese because there was a Chinese labor camp there, Saint-Omer, and Proven. Here they detrained and proceeded by lorry and on foot to Ypres, to join the 29th Division.

They spent a night behind the town here before going up the line into the salient, and in the evening Bill Saunders strolled off across a couple of fields to watch ammunition wagons going up the road. There was the continual sound of gunfire in the distance, but just where he was it was quiet, and in the evening light the scene was wonderfully peaceful.

There was a sound as of several express trains coming through the air straight at him at an incredible speed, all blowing whistles, and terror seized him. He fell flat on his face and immediately rolled up like a hedgehog; he became smaller and more compact till he felt he could have been tucked comfortably into a bucket; he pressed himself hard against the ground. The shell registered a direct hit on one of the ammunition wagons, which blew up in a shower of fragments. They were a hundred yards away, the shell was nowhere near him. The Germans were shelling the road, out here he was quite safe.

He got up feeling perfectly thankful that there was no one to see him making such a pitiable exhibition of himself, and walked back to the bivouac. Nothing in the way of shelling ever frightened him quite so much again.

When he got back he found that blankets had been issued during his absence and consequently there wasn't one for Bill Saunders, and for the first time in his life he was going to spend the night in the open. It was cold, and getting colder. He wandered dismally about in the half-dark, tripping over people and feeling very small and superfluous and very far from home. At last he kicked against two men who were sleeping together, sharing blankets, and one of them looked up.

"What's the matter with you? Ain't you got a blanket?"

"No," said Bill. "I wasn't here when they were given out."

The man considered this for a moment and then dug his elbow into the other man's ribs.

"Nobby," said he, "the pore little something 'asn't got a blanket."

Nobby roused himself. "Let 'im come in along of us."

"Look," said Blacker, the Good Samaritan, "you come in 'ere between us, you'll be nice and warm."

Bill hardly liked this; they were total strangers and probably inadequately washed according to his views, but there was nowhere else to go, so he thanked them and crawled in. They all settled down, and the two men promptly went to sleep. Not so Bill, for the night was full of unpleasant noises, everything was strange, and, what was worse, the men not only snored but scratched in their sleep, and he had a horrid conviction that they had good reason for scratching. Presently he heard three blasts on a whistle. Bill wondered if it was something of which they ought to take notice, so he dug Nobby in the ribs.

"What was that?"

"What was what?"

"Three whistles."

"Oh, that's nothing. Only Jerry up. Go to sleep."

"Jerry up? What's that?"

"Aeroplanes. It's all right. Go to sleep."

Nobby settled down again and some more time passed. Presently there came a series of resounding bangs, getting nearer and nearer till the last was only twenty yards off. Bill sat up with a jerk, dragging the bedclothes with him.

"Good Lord, what was that?"

"Only bombs. It's all right, go to sleep."

"B-bombs?"

"Yes. I told you, it's Jerry up. He's bombing us. It's all right, you ain't hit. Go to sleep, for 'evin's sake."

And these incredible men actually snuggled down and were sound asleep again at once. Bill thought this simply impossible, but a few days later he was sleeping peacefully through an artillery barrage.

The next night they went up the line into the salient. The troops they relieved passed down with their dead and wounded on stretchers leading the way, and the stretcher-bearers were pleased to ask the new hands if they would like a ride.

Bill Saunders found that the most trying aspect of trench warfare was not the nervous strain, nor even the intense discomfort, but the boredom of hanging about with nothing to do except wait for something to happen; even fourteen hours of it was too much. In the evening of their first day in a frontline trench he found himself volunteering to go out wire-cutting—anything sooner than just go on sitting there.

So they climbed over the parapet and came out on the expanse of stained slimy obscene mud which stretched for miles round beleaguered Ypres. Not a house, nor a tree, nor even a blade of grass, not even a bird, could live there, where the shell-holes met and merged and overlapped, continually filling with mud and water and continually renewed. Yes, one thing lived there and thrived, the rats, enormous rats.

All the other members of the party had been out in no-man's-land before and knew how to move and work quietly, but the ground was strewn with half-buried debris, particularly loose wire. Bill tripped and stumbled and seemed to himself to make enough clatter to awaken the whole sector, and repeated injunctions to make less noise were no help at all. He had no wish at all to make noises, they just happened. Nobody had told him to cut the wire close to a post and ease away the loose end, he cut it wherever he met it and the wire twanged like harp strings, sprang back and enmeshed him. He stepped back, tripped over something, staggered into a tangled snarl of wire, and was brought up literally all standing. At that moment someone in the German trenches heard something, sent up a Very light, and opened fire with a machine-gun.

Immediately the whole party went flat on the ground with the exception of Bill, who very unwillingly remained standing like Horatius defending the bridge.

"Lie down, you silly little blighter," said a hoarse voice behind him, "they're shooting at *you*."

Bill replied with the very first string of curses he had ever uttered, that he'd simply love to, were it not for circumstances over which he had no control, or words to that effect. He was surprised to find how fluent he was.

After a while the excitement died down, and by some miracle he was not hit. He disentangled himself and the party went on with its job, and when that was done Bill was sent out on listening-post with Blacker, as they could both speak German. Bill soon acquired the knack of moving quietly, since it is wonderful how quickly you can learn when your life depends on it. They lay in a shell-hole close to the German frontline trench and listened to the men in it talking. One of them had recently returned from leave and was telling the others about a revue called *The Pineapple*.

"There's some good numbers in that," he said, and hummed a tune.

"Any pretty girls?"

"Oh yes, lots of pretty girls."

"I don't want to see pretty girls when I go back," said an older voice, "I just want to go home. I have a new son, so I hear today. I should like to go and have a look at him, I should."

"Congratulations, Reinhardt."

"Thanks. I am not sure, though, that the little one is to be congratulated. It's not a nice world for babies to come to, just now."

"That's so, with everything so short and milk so hard to get—"

"Everything's hard to get. My aunt, who keeps a cake shop in Freiburg, says it's just terrible. The flour is bad and there's no butter, and eggs are short—"

"Yes, there's lots of business going *kaput* now—"

Blacker touched Bill, and they retired without advertisement.

"That's all right," said Blacker. "They're Saxons."

"What's *kaput*?" asked Bill. "That's a new word to me."

"Never heard it before. Well, the wire's cut and the Saxons are there, so tomorrow's little show shouldn't be too bad."

But at zero hour next morning, when the frontal attack began, they found to their disgust that the wire had been replaced and so had the Saxons—by the Prussian Guards.

It was to be a surprise attack—that is, there was no preliminary barrage—and they went over the top in a low morning mist which masked them from the German trenches. For some time there was no sound except the splosh-suck of boots in the mud and the hard breathing of men running. But at the appointed moment there came a shattering roar from the British guns behind them, and with a blinding flare that seemed to split the heavens and a deafening crash that shook the earth, the barrage fell on the German trenches ahead.

The next moment the men came up to the wire and began to cut and force their way through. Away to Bill's left an officer had found a gap and was swinging a gas-rattle violently and yelling above the din: "Come on, come on, me lucky lads! Walk up! Walk up! This way, come on!" The German artillery came into action and the shells began to fall among them; also they heard the steady tut-tut-tut-tut of the machine-guns from the trenches ahead, and the casualties began.

Bill's first thought was how very like the war pictures the scene before him was: bursting shells, earth flying up, and men falling. Then he saw a man go down whom he knew well, and another, and another, and some of them screamed, and the cry was passed back: "Stret-cher-bear-rer! Stret-cher-bear-rer!" on one monotonous note. Immediately the scene ceased to be a picture and became dreadful reality, and he knew that he was afraid. "I mustn't look round," he thought, "or I shall run back," so he kept his eyes on the ground and saw that it was alive with frogs, of all things, frogs hopping everywhere. The din increased as they went forward, and seemed to stun his mind. His tin of bully-beef fell out of his pack and he turned his head and watched it falling very deliberately like a slow-motion picture, to hit the ground and rise again, slowly turning in the air to fall to rest at last. He ran on, with a phrase from a song in *Maid of the Mountains* going round and round in his head: "When he fancies he is past love it is then he meets his last love when he fancies he is past love it is then he meets his last love when he fancies he is—"

So they reached the German trenches at last, and the Prussian Guards fought like fiends.

When they came out of the line, Bill Saunders was employed in interrogating prisoners. This was mainly a matter of getting men from as many different German regiments as possible and asking them how long they had been in the place where they were captured and where they came from before that. This provided data for the study of German troop movements, but any information on almost any subject was thankfully received. The great thing was to induce a man to talk.

This went on for some time, varied by spells in the unpleasanter parts of the line, for the 29th Division were emphatically what their opponents have since called "storm troops" and always used as such. Presently Bill found himself dressed as a German private, not only as regards uniform but right down to the skin, and sent into the cages—prisoners' camps—to study dialects, complete with papers proving that he really was Hans Hommell-hoff of Duisberg, and even some nice letters from home to show his fellow prisoners. He was sometimes in the room when other prisoners were being interrogated; it seemed to encourage them to talk if they saw an unhappy-looking little German private shivering in a corner.

In March 1917 Bill Saunders was told to proceed to London to interview someone at the War Office. He went through the usual performance of filling out a short form under the critical eye of the commissionaire and accompanying a small girl in a brown uniform up in a lift and along endless passages. At last he was admitted to a room where there were three officers sitting at desks. One of them summoned him, and Bill came smartly to attention and saluted.

"You are Private William Saunders of the Hampshire Regiment?"

"Yes, sir."

"Wait here a moment."

The officer left the room. Bill commanded himself to stand at ease and waited. Presently the officer returned and took Bill to another room which was merely down one flight of stairs and along two passages. Here in a room was one officer alone.

"You are Private William Saunders of the Hampshire Regiment?"

"Yes, sir."

"You have a note to hand in, I think."

He was perfectly right. Bill handed it over.

"Wait here a moment."

This officer also left the room, and Bill waited again. In a very short time he returned.

"Come with me."

This time he was taken to a room which was merely five doors away, and again found one officer alone, a big man with a heavy face and a nose that jutted out from his forehead.

"You are Private William Saunders of the Hampshire Regiment?"

"Yes, sir."

The man looked at Bill for a moment and then smiled unexpectedly.

"Sit down, Saunders. Not to beat about the bush, I have brought you here to ask you whether you would be prepared to leave the regiment for a time and engage in another sort of activity."

"Sir?"

"You are aware that it is imperative that we should have as much information as possible about the enemy; not only troop movements, but about conditions in Germany. Whether they are short of copper, for example, and food—we know they are short, but we must know how short—and, if they are getting supplies, where these supplies come from. All these things are of vital importance."

"Yes, sir."

"No doubt you know that there are men who make it their business to pass into Germany and bring us this—and other—information. Some of them live there permanently and pass their news to us through various channels."

"Yes, sir."

"I have to ask you if you will be one of these men. Not to beat about the bush, the work is delicate, very trying to the nerves—in short, it's extremely dangerous. You will work in touch with others, of course, but you must stand on your own feet. If you fail and are caught, no one can do anything to help you. In fact, you will probably be shot."

"Yes, sir," said Bill again.

"But there is this about it, that it is work of such value and importance as I cannot find words to describe. Compared with that, your job as an infantryman in France is about as important as pushing a perambulator round Regent's Park. Without Intelligence, the work of the General Staff is a fumbling in the dark. Without Intelligence, we are not likely to win the war. Why, damn it, man, with a little luck you might change the course of history!"

"I suppose so, sir."

"You understand, I cannot oblige you to take this job on, I have no wish to. I am merely here to tell you that those who have seen the manner in which you have carried out the duties assigned to you in connection with the German prison camps are of opinion that you might be useful."

"I see, sir."

"If you say that you do not wish to do this, but would rather return to the regiment, you are perfectly free to do so, and no one will ever hold your refusal against you. On the other hand, if you will accept you will be—er—not to beat about the bush, sir, you will be serving your country as few men can."

"Yes, sir."

"Would you like a few days to think it over? You have four days' leave, I understand."

"No, thank you, sir."

"What d'you mean?"

"I'll take it on, sir, please."

The officer smiled again, and said: "Splendid. I'm glad. I wish you luck." He gave Bill a cigarette, shook hands with him and told him to go into the next room and see a man in there. So Bill went in, and it was Tommy Hambledon, very smart in the uniform of a major of horse artillery.

"Congratulations, sir," said Bill, greeting him with delight. "I didn't know you'd got your majority."

"I haven't," said Hambledon frankly. "I just like the cut of these breeches."

CHAPTER FIVE
OUT OF THE FRYING -PAN

They sat over coffee in a private room at the Flying Lobster, and Tommy Hambledon talked.

"Officially," he said, "you are still with your regiment. You write to your people—how often?"

"About twice a week," said Bill Saunders.

"You will probably be away about six weeks this time. If you will write twelve letters in advance, I will tell you where to send 'em and they will be posted in France on the right dates. How right and wise was the imposition of a rigid censorship, which makes all our letters insufferably anemic anyway, even to our terms of endearment! 'Hoping this strikes you in the pink, as it leaves me,' you know. Got any use for terms of endearment, Bill?"

Bill blushed violently.

"Oh, lor'. Well, it doesn't matter so long as you don't tell her anything. You do understand, Kingston, that it is completely imperative that you keep your mouth shut."

"Of course, sir."

"You are two people now and you must keep them separate at all costs; in fact—you aren't doing badly at your age—you are already three. You are Michael Kingston at home, Bill Saunders in the army, and Karl goodness knows what on the job."

"I've almost forgotten what Michael Kingston feels like."

"You mustn't merely play a part, you must actually be the man you appear. You must not only act as he would, but think as he would. All this about spies making up their faces and wearing wigs is all poppycock. We can do things to your eyebrows which will make you look different, but mainly you look different because you *are* different. Consider the boy, the simple unsophisticated boy—if there is such a thing. Consider him proceeding to the pastry shop with form erect, chest thrown out, a gleam in his eye and sixpence in his pocket. Consider him proceeding to the head's study. His face is longer and narrower, his form shrinks—especially behind—and his whole appearance is marked by a strong conviction of the inevitable distastefulness of the immediate future. He is a different boy. Remember also that people only see what they expect to see. If your best friend, knowing beyond a shadow of doubt that you were immovably fixed in Saffron Walden, were to meet you face to face in the High Street of Nizhnii Novgorod, would he believe it? No. He would say to himself: 'If that's what vodka does to you, I'm signing off.' That's all. Pass the port."

"But we're drinking coffee," objected Bill, but he passed the port all the same.

"Perhaps you're right. A little more of this port and I shall deliver my celebrated lecture on Jezebel. She was a great lady, and much maligned.

Jezebel, your health, and I hope I meet you in the hereafter. Let's go some-where else."

"But," said Bill, "where are we going and what for?"

"I suggest the Clinging Codfish. Isn't that its name? The taxi-driver will know."

"No, no. I mean when we go abroad."

"We are going to Germany, my pippin, to ascertain the whereabouts of one Peter Collins, who seems to have gone away leaving no address."

"But who is he?"

"He is one of our men," said Tommy Hambledon, suddenly and com-pletely sober. "He is a good man, too—a very good man. It was he, in fact, who pulled off that stunt about the Kaiser's dispatch to Germans in America, and he has apparently disappeared. And I am going to find him if I have to pull down the Wilhelmstrasse stone by stone and throw the bits at von Hin-denburg." He stared across the room, and Bill did not venture to speak.

"So a-hunting we will go," went on Hambledon, returning from his mys-terious distance, "and what shall the harvest be? Selah, which is Hebrew for 'wait and see.' Tomorrow I will take you to a man who will tidy up your face, and to another man about some clothes, and as I already have the tickets and what's-its, we needn't go and see a man about that too, which is pleasant, isn't it? In the evening we might take your young woman out somewhere. Does she correspond with your people? No? How wise you are, how forth-looking beyond your natural years! Anything else you want to know you can ask me tomorrow, for now we are going to the Cheerful Conger. I don't like this place, I hate the shape of the chairs. Come on."

Three days later they crossed from Harwich to the Hook of Holland, and thence to Rotterdam. Here they entered the shop of a dealer in antiques, an old man and fat, with a cast in his eyes. They strolled about, examining this and that, till the old man asked if they would be pleased to see the things in his showroom upstairs, so they went up, and argued about the price of a copper bowl till a lady, who was the only other customer, went away. Hamble-don touched Bill's arm and led the way through a door into the private part of the house and into what was plainly an unoccupied spare room.

"Here we become Dirk and Hendrik Brandt," he said. "You are Dirk Brandt, my sister's son from South Africa, which naturally accounts for your ignorance of Europe and your well-intentioned but uncouth manners—have you ever kissed a lady's hand, Dirk? I thought not. But your sympa-thies, since you are of Boer descent, naturally tend towards the German side. At least, we can make it appear natural. I made it appear natural to be found asleep on a roof one cold night, I said I was Father Christmas and I couldn't identify the lady's chimney, so I was waiting for daylight."

"Do I really have to wear these boots?"

"You do. Pass my trousers, will you? The checked ones. I am your Onkel Hendrik, a Dutchman born in Utrecht but at present resident in Cologne, where I am a merchant connected with the import trade."

"I thought Germany was blockaded, so there wouldn't be any import trade, Onkel Hendrik."

"You'd be surprised," said Tommy Hambledon.

"I wish I knew a bit more about South Africa," said Bill thoughtfully.

"You've read *Allan Quatermain*, haven't you? And possibly *The Story of an African Farm*? Well, what more do you want?"

"My father was a transport-rider," began Bill, "and an explorer. He went with Jameson and Rhodes through what was afterwards Rhodesia—"

"No, he didn't, you Imperialistic owl, you're on the wrong side. He was a Boer farmer, and it was he who had the bright idea of feeding the captured Jameson Raiders in horse troughs on the racecourse in Jo'burg, to amuse the crowd. No, that was your grandfather, of course. Your father was out on a raid with Christian De Wet. Are you ready? *Vorwärts*."

They went to Amsterdam first, to do a little business, thence to Utrecht, "to see my aging parents," which they did; at least they saw somebody's; and from there by train to Cologne, as it was a simple matter for that obliging trader Hendrik Brandt to cross the frontier into Germany.

"You are being pampered on your first trip," said Tommy Hambledon, "it is not always so easy as this. But it is a lot easier than the spy books make out. There you either crawl for miles on your belly through wet turnips and under electrified barbed wire, or climb mountains inaccessible to the boldest mountaineer and come down on an avalanche. In actual fact, you'll probably take a streetcar. Here's the frontier, my innocent tourist."

So Hendrik Brandt passed the customs and passport officials with the uninterested manner of the habitual traveler, while Dirk Brandt from Lichtenburg stared about him with round eyes and had to be nudged and told to come on and not be a moon-calf. They returned to the train and went on into Germany; Bill thought privately that it was far too simple and not nearly romantic enough.

They reached Cologne rather late in the evening, and Dirk discovered that his uncle lived in the Dom Hotel, and not only that, but that he had an office in the Höhestrasse near the Café Palant. For he really was an importer, and, what is more, Dirk spent several very strenuous days learning the business. He had a small desk in the corner of his uncle's room and heard Hendrik Brandt interviewing customers; it was interesting but rather dull. The evenings, however, were better; they went to theaters and cabaret shows, and Dirk made many acquaintances. The men, of course, being mostly officers on leave, came and went and he never got to know them well, but the womenfolk remained and were very friendly. He was flattered by this at first, then puzzled, and finally horrified when he realized that he was mainly popular because Onkel Hendrik sometimes brought food into the country, and these people, nice people, people who at home might have been his aunts and sisters, were nearly starving.

Tommy Hambledon asked him one day if he knew a man named Max von Bodenheim.

"Yes," said Bill. "I've met him several times. He goes about in a wheel-chair—his legs are paralyzed since '15—but he goes everywhere. He's by way of being rather hot stuff, you know, or he would be if he weren't crippled. He sees everything with those flaming dark eyes of his, and he doesn't seem to like any of it. He doesn't believe in anything and he hates the English like poison."

"I think it would be a good idea if you got to know him better," said Hambledon. "He has certain connections in Berlin—he might be useful."

"Very well, I will."

Late that night Dirk was watching the cabaret at the Rosenhof and strolling about between the acts with a glass in his hand when he came across von Bodenheim. It may be said that Dirk was not entirely surprised at this, he had reason to think the man would be there. Dirk stopped and said: "Good evening."

"I am glad you find it so," said von Bodenheim.

"Oh, I don't think it's too bad," said Dirk, with his usual ingenuous look. "Good show, isn't it?"

"If you admire the antics of a dozen half-clad sailors' delights posturing before a crowd of semi-imbeciles, it is an excellent show."

"I do think," said the boy from Lichtenburg earnestly, "that they might have rather more clothes on."

"I agree," said von Bodenheim. "If they had so many clothes on that one couldn't even see their faces, it would be much better. If they were all enclosed in oblong boxes with the lids screwed down, it would be better still. Waiter! Bring me some more Berncasteler."

"People seem to like them," said Dirk, as the applause died down, but as he got no reply he changed the subject. "Is there any news—" he began, but broke off as von Bodenheim spun his chair round and looked at him attentively.

"How old are you, Brandt?"

"Seventeen."

"And you come from—?"

"Lichtenburg, in the Transvaal," answered Dirk, dropping his voice in deference to the next item on the program. Max von Bodenheim, however, paid it no attention. "Good life out there?"

"Oh, it's grand. My father had an ostrich farm," said Dirk, hoping that the Transvaal was one of the places where ostriches grew, "That is, it was my father's. My brothers have got it now. We have horses to ride, and plenty of shooting and all that. But there are such a lot of us, and one doesn't make much money, so when Onkel Hendrik Brandt wrote and suggested one of us going into his business, Mother sent me."

"Think you're going to like it?"

At this point several people said: "Sh-sh-sh," and von Bodenheim swung his chair round, stuck an eyeglass in his eye, and stared at them.

"What's the matter with the people?"

"There's a lady singing," said Dirk in an apologetic manner.

"Is there? I don't think I see a lady and I'm damn sure I don't hear singing."

If Dirk really felt as uncomfortable as he looked, it must have been a painful moment.

"I'm sick of this farmyard anyway, let's go somewhere else," said von Bodenheim, and wheeled his chair out of the room with Dirk following.

"Would you care to come to my house?" asked the German.

"I should be honored," said Dirk, with a formal bow. His manners were improving daily.

A manservant with a wooden leg was waiting outside to push the chair, and Dirk walked beside it till they reached a house with a garden round it, in the Blumenthalstrasse.

"Come in," said von Bodenheim, as the servant opened the door, and he led the way into a room at the back with french windows presumably leading to the garden.

"Do you drink whisky?" he asked, to Dirk's surprise, as the servant put decanters and glasses on the table. "The one good thing that comes out of the British Isles—this is Haig and Haig."

"Thanks," said Dirk. "There's one other good thing comes out of England—beer. English ale."

"Perhaps you're right, though personally I don't like the stuff. Have you ever been in England?"

"For three days on my way from Africa. We landed at Plymouth. I had a couple of days in London, and then sailed from Harwich for Hook of Holland."

"Of course," said Max von Bodenheim slowly, "you are a British subject."

"Yes, but I'm taking out Dutch naturalization papers as soon as my uncle definitely decides to keep me."

"Oh yes. Did you like England?"

"No, not at all. Officials came on board at Plymouth, demanded endless papers, and asked endless questions. They also went through every scrap of baggage I had and repacked it so atrociously I had to pack it all over again. Not content with that, we had the same performance all over again when I arrived in London, and much the same again when I left Harwich. Besides, there's a rationing system in force there, you have to have tickets for meat and butter and sugar, and something went wrong so I didn't get any. So I lived for three days on bread and jam and savories, and no sugar in my tea. And there was an east wind all the time, and bits of paper and dust blew about the streets. And when the sun did shine, it wasn't even warm. No, I don't like England."

Von Bodenheim was considerably amused by this tale of misery.

"Didn't you know anyone?"

"My brother Jan wrote to our importers and asked them to do something for me, and the old man's son met me and took me about a bit in the evenings. He was busy all day. We saw one jolly good show," went on Dirk, visibly brightening, "at a theater called Daly's. It was *Maid of the Mountains*, it had some dashed good tunes in it. Everyone was whistling them."

"And the English, did they seem fairly cheerful, or depressed, or grumbling?"

"Oh, they grumbled a lot, I thought, but Frank Micklam—that's the man who took me about—said the English always do that, and that, as a matter of fact, there was less grumbling than there generally is in peacetime. But I wasn't very interested in the English," said Dirk, with rather a sneer. "The fellow who met me was very nice and all that, but so dashed condescending. 'You colonials, what?' he said. You know, not—well, not like one of us at all."

"So you weren't impressed?"

"Why should I be? What are they to me? They conquered my country, but that doesn't make me English. I am half Boer and half Dutch, even if I am a British subject—subject!" said he with a snort.

Von Bodenheim laughed aloud.

"You are positively refreshing," he said. "I thought all the English colonials regarded themselves as the Lion's cubs, so to say."

"You'd be surprised," said Dirk mysteriously.

"So you think you'd be more at home as a Dutchman, do you?"

"Well, yes, you see it's my mother's country, and I do think blood tells, don't you? But what I'd really like—no. You'll think I'm posing."

"Believe me, I shall not. I know fast enough when anyone's posing with me. Tell me."

"Well, what I'd really like—I know you'll think this awful cheek—I'd like to become a German and fight in the German army." Dirk sat back and looked at von Bodenheim like a child expecting to be snubbed.

"Oh, would you? Well, really, I don't see why you shouldn't—"

"Oh, could I? Where do I join up? Do I have to be naturalized first? How old do I have to be? How long training do I get? Can I choose what regiment I join? I'd like—"

"Heavens, boy," said the German, laughing, "one at a time! Age, eighteen. About the naturalization, I don't know, but I'll find out. But I think you'd have to get your uncle's consent. If you joined up without it he could haul you out again, as you are not a German subject, and I think you'll want his consent to be naturalized too, as you're under age."

Dirk's face fell noticeably.

"Tell me, why do you want to fight for Germany?"

Dirk stared into the fire.

"When I was quite a little boy, somebody gave me a picture-book about Germany. At least, they were German legends, all about Siegfried and Wotan, and Valkyries riding down the wind, and shining swords, and dwarfs in the—the Harz Mountains, I think—" he hesitated. "I've forgotten, rather. They made armor for the heroes, didn't they? Anyway, it was all wonderful and—and sort of shining, do you know? There were pictures of great castles, and dark forests. Then, when I was older, some German officers came and stayed at our place. They were on a shooting expedition"—von Bodenheim smiled—"one of them used to talk to me and tell me about the German Army, and I remember I used to ask him strings of questions. I expect I was an awful worry, really. He belonged to the Death's Head—Hussars, are they?"

Von Bodenheim nodded.

"So I made up my mind then that some day I'd go to Germany and join the Death's Head Hussars, and I've always stuck to that. And now I'm in Germany at last"—his voice rose—"and—well, you see now, don't you?" he ended lamely.

"Yes, I see," said Max von Bodenheim, in a voice so gentle that few of his acquaintances would have recognized it. "Well, we'll see what we can do. Even if you can't join the army—"

Dirk looked disappointed.

"Don't look so dismal. There are other things you might do."

"What other things?"

"There are other ways of serving a country besides fighting for it, boy. Even I, crock as I am—" he stopped.

"I don't understand, sir."

"Never mind. We'll talk about it some other time, perhaps."

Dirk glanced at the clock and sprang to his feet.

"Heavens, sir, it's nearly two! What must you think of me?"

"Quite a lot that's pleasant, believe me. I am very glad you came tonight—I had the blue devils and you have chased them away. I shall sleep tonight."

"I hope you will, sir."

"One last toast before you go."

Max von Bodenheim pushed the rug off his knees and sat very upright. Dirk, following some instinct, stood erect.

"*Hoch dem Kaiser! Hoch!*"

Dirk drank.

"Good night, Brandt, come again soon. Don't lose yourself on your way home and wander into the Kammachgasse."

"What's that?" asked Dirk, genuinely puzzled.

"Never mind," said von Bodenheim, laughing. "I don't think you'd like it."

When Bill Saunders got back to his room at the Dom he found Tommy Hambledon there, smoking a long cigar, waiting for him.

"Well?" said he.

"You were quite right, sir. He is in German Intelligence, and I think he's going to offer me a job in it too."

"Well done, boy."

"I told him the tale," said Bill Saunders, yawning, "about my hopes and aspirations for Germany from my youth up till on my honor I began to believe it myself."

"When you quite believe it," said Tommy Hambledon, "you'll be a real agent, my son."

CHAPTER SIX
PRIVATE ON LEAVE

When Bill had been in Cologne about a fortnight, Hambledon told him one morning that there was a little job on hand that night.

"There is a courier leaving Mainz Station at eight fifteen tonight for here," he said. "He has some papers in his little brown bag, and we are going to get them."

"How?"

"Goodness knows, it all depends on circumstances. I don't know anything about him, whether he's a big man or a little one, whether he'll have an escort or not—they don't as a rule, but these papers seem to be something special—whether he'll travel in a car with other people or in a first-class in lonely majesty, or, as they say, what."

"Then you haven't got any plan?"

"Of course not, how could I have? Do get out of your head these ideas about elaborate plans which are so popular in fiction. You know: At eight forty-four and one half precisely you will walk past the automatic weighing-machine on the down platform, and a man in a pale blue Homburg hat will pass you and murmur either 'Catfish,' 'Plaice' or 'Cod,' or 'Salmon.' 'Catfish' means the courier is a large savage man armed to the teeth who never sleeps, with an escort of eight of the Prussian Guard so alert that they take it in turns to breathe. That's to let you know it's going to be a little difficult. 'Plaice' means that he will have a girlfriend with him, so look out for squalls. That's rather a good one, pass the beer. 'Cod' means that, though he travels alone, he is a dangerous homicidal maniac who is quite sane till anybody touches his luggage, when a violent complex is suddenly released and he is possessed with a passion for peritoneotomy—"

"What's that?"

"What Jack the Ripper did. 'Salmon' means that he is a weak little man suffering from incipient sleeping sickness. Salmon is never served up on our job. Even if you could remember all that, he wouldn't; your watch would be fast—his slow, so you'd never meet; and his pale blue Homburg would be blown off his head at a corner and run over by a street car and the only other one he could buy would be a dark green one. Then we should naturally conclude that X 27 has been snootered and that this one was a counterfeit, whereupon it would be the stern duty of one of us to follow him out of the station and assassinate him without sound or trace in a town you don't know, if possible without leaving so much as a body to mark the spot. The best way, of course, would be to push him under a street car at the exact spot where his blue Homburg was run over, leaving it to be inferred that grief at his loss had driven him to suicide. Pass the beer."

"But haven't you any ideas?" asked Bill.

"Oh yes, lots. We could merely hit him on the head with a blunt instrument, take his bag, and just walk away with such ineffable dignity that anyone who saw us do it wouldn't believe their eyes. Or we could crawl along the footboard in the middle of the night somewhere between Coblenz and Bonn, open a car door, which is sure to be locked, by pushing down a window which is certain to be securely shut, and once more produce the blunt instrument. After all, an automatic is a blunt instrument, isn't it? We may find ourselves doing that, it's quite possible. On the whole I think the best thing would be for you to sing to him, and perhaps he would give you the bag to go away."

Friedrich Lunden was a Schleswig-Holsteiner on leave from the western front. He did not go home to the farm in Schleswig, he went to Mainz to see his Katje, who was in service there, good service in a big house, where she would learn how to do things in style, though, of course, economically, till the happy day should come when he would make her Frau Lunden. Then Father would retire from farm work to sit in the sun, smoke his big pipe, and tell everybody how much better the farm was run in his day. Friedrich and Katje would keep cows and pigs and poultry, and she would stand again in a blue apron under the flowering apple trees, with the blue sky above her and the blue waters of the Kattegat behind. No doubt in due course there would be little Friedrichs in peaked caps, and little Katjes with flaxen plaits, and the world would be a wonderful place when the war was over and they could go home together. There would be expenses, of course, but he had saved out of his pay so they could have a fine wedding and she should wear the silver crown.

He went round to the back door and rang the bell. It was answered by a sullen-looking wench who was the kitchen maid, so he saluted politely and asked for his Katje.

"Oh!" said the girl, and gaped at him. "Aren't you the soldier she was engaged to?"

"Was engaged? She still is. Can I speak to her?"

"She's gone away."

"Gone away! When? Why? Where to?"

"To Berentzhausen in Bavaria. Because she got married. Last week," said the girl.

He just stared at her in silence.

"Oh, she's all right. It's a nice place, I come from there."

Still Friedrich did not speak.

"In fact, she married my cousin. He used to come here to see me, and then Katje saw him, and then—then she married him—the cat! And they've gone home together, and I wish—I'd like to claw her eyes out—oh dear!"

The girl burst out crying and leaned her head against the doorpost. Friedrich felt dimly that he ought to say something appropriate, but as nothing presented itself to his mind, he turned on his heels and walked away. The girl lifted her face and stared after him, but he never looked back, and very soon his dejected little figure passed out of sight under the leafless lime trees.

He walked aimlessly on and on till his feet ached with the hard pavements, and then drifted into a beer-house for a drink. He had several and began to get angry. That Katje should do this to him for the sake of a lousy Bavarian, and she a Dane. He remembered that he was a Dane, too, though he lived in the Stolen Provinces; damn all Germans, first they stole his country and then his girl. So now there would be no happy homecoming and no Katje under the apple trees, and it didn't matter whether the war ever came to an end or not, and it would be much nicer if he went back and got killed, because he was very ill-used and horribly unhappy. He put his head on the table and wept.

The tavern-keeper was a good-hearted fellow with boys of his own at the front, so he went over, patted Friedrich on the shoulder, and asked what was amiss. Friedrich, forgetting that he hated all Germans, told him all about it between sobs and gulps of beer, and suddenly fell asleep in the middle of a sentence, so the innkeeper laid him on the bench and covered him up with an old coat.

Some time in the afternoon he woke up again and remembered all about it, and the innkeeper, who had been watching for this moment, stood him a drink and advised him to go home to his people. Friedrich thanked him, said that perhaps he would, and walked out.

Shortly before eight he arrived at Mainz Station very much the worse for drink, tearful, quarrelsome, and sleepy. The train for Cologne was standing at the platform, so he decided to get in, but all the cars were full of the sort of Germans who had stolen his girl and he wanted to lie down somewhere comfortable and go to sleep. He wandered up and down the train, twice passing two shabbily-dressed men, also walking up and down and waiting for providence to do something. Friedrich did not notice them. There was also a dapper little man, very important-looking, and holding a dispatch-case in his hand, who was talking to the stationmaster. Friedrich did not notice him either. He mooned on till he came to an empty compartment, quite empty, brightly lit and warm. It had a long stuffed seat in it, one of those mattress-looking seats, all soft bulges with buttons between. He got in, lay down, and went to sleep.

Five minutes later he was aroused by someone shaking his shoulder. He stirred, groaned, and said: "Go 'way."

"Get up, my man, get up."

Friedrich looked up and saw a little man with a dispatch-case.

"Go 'way, I tell you," said the soldier. "I want go sleep." He snuggled down again, and two shabbily dressed men glanced in as they strolled by.

"You can't sleep in here, I tell you," said the courier. "This compartment is reserved for me. Get out *at once.*"

Friedrich rose slowly to his feet, opened his eyes, and saw a face just in front of them—a pink face with a cross expression. It annoyed him, so he raised his right hand quite slowly and pushed the face—hard. It disappeared backwards out of the car door, and Friedrich, with a sigh of relief, sank again on the padded seat.

The courier picked himself up boiling with rage, reentered the carriage with more haste than wisdom, put his bag down on the seat in order to have both hands free, and hurled himself on the soldier. He seized him by the collar and shook him violently.

This time Lunden woke up in earnest. Another blasted German; they had stolen his country and his girl, and now they wouldn't even let him have a bed. He rose in his wrath and attacked the courier with joyful abandon. The car filled with battle and presently overflowed, as the two men rolled out of it onto the platform, and again the two shabby men passed by.

Railway officials and sentries rushed to the scene of battle. Railway officials picked up the courier and dusted him, while sentries picked up the soldier and shook him. And just at this moment a shabbily dressed man registered a suitcase through to Cologne.

The courier resumed his dignity and straightened his tie. Then he indicated Friedrich.

"The disgusting fellow is simply beastly drunk," he said.

The fire of battle died down in Friedrich, who drooped like a fading lily in the arms of his captors.

"I'm not," he protested, "I only wanna go sleep."

At this moment the guard was bestowing the suitcase in the baggage car for Cologne. He locked the doors.

The courier turned to the car and looked on the seat for his bag. It was not there.

This was just plain impossible, it must be there. He looked on the floor and then on the seat again, but the bag had not returned. He let out an agonized howl which brought officials running.

"My bag! It is gone. I put it on this seat."

"It cannot have gone, Herr Kurier," said the agitated stationmaster. "It must have slipped down."

But it had not.

"That man," said the courier, pointing at Lunden, "has taken it."

Friedrich, who had gone to sleep in a leaning position, took no notice, but the sentries examined him.

"It is not here, Herr Bahnhofvorsteher," they said truthfully. "Wake up, pig of a Schleswiger, and tell us what you've done with the gentleman's bag."

"I never touched it," wailed Friedrich, who had reverted to the tearful stage. "I never saw it. I want beer. I want Katje. Ooh, don't hit me! I want to go to sleep."

"You look like getting put to sleep for good over this," said one of his guards, and Friedrich wept bitterly.

They held up the Cologne express for nearly two hours while they searched every compartment and questioned every passenger. They saw a rather silly-looking boy in the fourth class eating a horrid meal of blood-sausage and onions, but no one would suppose for a moment that he had had anything to do with it. They did not even see the older of the two shabby men, for he thought it wiser to travel on the wide shelf in front of the engine, among the jacks and breakdown tools. The only place where they did not look was through the registered baggage, which was in a sealed car; the thing couldn't possibly be in there.

"You see," said Tommy Hambledon later, piously pointing the moral, "how Heaven helps those who help themselves."

"I trust Heaven is helping the courier, too," said Bill Saunders grimly. "I think he'll need it."

Dirk Brandt saw a good deal of Max von Bodenheim in the ensuing weeks, and sometimes he strolled beside the chair along the quays in the morning sunlight; it was a favorite resort of the German's. After a time von Bodenheim would dismiss the servant, Dirk would lean on the push-bar at the back of the chair and ask endless questions merely to evoke von Bodenheim's caustic comments. One morning they went as far as the New Bridge, which was being built at that time by British prisoners of war to replace the old Bridge of Boats.

"There are some of your cousins," said von Bodenheim.

"They are not my cousins," said Dirk in an obstinate tone.

"They are an arrogant race of bandits," said von Bodenheim, "and one day soon we will smash them. They cannot be allowed to dominate practically every part of the world which is worth having. But they are our cousins, all the same; perhaps that's why we dislike them so much. It takes a relative to arouse that soul-searing hate one feels for one's aunts—have you an aunt?"

"No," said Dirk, who felt too much at peace with the world this lovely morning to harass his brains by inventing Dutch aunts.

"You are spared something. When we are young they harrow our finer feelings by telling us we have not washed behind the ears. When we grow a little older they abash us by telling in company indelicate stories of our infancy. When we grow up they dissect the lady of our choice into her component vices, and, disregarding any few shreds of virtue she may still possess, they force the revolting spectacle upon our attention, usually before breakfast. I was never at my best before breakfast."

"You don't seem to have been lucky in your female relatives," said Dirk. "Why didn't you tell them where to go?"

"Because in Germany one is brought up in a rigid code of outward respect for one's elders. One kissed their arthritic knuckles, spoke when one was spoken to, and never answered back."

"I think that is a very accurate description of how England expects to be treated," said Dirk.

"That is true. All the same, it is a mistake to underrate them. I have no patience with the fools who call them stupid; one hears it rather often. It is not true."

"My people used to call them that," said Dirk.

"Yes, and were defeated. The English don't mind appearing stupid, but it is a pose. They are financially astute—they owe that to the high proportion of Jews in the country—they are politically clever, and they know how to wait. Also their Intelligence service is second to none."

This was so unexpected that Dirk was glad he was behind the chair and not in view of von Bodenheim's observant eyes.

"Really, you surprise me," he said as casually as he could. "One never hears much about it."

"Of course not. But I imagine that even you in South Africa must have heard of the Kaiser's dispatch to the German population in the United States."

"I don't think so," said Dirk, feeling his palms grow hot. "We didn't get papers very regularly on the farm. What happened?"

"The Kaiser wrote instructions to the Germans resident in America regarding their activities in the event of the United States coming into the War. It was drafted in His Majesty's private study, kept in the safe there, and never left the room till it was entrusted to four men to take to America. On the journey one of them was always on guard. But on the very day they landed in New York the full text of the dispatch was published in every newspaper in America. It is no secret, you see."

"But," gasped Dirk, "the thing's impossible."

"Nevertheless," said von Bodenheim, "it was done."

"But how? Was—could one of the four men have been a British spy?"

"No, no, you are too romantic, my dear Brandt. It was copied before it left Berlin."

"But how?"

"Don't ask me. I doubt if anybody knows except the man who did it, and he'll never tell."

"I suppose he wouldn't dare to."

"He can't. He is dead."

"Oh, really?"

"Yes. He was indiscreet—he got careless, I suppose. One night he went to see a lady in the Elizabethenstrasse in Wiesbaden. We waited for him outside, and when he came out we got him."

"But—but how did you know he'd done it?"

"We knew. I told you, he got careless. I regretted the necessity, he was a brave man."

"Clever, too," said Dirk.

"Yes. They have no one so able now."

Dirk felt like a germ under a microscope.

"I thought you hated the English."

"I do, but I don't despise them. It will be interesting to see if they get hold of the next little surprise we have got for them."

Dirk made interested noises, and von Bodenheim went on:

"About the Hindenburg Line. Our new line of immensely strong fortified trenches to the east of the Somme. It runs from the Vimy Ridge to the Chemin de Dames, before Cambrai and by Saint-Quentin and La Fère to rejoin the old line near Reims."

"But—what about it?"

"We are evacuating the whole Somme area."

"Great heavens!"

"Wouldn't the British love to know that? You see how I trust you, Brandt."

"You may," said Dirk proudly. ("I don't believe a word of it," he said to himself.)

"All the same, if it got out I would attend to your affairs myself," said von Bodenheim grimly.

"It looks as though it's going to be a little hard on me if some British spy does get hold of it," said Dirk with a laugh.

"They won't. Only Collins could, and he's dead."

Dirk found nothing to say to this, and von Bodenheim changed the subject.

"Are you going to see that Ibsen play at the Schauspielhaus next week?"

"*Gespenster*? I am not sure. It is possible my uncle will want me to go into Holland for him next week. About wheat, I believe."

"We cannot have too much wheat," said von Bodenheim gravely.

"The food is getting very bad."

"It has got bad. The bread is appalling stuff, all hard crust on the outside and a soggy mess in the middle."

"There is a scandal about the so-called veal loaf," said Dirk, "have you heard it? That provision shop at the corner of the Höhestrasse and the Brückenstrasse was selling a veal loaf which was very cheap, quite palatable, and really nourishing. So naturally everybody rushed out and bought as much as they could. Now the rumor has gone round that the manufacturer puts anything into it that he can find in his factory—even the rats. But the poor devils who have bought it must eat it, they can't afford to waste it. I heard about it from the Bluehms, you know?"

"It is the British blockade," said von Bodenheim. "They starve women and children to unman the frontline soldier. That is modern war."

"I should like to do the same to them," said Dirk.

"Our submarines will worry them a little yet. Already, you tell me, their beefsteaks are rationed."

"Mine was rationed out of existence," laughed Dirk.

"Tell me," said von Bodenheim. "If you wished to return to England, you could, eh?"

"Oh, I suppose so, but I don't want to."

"You would, perhaps, go if there were a good enough reason?"

Dirk thought this over, and said: "You mean, if I could in any way serve Germany?"

"Precisely."

"I'd—I'd do anything! But what use should I be?"

"We'll see. I shall see you again tomorrow?"

"I'm going to the Metropol tonight, there's a new show on there."

"Perhaps I shall see you then. *Auf wiedersehen*, Brandt."

Bill Saunders strolled back to the Dom Hotel and unfolded his tale to Tommy Hambledon.

"So that's what happened to Peter Collins," said Hambledon. "God rest his soul. At least they shot him outright and did not try to make him talk— ugh! I wonder where he slipped up. We all do it, you know, sooner or later, if we keep on long enough. I shall, one day. I've lasted longer than most of 'em."

"Shur-rup," said Bill, quoting one Robey. He went on to repeat what von Bodenheim had said about the retirement from the Somme to the Hindenburg Line.

"It's a trap," said Hambledon decidedly. "I'm sure it's a trap. We pass on the news, and it's you and me for the high jump. Does it sound likely?"

"No," said Bill. "I didn't believe it myself."

" 'In vain is the net spread in sight of any bird,' " said the British agent. "We'll leave it at that."

"Talking about birds," said Bill, who was getting more sophisticated every day, "I'm going to see the new show at the Metropol tonight, and von Bodenheim is probably going too. If he wants me to go to England for German Intelligence—"

"Take it on. Has it occurred to you that you are a subject of interest to German Intelligence already? You could not easily return to England now unless they send you. You will be tailed wherever you go in Holland. They would know if you crossed to England."

A queer little thrill ran through Bill Saunders and his eyes brightened. This was Life. Tommy Hambledon watched him ruefully.

"Yes, it's got you now, and it will never let you go. When once the job has taken hold you'll find that nothing else in life has any kick in it, and apart from the job you're dead. Neither the fields of home nor the arts of peace nor the love of women will suffice."

CHAPTER SEVEN
THE EARS OF THE ENEMY

In the Cathedral Square in Cologne there is a garden which is bisected diagonally by a footpath, as well as having roads all round it, and in this transverse path an old match-seller was usually to be seen. He was obviously very poor, as his clothes were colorless and ragged, but perhaps he had a family to keep, because any observant person could see that he did a fairly good trade. He used to advertise his goods by a monotonous cry of "*Striken! Striken! Striken!*" on one melancholy note. He did not always stand in the same place. Sometimes he was at the southwest end, near the Erzbischofliches Museum, and sometimes at the Cathedral end, on the corner, whence he could be seen from some of the windows of the Dom Hotel. Hendrik Brandt looked out of his window on the second floor and saw the old man there.

"I think we are running short of matches, Dirk."

Dirk nodded, picked up his hat, and went out.

He turned right on leaving the hotel and walked up on the north side of the Cathedral, across the west end, and into the Höhestrasse, where he bought a paper and a tie. He returned through the Sporergasse into the Cathedral Square, naturally crossed the gardens by the transverse path, and passed the match-seller.

"Striken! Striken!"

"Two boxes, please," said Dirk, and gave him a mark.

"*Danke schön,*" said the match-seller.

"*Bitte schön,*" answered Dirk, and strolled nonchalantly back to the Dom Hotel.

Tommy Hambledon turned the contents of the matchboxes out on the table. One of them had a strip of thin paper underneath the matches, and on it was written: "Apples unobtainable, am sending onions."

"Leave canceled, am sending instructions," read Hambledon.

"I thought we didn't use codes."

"We don't, if you mean the kind you sit up at night with a wet towel round your head to decipher with the help of columns of figures. We have experts who do that, if it's necessary, but we do occasionally replace one simple word by another. 'Leave' is 'apples' because you hope there'll be an Eve or two about, and 'instructions' are 'onions' because we hope they'll be more unpleasant to other people than to the recipient. 'Best quality fertile eggs for setting' would of course mean 'a supply of bombs is being forwarded per passenger train.' If I assassinated the Kaiser I should write: 'Send no more umbrellas,' and they would know at once that the reign was over."

"Are you serious?" asked poor Bill.

"Seldom. Anyway, this means you, my lad. No journey to Holland to buy potatoes or whatever it was—at least, not on Wednesday."

"Wheat," said Bill. "At least, that's what I told von Bodenheim."

"Seriously, I don't think it would do any harm for you to become a little better known in Cologne. You are the favorite nephew of a rich uncle, you have money to burn for the first time in your life, and it goes to your head. You are young, impulsive, and silly. You have attacks of paralytic shyness followed by shattering exhibitions of misdirected energy. You are fairly easily affected by drink at present—you can become hardened to it by degrees if convenient—it may take the form of beaming upon everyone, retiring to some quiet spot and going to sleep. That's always a good idea, for if people think you are wrapped in a drunken slumber, they won't worry about you. Let no man, and especially no woman think you have a single idea beyond having a good time. When in doubt, put on that boiled-codfish expression which seems to come so naturally to you, and in moments of embarrassment think of cold pickled pork."

"Why?"

"It takes your mind off," said the man of experience.

About nine that night young Dirk Brandt drifted into the Metropol. There was a cabaret show in progress and the place was well filled with apparently cheerful people making a good deal of noise; officers on leave mostly, and ladies who, generally speaking, were not their sisters. The air was hazy with smoke and the conversation with drink, there were many bright lights reflected in numerous mirrors, and much sumptuous gilding; in fact, the whole effect seemed to overpower the boy who came in and stood blinking inside the door, looking like a rather cross rabbit. After a moment an acquaintance called across to him:

"Hullo, Brandt! Come and talk to us."

The boy cheered up visibly and went to the table where a man and two dazzling blondes were sitting.

"Leutnant Bluehm! I'm so glad to see you again."

"May I present Herr Dirk Brandt—Fräulein Elsa Schwiss, Fräulein Hedwige Schwiss."

Dirk bowed from the hips and kissed their hands in the prescribed manner.

"They are the Bavarian Nightingales you see on the posters," continued Bluehm. "They sing, I believe. You do sing, don't you?"

"We try to, Herr Leutnant," they said more or less together, and giggled.

"Do you do anything else besides sing?"

"Oh, Herr Leutnant!"

"I mean, do you dance too?"

"Sometimes, Herr Leutnant."

"Charming, charming. Do you do anything else?"

"We play duets on the piano, Herr Leutnant, when we are quite alone," said Fräulein Elsa, and the girls held hands and giggled again.

"I shouldn't think that often happens, does it?"

They evidently considered this the height of wit, for they leaned their heads together and pealed with laughter.

"Not very often, Herr Leutnant," said Fräulein Hedwige when she had recovered enough to speak.

"Sit down, Brandt, and have a drink—will you join us?"

"Thank you," said Dirk, and sat down. "Tell me, Fräuleins, are you really sisters?"

"Of course, Herr Brandt," said Elsa.

"Can't you see the likeness, Herr Brandt?" asked Hedwige, and again they leaned their heads together and looked coyly at him.

"You make me wish I were a photographer," said Dirk, "when you sit together like that."

"We had our photograph taken like this once," said Elsa. "It was much admired."

"Somehow," said Bluehm indulgently, "I was beginning to think you had."

This struck Dirk as funny, and he laughed uproariously. The Bavarian Nightingales, for once, did not.

"I've got a horrid 'ickle feeling he's laughing at poor 'ickle us," said Elsa to Hedwige.

"So have I," agreed Hedwige, and they nodded at each other and then looked reproachfully at Bluehm.

"Have another drink," said he.

There was a burst of laughter and babble from a party at a nearby table, and they all looked round to see what was happening.

"You can't expect me to believe that!" said a girl.

"It's true, upon my honor," said a dark saturnine officer in Flying Corps uniform, who had evidently been telling a story.

"So what did he do then?"

"He sort of looked round, don't you know, for something to brain her with," said the flying man, in a tired drawl, "and he saw one of those poker-work outfits on the table ladies play with, don't you know? Pictures of Ehrenbreitstein on milking-stools. So he got it going and drew the Hussars' skull-and-crossbones on her. It was his old regiment, you know."

"Where?" asked another man at the table.

"At Minden on the Weser," said the flying man solemnly, and drained his glass.

"Minden," thought Dirk, and the Hampshires wear red roses in their caps every first of August for Minden, when they and the Hanoverians beat the French. And he was a man of the Hampshires here among this rowdy crew, if only they knew it, and a man must speak of Minden. ...

"What are you thinking of, Brandt?"

Bill Saunders returned with a jerk.

"Only wondering if it hurt," said he, with his most innocent look.

("You're not Bill Saunders of the Hampshires, you're Dirk Brandt from Lichtenburg," he said fiercely to himself. "Never do that again.")

"I'm afraid it must have done," said Fräulein Elsa with a graceful shudder.

"The lady was past noticing a little thing like that," said Bluehm.

"How do you know, Bluehm?"

"Oh, I've heard it before. Knirim always tells that story when he gets tight."

"Tell Herr Brandt about it," urged Hedwige, "it's simply screamingly funny."

"No," said Bluehm slowly. "I don't think I will, it isn't a very nice story." And, oddly enough, he looked, not at the two girls, but at Dirk Brandt's wide blue eyes.

"Have another drink," said Bluehm.

"What's the time?" asked Elsa. "Oh, we must go, Herr Leutnant, we're on in five minutes. We shall see you afterwards, shan't we?" she said, and got up.

"Maybe," said Bluehm, "we'll see."

"Oh, do let's," said the lovely Hedwige, leaning across the table, "we shall be so disappointed if we don't!"

"Fräulein, the disappointment will be all mine," said Bluehm, bowing over her hand, "and it will be almost more than I can bear. But it is the last night of my leave," he went on in a lower tone while Dirk pretended not to hear, "and my mother and my sisters are at home—"

"I understand," she said, but looked at him wistfully.

"I will come if I can," he said hastily. "You know that," and she smiled, pressed his hand, and hurried away.

"Rather nice girls, those two," said Bluehm carelessly. "Unlike most of these cabaret singers we have here, who are just out for what they can get. Daughters of the horseleech, most of 'em," he went on biblically. "Children of Erebus. Vestals of Aphrodite."

"Rather hot stuff, in short," said Dirk cheerfully.

"You let 'em alone, young feller," said his senior by nearly four years, "or you'll regret it."

He emptied his glass; Dirk said: "Have one with me now," and ordered it.

"I expect you think," said Bluehm, whose speech was becoming a little careful, "that I am not old enough to advise you. It is true that in years I am only just twenty-one, but I have had nearly three years of war, and in experience and—er—wear and tear, as it were, I am middle-aged. It's sad, isn't it? A whole generation, and all middle-aged." He stared gloomily across the room at the Bavarian Nightingales, who tripped prettily onto the stage and began to sing.

Flying Officer Knirim came from the other table to sit at theirs, and said: "Hullo, Vi'let, still here?"

"Till tomorrow," said Bluehm. "May I present Herr Dirk Brandt? Nephew of our benefactor, Hendrik Brandt, to whom we owe most of what food is really edible in Cologne."

"Welcome, nephew of our uncle," said Knirim. "Been here before?"

"Never," said Dirk shyly.

"And what do you think of Cologne? Have you visited the Cathedral? And the Wallraf-Rickarts Museum?"

"No," said Bluehm, coming to the rescue, "but he is much impressed by our Kammachgasse."

Dirk laughed, and Knirim said: "I beg your pardon. I have had too much to drink and I am always rude when I am drunk. I hope you will be very happy here."

"Thank you," said Dirk, and blushed becomingly. "Have a drink?"

"What is it? Goldwasser? Heavens, yes. Far better than what we've been having. Thank you."

"How's things, Knirim?"

"Oh, not going too badly. We should finish the job by next Thursday."

"So soon? When I was there about a week ago it looked as though they'd never get all that stuff back. The transport was everlastingly getting bogged."

"Oh, you were on the Somme so lately, were you? Well, you'll be more comfortable when you go back."

"I hope so," said Bluehm.

"You'll be able to flower in comfort, my Vi'let."

Knirim saw Dirk's look of surprise and deigned to explain.

"You see, his name sounds rather like 'bloom,' so we call him Violet because he shrinks. Do you still shrink, Vi'let?"

"Habitually," said Bluehm. "In fact, I shrink from the row that's going on here; you can't hear a note of the songs. Let's go somewhere else."

Max von Bodenheim came from the other end of the room on his way to the door and paused at their table.

"Good evening," he said. "Enjoying yourselves?"

"Not particularly," said Knirim. "In fact, we were thinking of trying our luck elsewhere."

"Let's go to the Palant," said Bluehm.

"Have a drink, sir?" said Dirk.

Von Bodenheim glanced at the bottle and said: "Please. Who told you to order that?"

"My uncle recommended it," said Dirk modestly.

"Your uncle has damn good taste," said Knirim. "Let's finish the bottle before we go on. Here's to—to a lucky move, eh, Bluehm?"

"Let's go to the Palant," said Bluehm.

"And that's better still," said Knirim. "Heard the news, von Bodenheim?"

"Probably," he said, turning a repressive stare on Knirim, but the flying man was past noticing details.

"About the new line," he said. "We move back on Thurs—"

"You blasted fool," said von Bodenheim in a tone of biting scorn. "How many times have you blabbed that about tonight?"

"Not at all," said Knirim indignantly. "What's wrong? We're all friends here."

"How long have you known Brandt?"

Knirim glanced at the clock and said casually: "Oh—about half an hour."

"It's lucky for you I can answer for Brandt," said von Bodenheim. "Do you see that notice on the wall?"

Knirim read it aloud. " 'Guard your tongue, the ears of the enemy are open.' Oh, they stick that up wherever one goes."

"Yes, and it's meant for fools like you."

"Let's go to the Palant," said Bluehm.

"Will you come too, sir?" said Dirk to von Bodenheim.

He recovered his temper with an effort, and said: "Yes, let's go. Coming, Knirim?"

"No, I think I'll stay on for a while," said Knirim sulkily, and strolled off.

"Just a moment," said von Bodenheim. He wheeled his chair across the room and signaled to an officer sitting at a table in the corner. The latter got up and exchanged a few quiet words with von Bodenheim, who returned to Bluehm and Brandt and said: "Well, shall we go?"

They walked past the Neumarkt and down the Schildergasse, with Bluehm and Dirk on either side of the chair which the one-legged soldier was pushing. Just at the corner of the Herzogstrasse a car overtook them, and the light of a street lamp fell on the faces of its occupants.

"Why," said Bluehm, "there's Knirim."

"Yes," said von Bodenheim.

"It's a staff car, too," said Bluehm.

"Yes," said von Bodenheim again.

Dirk glanced at Bluehm and saw that his face was white. They went on without speaking to the next corner, where Bluehm stopped and said: "I think, if you will excuse me, I should really go home. It is, after all, the last night of my leave, and there are my mother and my sisters. It was thoughtless of me to stay out so long."

Max von Bodenheim shook hands with him and said: "Of course, as you wish. Good luck, Bluehm."

"Good luck, Bluehm," said Dirk. "*Auf wiedersehen.*"

Bluehm saluted and marched off perfectly steadily down a side turning, and von Bodenheim watched him till he was out of sight.

"Wonderfully sobering effect the night air has," he said.

"Yes," said Dirk.

Von Bodenheim looked up at him and laughed.

"Have you got the wind up too?"

Dirk had and, what was more, thought it politic to show it.

"What will they do to him?" he asked nervously.

"What do you think? Shoot him?"

At that moment they heard rapid steps coming towards them, and Bluehm came up to the chair again.

"You know," he said, "I don't think Knirim talked to anyone but us. He wasn't so bad till he got to our table—it was Brandt's Goldwasser that finished him off."

"Thank you, Bluehm," said von Bodenheim. "Good night."

"Er—good night," said Bluehm. He hung hesitantly upon one foot for a moment, then turned on his heel and went.

"No, they won't shoot him," said von Bodenheim. "They won't waste a good man like that. He will wake up tomorrow to find himself a private in a line regiment on his way to the front, that's all. He won't like it, of course, after the Hussars and the Flying Corps."

"I see," said Dirk dubiously. "So that's all."

"Well, shall we go on to the Café Palant in spite of having lost our Violet?"

"Yes, if you would care to. By the way, I wanted to tell you—my trip is put off for a few days after all. The wheat ship I was after is at the bottom of the North Sea; one of our U-boats made a little mistake, apparently."

"Oh, that's too bad," said von Bodenheim with a laugh. "These accidents will happen. I told you there would be some fun with them soon. After all, they could not label her 'For the Fatherland—do not touch!' "

They entered the Café Palant, the soldier servant stood back at the door, and Max von Bodenheim led the way to a table in an angle between the wall and the foot of the stairs.

"I generally sit here," he said, wheeling himself into the angle as the waiter cleared chairs out of his path. "One is less likely to be in the way."

"One is less likely to be overheard, too," thought Dirk as he sat down with his back to the wall and picked up the menu. "Believe it or not, I'm hungry," he added aloud.

"So you won't be going away just yet," said von Bodenheim, when they had given their order.

"I suppose not," said Dirk. "I shouldn't, unless there were anything to go for. There's plenty to do in the business here."

"I expect there is." Von Bodenheim leaned forward across the table as though he were trying to look round the square pillar in the middle of the room at the orchestra opposite. "Unless we asked you to go?"

"But my uncle?"

"He would raise no objection."

"Oh, wouldn't he? I should have thought he would."

Von Bodenheim laughed. "In the first place, I don't think he'd want to. We have a—a little influence over him."

Dirk raised incredulous eyes to the German. "What, you mean—er, your people—" he said, in awed tones.

"The department, yes. You see, he did a little job for us in England once."

"You do surprise me," said Dirk truthfully.

"Yes. He didn't want to, and he got badly frightened. In fact, I believe he was nearly caught. He left England in considerable haste, and refuses flatly ever to go back again."

Dirk laughed, he had to.

"It sounds so comic," he said. "He's so—so dignified and all that, isn't he? I can't imagine him hareing towards the docks with the police hot on his trail—"

"You idiot," said von Bodenheim, laughing. "I didn't mean he actually ran in the physical sense—"

"With an attache-case bearing his initials in one hand and an umbrella in the other, covering the ground like a startled antelope—"

"Here's your Wiener schnitzel," said his amused companion. "What are you drinking?"

"Lager," said Dirk. When the waiter had gone, he said: "I had no idea of anything like that."

"You'd better not remind him, it might be tactless."

"I didn't know you knew him."

"I don't; as it happens, all this happened before I came to Cologne. If I met him now, it would be as an ordinary acquaintance."

"Of course," said Dirk submissively.

"But, naturally, things would be much easier for you. You are a British subject and have a perfect right to be there."

Dirk made a little grimace, as though the reminder were distasteful, and said: "Yes, but what good could I do? I don't know anything about guns or fortifications or aeroplanes."

"Lots of good. You can talk to soldiers everywhere and find out all you can about troop movements, how training is going on, are they short of equipment, and so on. You can find out what effect the air raids had on the civilian population. Are they short of food? Is there much shipping laid up round the coasts? What do they think of the submarine campaign and—if you have the luck, which I doubt—what are they doing to combat it? You'd better go to Chatham and Portsmouth and talk to sailors in taverns. You see, we are so short of news from England that almost anything is of value."

"I see. Well, sir, I'll do what I can."

"Good lad."

"What about my uncle? Do I—"

"Do nothing. Wait, and you'll find things will arrange themselves."

"Talk of the devil," exclaimed Dirk, "there he is! Not the devil, far from it. I mean my uncle. Gay old bird, who'd expect to find him here? That man who has just stood up, in the far corner. May I present him, sir?"

"Please," said von Bodenheim, and Dirk crossed the room to meet Hendrik Brandt.

"The news we heard about the Kluges is true," said Dirk, without attempting to lower his voice as they edged their way between the tables. "They go on Thursday."

"Really," said Hendrik Brandt calmly. "Frau Kluge will be pleased, it's much pleasanter in the Siebengebirge."

"Much," said Dirk. "Von Bodenheim is over there by the stairs. He says he always gets that table."

"Epitaph for a great man," murmured Brandt. " 'He always got a table.' "

Dirk presented his uncle to Max von Bodenheim, who said: "I cannot think why we have never met before."

"I do not go out a great deal," said the importer mildly. "Socially, I mean; indeed, I came here tonight to meet a business acquaintance—my business occupies most of my time and all my energies. Things are very difficult. Difficult and disappointing. There is this little matter of a cargo of wheat—"

"Your nephew told me," said the German gravely. "It is a serious matter."

"It is indeed. Not only the financial loss, which is serious, but the thought of all that good food being wasted when it is so sorely needed. But I must not talk business here at this hour, it is most out of place. Dirk, my boy, what are you drinking?"

"Lager, Onkel Hendrik."

"That's right, lad. Lager is quite enough for you at your age."

Von Bodenheim, who had noticed on various occasions that Dirk could manage quite a quantity of assorted drinks without becoming more than amiably sleepy, smiled and said: "Quite right."

"I am glad you agree with me, Herr Kapitan. It is a responsibility, believe me, to be in charge of a young relative for whom one is answerable to one's sister, especially in a city like Cologne in times like these."

"It must be," said von Bodenheim, fidgeting slightly.

"In fact, were it not for the confidence I feel in his mother's strong moral influence and sound upbringing, I should hesitate to expose so young and inexperienced a lad to the temptations inevitable to such a situation as his."

"Quite," said von Bodenheim, and yawned irrepressibly. "I beg your pardon."

"I weary you," said Herr Brandt unerringly. "Come, Dirk. If the Herr Kapitan von Bodenheim will excuse us—"

"It has been a pleasure," said von Bodenheim.

"It has been an honor," said Hendrik Brandt.

CHAPTER EIGHT
T-L-T MÜLHEIM

They walked the short distance to the Dom Hotel talking of indifferent matters and enjoying the cool night air in the empty streets. They went into Hendrik Brandt's room and Bill said: "What do you think of von Bodenheim?"

"Hot stuff, very. So much so that I hope he'll never want to see me again. I do not desire that he should cultivate my acquaintance. He is too intelligent."

"You took care he shouldn't think that of you."

"Great care."

"I only hope he didn't see that your business acquaintance had wonderful golden hair."

"He wasn't standing up," said Tommy Hambledon, "you were. Now, what's all this?"

"It's true about the retirement to the Hindenburg Line," said Bill. "They hope to move back on Thursday." He repeated Knirim's indiscretions.

"Slogan for teetotalers," said Hambledon. " 'Beware of drink, it is a friend to the enemy.' Today's Monday. No, it's now Tuesday morning. Heavens, the time is short. Old Reck is our only hope and I fear he'll be too late."

"Old wreck?"

"R-e-c-k. He's not so very old, either. He is the science master at that big school at Mülheim—the one with the tower."

"What does he do?"

"Spark wireless. He transmits messages in Morse. In code, of course, that's a case where code is absolutely necessary."

"A transmitting wireless station—at Mülheim?"

"Certainly. Why not? There was one in Berlin at one time, close to the Wilhelmstrasse, a building with a copper dome. The dome served as an aerial, I believe; I am a child in these matters."

"It's incredible!"

"It's true. What's more, it was months before the Germans found it, though it was so loud it drowned nearly every wireless station in Prussia."

"And what's-his-name runs one at Mülheim?"

"Reck. Yes. It's too late to do anything now, he only transmits at night, of course. I'll send him a message to meet us at the Germania tomorrow. Old 'Striken' will take it. We will draft a message and Reck will code it and send it off. With luck, they'll have twenty-four hours' notice. We can't do any more."

"Can't I go out to Mülheim tonight?"

"No good. It'll take him some time to code it, and by the time you've got there and he's done that, morning will have gilded the skies and all his dear scholars will be buzzing round and hanging with reverent awe upon every word that falls from his lips—I don't think. He keeps silkworms."

"Why?"

"A useful and paying hobby. He corresponds with fellow enthusiasts in neutral countries—no doubt they exchange pedigree sires and things. Besides, it's always nice to have a few boxes nobody wants to look into. Besides again, it makes a pleasant outing on a summer's day to hop on your bike and buzz off somewhere to collect mulberry leaves. One meets quite interesting people sometimes, collecting mulberry leaves. Strange, isn't it, to think of Intelligence keeping a list of all the addresses of all the mulberry trees within a thirty-mile radius of Mülheim?"

"Sounds like a popular song," said Dirk. " 'Meet me by the mulberry tree, For I would have a word with thee.' " He yawned suddenly. "I beg your pardon. By the way, I was most interested to hear that you had done a little job for German Intelligence and made England too hot to hold you."

"Von Bodenheim tell you that? Good. I started that little story myself," said Hambledon. "Glad it's got round."

They left the office in the Höhestrasse in the middle of the afternoon for coffee and cakes at the Germania. The place was fairly full, and they found themselves obliged to share a table with a nondescript little man who was sitting alone and reading a technical magazine.

"May we sit here?" asked Hendrik Brandt. "I am so sorry, but the place seems crowded today."

"Oh, please do," said the man, and removed his literature from the sugar-basin.

"I am distressed to interrupt your reading," said Brandt.

"It is of no consequence," said the man politely. "I had finished the article in which I was interested." He shut the magazine and put it on the corner of the table. The waitress took their order and retired again. There was a longish pause.

"The weather is lovely for the time of year," said Herr Brandt.

"It is, indeed, beautiful," agreed the man.

"It is pleasant to find the days drawing out."

"Spring is, in fact, here."

"That is true. One hopes the winter is now over, for the sake of our poor boys at the front."

"Yes, indeed."

"One fears their hardships must have been terrible."

"As to that," said the man, "I have no information."

"I am no better informed than the next man myself," admitted Brandt. "But one hears stories from soldiers on leave—"

"Sir," said the stranger, "I am convinced you mean no harm, but there is a notice on the wall to which, I am sure, we ought all to pay attention." He pointed it out; like the one at the Metropol it ran: "Guard your tongue, the ears of the enemy are open."

"Sir," said Brandt admiringly, "how right you are! If only everyone were as careful—"

"It is only our duty," said the man, and at that moment the waitress returned with a loaded tray. Hendrik Brandt, always thoughtful, hastened to help her by moving some of the things on the table, and in so doing knocked down the magazine. Apologizing for his stupidity, he handed it to the stranger, who said it was of no consequence, and tossed it carelessly on the spare chair. Uncle and nephew confined their interest and comments to the cakes, the room began to clear, the stranger picked up his magazine, bowed, and went.

"Won't he know if he's successful?" asked Bill.

"No. He can't receive, he only transmits. Must be a queer life, sitting up at night popping out disconnected letters into the blue, with one ear cocked for a stealthy step on the stairs, and never an answering sound from the outer darkness to cheer his shuddering soul."

"You are making my flesh creep," said Bill.

Late that night the inconspicuous man crept from his bedroom to the closet off the physics laboratory where he kept his silkworms, opened a box, pushed his arm under a branch of mulberry covered with sleeping innocents—presumably even a silkworm sleeps sometimes—and drew out an electrical coil which once formed part of the works of a car. He took it into the laboratory and fitted it into its appropriate place in a polished wooden box such as usually contains a laboratory balance. He shut the box up and rattled the catch a few times to see if it was in working order. The catch looked ordinary enough, but it was not. It was, in fact, a tapping key.

He carried the box across the room and put it on a workbench close to a window which was a few inches open. He put his hand out, felt about in the ivy outside, and drew in a wire which he connected to the box.

The other end of the wire would have interested anyone in the school who was afraid of thunderstorms, for it was connected to the lightning-conductor which came down the tower, and the conductor had been cut at that point and carefully insulated. It had become, in fact, a wireless aerial.

The man pulled a stool up to the bench, sat on it, drew the box towards him, and began tapping out dash—dot dot dot dot—dash, pause, dash—dot dot dot dot—dash, pause, TLT, pause, TLT, to those whom it might concern, the call-sign of Reck of Mülheim. There followed a string of apparently meaningless letters.

The wireless operator on the destroyer pushed up his earphones for a few minutes' rest as the sublieutenant came in with a message from the bridge.

"Yes, I'll send it," he said, "but I'll eat my aunt's galoshes if anyone gets it. The atmospherics tonight are simply deafening."

"The old man wants to know if you've heard anything from the flagship yet."

"Nothing, and I'm not likely to till this electrical storm eases up. If the whole German fleet was out tonight talking all round us I shouldn't know it." He pulled his earphones on again.

"TLT," said the Morse, "TLT. BXAN—" The rest was lost in bangs and crackles.

"TLT," said the operator. "I've got that half a dozen times in quiet moments, but the dear knows what the poor old buffer is trying to say."

"Who is he?" asked the sub.

"Some chap in the Fatherland with a spark transmitter."

"Wonder if it's anything important."

"He wouldn't wake up half Germany to tell us baby'd cut a tooth, you know. Tell the old man it's hopeless at present, but may improve later."

On Saturday in that week Bill Saunders walked out of Liverpool Street Station and was confronted with a row of screaming posters.

"Great British Advance," they said. "Germans retreat on 100-mile front. Australians capture Bapaume. Great Allied Victory." He bought a paper and read hastily down the leaded paragraphs, evidently the affair was a complete surprise.

"So it failed after all," he said. "Damn."

He went to an inconspicuous restaurant with a markedly Eastern atmosphere up two flights of stairs from Piccadilly Circus, to meet a friend from the War Office. They had an excellent lunch without being asked for meat coupons, which was the singular achievement of this establishment, and over strong black coffee poured from a brass pot by an impassive Oriental, Bill Saunders unfolded his tale.

"I came over," he said, "principally because Hambledon wanted to know if you heard anything over here about a new valve of some kind in the envelopes of the latest Zepps. Our information is of the sketchiest, but apparently this new device enables them to climb at a much steeper angle than the previous ones could, and to reach a much greater altitude."

"We knew," said the man from the War Office, "that if they climbed too steeply or went too high they had trouble with the hydrogen expanding. I believe they had some bursts."

"I don't know any details. The fellow who talked was in the boastful stage of drink. He merely said that now the Zepps could come in at a height where none of our planes could reach 'em even if they knew they were there. Then they could come down, lay their eggs, and off up again like a rocketing pheasant. He said their new valve would teach the *verdammt* English something, and then one of the other men dug him in the ribs and he dried up finally."

"And where were you while all this was going on?"

"Oh, only washing up glasses behind the bar. It's a foul little pub on the outskirts of Ahlhorn; the mechanics go in there for their half-pints. I was supposed to be walking from Osnabruck to Wilhelmshaven to join the navy."

"What's put you on to this?"

"Something von Bodenheim said about recently increased efficiency, so

I dropped in there on the way home, as it were, and had a chat with Hamble-don over the phone about it. We talked about a new kind of self-raising flour, and Hambledon said I had better speak to our importers about it."

"We haven't heard anything here, but I will have inquiries made. Anything else?"

Bill Saunders went on to give the rest of his news, adding: "Von Boden-heim seems to be quite important."

"We have heard of von Bodenheim from Berlin," said his hearer. "He is definitely important. You have done well to get into touch with him, and to have been asked to work for German Intelligence should prove useful. Very useful. Not to beat about the bush, I consider you have done well."

Bill Saunders made suitably deprecatory noises.

"It was unfortunate that the news about the German retirement did not reach us, but the electrical storm which covered a large part of southeastern Germany and the North Sea that night paralyzed wireless communication over a wide area."

"So that's what happened. I wondered if the poor chap had come to grief."

"His call-sign, TLT, was picked up by a destroyer off the Scheldt that night, but the rest of the message was lost. Unfortunate."

"About von Bodenheim—"

"You shall be provided with useful information to give him—information which he can check and find correct—that is, if he has anybody to check it. He would be pleased if you could arrange an agent or two for him in England, I think."

"He'd be delighted, but how can I do it? I am not supposed to know anybody in England."

"You met a German woman in Holland—where did you go? Utrecht? Of course. In Utrecht—whose husband is an Irishman named, let me see, Butler is a name of no particular nationality, but common in Ireland. She lay doggo here when she found all her fellow countrymen being gathered in, and remained undiscovered. She went across to Holland—what for?"

"To see her aged aunt?" suggested Bill.

"Would anybody cross the North Sea at a time of unrestricted submarine warfare to see an aunt? She went about money. Her father, who was a prosperous market gardener in Westphalia—I'll give you his name and address later on—died recently, and she went to see a friend in Holland about the expected legacy. Butler works as a porter at Euston, he is over military age. What more natural than that you should go and see him? He does not like the English. I think that is good enough even for von Bodenheim, especially if he looks up the recently lamented and finds he has a married daughter in England. Yes. Armed with that and some information which I will give you later, you should be a godsend to von Bodenheim."

"What do I do at the moment?"

"Keep quiet. You realize that you aren't supposed to be in England at all? Privates of the line don't get leave at the end of only six months. I'm sorry, but you mustn't be seen by anybody who knows you, nor must you go back too soon or von Bodenheim won't believe you've seen all you say. Let me see, do you fish?"

"Yes, sir," said Bill, remembering Itchen and Test.

"Good. Go to a quiet hotel for tonight and come and see me at ten thirty tomorrow morning. I think I can fix up something for you. There are lots of hotels in Bloomsbury; any one will do."

"Where's Bloomsbury?" asked the British agent from Cologne.

Ten days later he returned to the Dom Hotel and rang up von Bodenheim's house. The German was at home.

"I should like to see you," he said. "Can you come here now?"

"I'll see if my uncle can spare me," said the dutiful Dirk Brandt. "I'll come at once if he can; if not, I'll ring again."

He put the receiver down and said: "He's there. Shall I go at once?"

"I think the enthusiastic young Intelligence agent would leap on the first tram," said Tommy Hambledon. "You know what to say to him."

"Yes, that's all right," said Bill Saunders. He crossed to the cupboard, took out a decanter and a glass, and poured himself out a drink.

"Have you come to that already?" asked Hambledon in a flat voice.

"What do you mean? I've practically been on the water-cart in England."

Hambledon said nothing.

"Besides, one wants to be on one's toes with the Herr Kapitan Max von Bodenheim."

"Quite," said Hambledon.

"Well, here's luck," said the boy. He emptied the glass, picked up his hat, and walked out of the room with a slight swagger. Hambledon watched him go, sighed faintly, and went on checking invoices.

Von Bodenheim greeted Dirk with obvious pleasure. "I am very glad to see you again," he said. "What will you drink? There is still some whisky. How did you get on? Do you like England any better?"

"I did my best," said Dirk modestly, "but I'm afraid I haven't got much for you. It's difficult to make soldiers and sailors talk, now one can't stand them a drink—there's what they call a no-treating order in force."

"Perhaps that's why they introduced it," said von Bodenheim.

"I went down and had a look at Southampton Water, nobody seemed to mind. They've had so many ships damaged by torpedoes lately that the shipyards can't cope with the rush, so they beach them on the mud to wait their turn. There are lots of 'em on the Beaulieu shore—I saw the *Gloucester Castle* with a hole in her side you could have driven a tram through."

"So," said the German. "It seems that they by no means invariably sink."

"Oh, quite a lot of them do," said Dirk cheerfully. "I couldn't find out what they were doing about it, though. I did notice, by the way, that they were restringing the overhead wires of the Southampton trams with real copper wire."

"No shortage of that."

"No, but they're terribly short of sugar and meat. You see long queues waiting for the shops that are open, but quite often the butchers put a notice up: 'No meat today,' and just shut."

"So. You say the shipyards are busy?"

"Yes, on these repairs, and building new ships. One man told me that even some of the smaller shipyards are turning out one destroyer a month."

"Let me refill your glass," said von Bodenheim. "It seems to me you have used your eyes to extraordinary good purpose. Please go on."

"What else? I think you asked if they were short of arms and equipment. I couldn't find out what was happening in any of the factories, except that they are working day and night."

"The devil they are!"

"There are a tremendous lot of Americans coming over now."

"And the English, how are they taking it? Are they weary of the war?"

"There are some—what do they call 'em?—conscientious objectors," said Dirk. "Men who feel that war in any cause is wicked, so they won't take any part in it. They are sent to prison."

"Are there many of them, and what do the public think of them?"

"The public jeer at them and call them cowards. There must be a pretty good system over there now; I was told they could turn a plowboy into a soldier in three months, including ten days' draft leave."

"They must have some first-class noncommissioned officers, then," said von Bodenheim appreciatively.

"I can't think of anything else except that they are desperately short of matches; I couldn't buy a box. Everyone is using those tinder lighters for cigarettes—I brought you one, sir, as a memento, here it is—they are useful in the open air, as wind only makes them glow all the better. Look. You pull the tinder wick up to the level of the flint and then spin the wheel on the palm of your hand; that's got it, do you see?"

"Very ingenious," said the German, playing with the lighter. "Very clever. Thank you, Brandt, I shall value this, from you."

Dirk colored up and said: "It's nothing—I'm glad you like it. There was one other thing I did. I don't know whether you'll approve; if not, we needn't go on with it." He unfolded his story of Butler, the Euston porter and his German wife. "I thought he might come in useful, sir; you said we were terribly short of people over there. They seemed genuine to me, but you can verify the woman's father at Soest, Muller was his name, I've got his full address somewhere," he went on, looking through his wallet. "She wrote it down for me. Here it is." He pulled out a piece of thin bluish paper with unmistakably German writing on it and handed it over. As he did so a small piece of paper fell out and he picked it up. "What's this? Oh, Southampton tram ticket, that's all." He twisted it up and threw it in the ashtray.

"My dear boy," said von Bodenheim, "you have done extraordinarily well, especially considering that you did not know anyone and had no contacts. I am very pleased. You must have a natural gift for this kind of thing—I am glad you're not working for British Intelligence." He laughed easily, but his eyes never left Dirk's face.

But the boy never turned a hair. "You flatter me, sir," he said earnestly. "I was lucky, that's all."

Von Bodenheim lifted his glass. "Luck comes to those who deserve her," he said. "Your health, and may this be the forerunner of many more successes."

"Here's to you, sir," said Dirk, "who showed me the way."

"I must report all this," said the German. "I will have enquiries made about this Butler woman."

"I should go back," said Dirk, rising. "I had only seen my uncle for ten minutes before ringing you up. I have to report to him on some business I did in Holland."

Dirk had gone about fifty yards down the road when he remembered he had left his hat in von Bodenheim's room, so he went back for it, and then returned to the office in the Höhestrasse.

"Well, that went off all right, so far," said he. "He was particularly pleased about Butler."

"He would be," said Tommy Hambledon. "They are so short of agents in

Great Britain that a semi-imbecile deaf-mute would be welcome. But what did you mean by 'so far' in that doubtful tone?"

"I dropped a Southampton tram ticket," said Bill, "so I screwed it up and threw it in the ashtray. Then after I'd left I went back for my hat—"

"Which you'd forgotten on purpose?"

"*Näturlich*," grinned the boy. "And the ticket was screwed up differently. He does not quite trust me."

"When you've been on the job for as long as von Bodenheim, you'll find you don't trust anybody. You'll find you can't trust anybody, not even when you want to. That's the hell of it. For the rest of your life you'll find yourself laying little traps for the people you most care for, to see if they fall—" Hambledon's voice tailed off.

"Don't you trust me?" asked Bill Saunders, thoroughly taken aback.

"At present," said Hambledon sternly. "I merely expect to be able to trust you. Understand?"

"Yes, sir," said Michael Kingston from Chappell's School.

CHAPTER NINE
SALUS POPULI SUPREMA LEX

Some months passed during which nothing happened of any particular moment, and Dirk Brandt became gradually absorbed into the daily life of Cologne. They observed troop movements and ration restrictions, and passed harmless but interesting news to von Bodenheim from the helpful Butler. It was all quite easy but rather dull, and Bill Saunders was rash enough to say so one day.

Tommy Hambledon looked at him with marked distaste. "I suppose you had to choose this morning to make an ill-omened remark like that," he said. "I have just heard that a horrid rumor has reached the ears of authority to the effect that Germany proposes to bring Great Britain to her knees by strafing the civil population. The idea, apparently, is to drop cholera germs in the various reservoirs round London and leave nature to do the rest."

"How increasingly beastly!" said Bill Saunders. "How is it going to be worked, and where do they get the bugs from?"

"They are going to be dropped from aeroplanes, and it's the question of where the bugs come from that concerns us. Our informant only says that he gathers there was a technical difficulty about dropping cholera bugs a couple of thousand feet, or they would have done it long ago. Now, it appears, some ancient retired professor has solved the problem, and it is up to us to find and discourage him. When I say 'us' I don't mean only you and me. Every British agent in Germany is going through all the retired professors on his visiting-list with a fine-tooth comb, all other activities being laid aside for the moment. It is as serious as that."

"So," said Bill, who had picked up the expression from von Bodenheim and used it even in English. "Have we any professors in stock?"

"Quite a lot, not in Cologne, but around. This is rather a favorite district for retiring to. Let me turn them up. There's Paffrath at Düren. He's a— one moment. Research into Industrial Diseases. Possible, though I shouldn't call cholera an industrial disease; in fact, you don't get it if you are industrious—at keeping the sanitary system in order. There's Rötlander of Bonn. Professor of Tropical Diseases. That's more likely, we will investigate the Herr Professor Rötlander of Bonn. There's the Herr Doktor Bauer of Siegburg. He isn't a professor but he has a great reputation in medicine. I don't know any of these people personally."

"I say," said Bill Saunders, "I hate to be so optimistic, but couldn't it be almost any doctor?"

"No, thank God," said Hambledon, and meant it. "It's a little more limited than that. Our man is positive that it's some quite old gentleman of considerable reputation, but long retired, who has been persuaded to come out of his shell. Finally, there's old Professor Amtenbrink of Remsheid, but I should hardly think it's he. I know him quite well; I don't believe he'd lend himself to a scheme like this, even for the Fatherland. He grows roses, and I get him all sorts of weird chemical manures from Holland. I don't know why I bother, unless it's because I like him."

"Have I seen him?"

"No. Now you mention it, he hasn't been in lately, and that's odd, because he used to come here rather a lot. He did write to me for some gelatin. Gelatin. I wish I had a larger store of general knowledge. I took it for granted he wanted to catch greenfly with it. Would one? I don't know, I never thought about it."

"If he wanted it officially," said Bill, "wouldn't he get a supply from a government chemical factory?"

"Very true," said Hambledon, cheering up. "Of course he would. So it probably isn't he, I'd hate to think it was. We will start on Rötlander of Bonn."

But Professor Rötlander would do nothing but sit on the sofa beside Dirk and recite over and over again the *"Benedicite omnia opera,"* which is in English the canticle beginning: "O all ye works of the Lord," while Hendrik Brandt talked to the Frau Professor about flour and butter.

"After the needs of the fighting services have been met," said he, "there follows on the list for preferential treatment in the matter of supplies the names of those who have deserved well of their Fatherland. Your husband's name is high upon that list."

"That is as it should be," said the lady.

"Undoubtedly."

"He wore out his great brain in the service of humanity, Herr Brandt, and it is a comfort to me to be assured that now he is not forgotten. For he is like a child now, Herr Brandt, and can no longer help anybody, and sometimes he cries because I have to stint him of butter."

"You shall have some, if I go short myself," said Hendrik Brandt, and kept his word.

Professor Paffrath of Düren died, and the two importers were so unfortunate as to choose the day of his funeral to call upon him.

"If he's the bloke," said Bill Saunders as they walked back to the station, "the practice will cease forthwith."

"Unless he's left explicit directions on several sheets of foolscap," said Hambledon. "We will put his case back for further consideration if we draw blank elsewhere. Dr. Bauer of Siegburg."

Dr. Bauer proved to be a fat little man with a strong Bavarian accent, and very ready to talk. He soon made it clear that he regarded war between nations as an abominable exhibition of mass insanity, when there remained the so greater and so more enthusiasm-inspiring battle against disease.

"In this my war, in which I have fought all my life," he cried, "there are no nations nor frontiers except that between Man and Bacillus, and from every civilized country men of skill and intellect stand shoulder to shoulder against the foul invader!"

"How right you are!" said Hendrik Brandt, while his nephew remained in the background in an attitude of respectful admiration.

"We can mark him off," said Hambledon. "The true internationalist. There remains Professor Amtenbrink; I don't believe it, but we'll go tomorrow. In the meantime, I think it is time we knew a little more about the subject. Let us see if the Public Library will help us?"

The Public Library proved to be short on medical works, apart from nursing manuals, good advice to mothers, and handbooks on the identification and treatment of the commoner diseases.

"If I wanted to know," said Tommy Hambledon, "whether what my orphan child had got was mumps or whooping-cough, these works would be invaluable. If, as is highly improbable, I ever become a mother—"

"Here's something," said Bill, and indicated an encyclopedia in a dozen volumes. They turned up cholera and read a vivid account of its horrible symptoms. Bill turned green, and even Hambledon ceased to jest.

"So they infect the drinking water, do they," he said, "and women and children, and men on leave, and soldiers training, and men at home working their hearts out to keep the country going, will scream for hours with cramp till they can't scream any more? Then they shrivel up from the effects of humiliating and indecent paroxysms, turn a greenish clay color, and get colder and colder until they die. Mortality, seldom less than twenty-five per cent and usually much more. My God, if the fellow doing this were my own brother, I'd shoot him in the stomach and laugh at him while he died!"

He lit a cigarette, forced a laugh, and said: "Sorry to be so dramatic. I was getting all worked up."

At once an attendant arrived from nowhere in particular, and silently indicated a notice saying: "*Rauchen verboten.*"

"Your pardon, gracious sir," said Hambledon earnestly, and stubbed the cigarette out.

"Here's a cross-reference," said Bill pointing to a footnote on "Koch's 'comma bacillus,' *see* 'Bacteria.',"

They turned up "Bacteria" and found that this was a term applied to the lowest division of that form of vegetable life known as fungi. That "bacillus" means a "little rod," and that Koch called his discovery the "comma bacillus" because it was a curved rod. That bacteria multiply by division. That they contain no chlorophyll, and therefore cannot obtain carbon from carbonic-acid gas, but must be parasites, feeding upon organic matter and in some cases attacking living organisms. That it is in this manner that certain bacteria cause certain diseases.

"This is where the demon king pops up," said Tommy Hambledon. "Enter the villain in a graceful spiral, provided with a whiplike flagellum."

They turned over a page and came upon a paragraph headed: "Cultivation of Bacteria."

"The study of bacteria," it said, "has been greatly facilitated in recent years by the discovery of suitable methods of germ-culture. The use of aniline dyes in staining bacteria permits of their characteristics being readily observed. The customary culture media is a sterilized mixture of gelatin and broth—"

"Gelatin," repeated Hambledon. "Gelatin. Thank you, Bill, that will do. Will you put the book back?" He sat and looked straight before him for some moments.

"Tomorrow," he said in a cold voice, "we will go and call upon the Herr Professor Amtenbrink."

They went by train through Opladen and Ohligs to Remscheid and found the professor among his roses. He had bush roses in round beds, and standard roses in crescent-shaped beds cut in a wide lawn, which had screens of ramblers on three sides of it. The fourth side was the white wall of the old gentleman's house, with climbing roses on a wooden trellis. Professor Amtenbrink was walking slowly round his beloved roses looking for the folded leaf which indicates a caterpillar. When he found one he squeezed it firmly between finger and thumb, removed it carefully, and dropped the debris into a small basket on his left arm, since there are few more futile ways of wasting one's time than by squashing again and again an already flat caterpillar. He greeted Hendrik Brandt with evident pleasure and received Dirk very kindly.

"I had to visit Ohligs on business," said the importer, "and it is so long since I last saw you that I could not resist the temptation to find out if, perhaps, you were ill. I am delighted to see you looking so well."

"Never resist the temptation to come and see me, my dear Brandt, I cannot tell you what pleasure it gives me. I have not been ill, only—well—much occupied of late."

"Roses been behaving badly? They look well enough."

"No—no, though indeed I have had much trouble with mildew. It has been a wet summer, and among our woods the damp hangs in the atmosphere. Mildew is, of course, our most persistent trouble, and now it is so difficult to get the necessary chemicals. Crepuscule, on the wall yonder, is covered with it."

Dirk looked at the masses of copper and yellow which reached to the upper windows, and said: "I think it looks wonderful. Can there really be much the matter with it?"

"You will see when you get closer," said Amtenbrink grimly. "Are you a gardener? No? Nor was I at your age. Gustav Grunerwald here is nearly as bad."

"What do you have to do to it?" asked Dirk, examining the velvety gray film. "It seems to stick so tight."

"You mix a weak solution of sulphate of potassium in a bowl, carry it round in your hand, and dip the affected branches into it. If you are not careful, they break off, especially in wet weather."

"I'll get you the potassium sulphate if you want it," said Brandt. "I cannot have the peace of this garden disturbed by unsatisfied longings."

"You are always kind," said Amtenbrink. "I was, indeed, thinking of asking you to get me some. But I am at the moment attacking the problem from another angle. You are probably aware that mildew, being a fungus, is allied to the bacteria, which are also fungi. It's odd, isn't it, to think of the germs of tuberculosis, of smallpox and of cholera as being vegetables? But they are."

"This is interesting me beyond words," said Brandt with perfect truth. "Please go on."

"It had occurred to me to wonder whether it were possible in any way to inoculate rose trees against the onset of mildew. Perhaps you'll think it an old man's foolish hobby, but I have approached the subject in the usual manner of research workers, with a gelatin culture in my laboratory—God bless my soul, my dear Brandt. You are ill, take my arm. My boy, you will find some chairs on the veranda; go and fetch one."

"It is nothing," said Brandt. "A momentary giddiness, that's all. The sun is hot—"

"And I have kept you here while I chatter. Let us walk slowly to the house and sit in the cool. You will drink a glass of wine with me; it will restore you."

"Thank you," said Brandt with a queer little smile. "I shall be pleased to."

They sat in long wicker chairs while the old gentleman brought glasses and a decanter from a cupboard. The glasses had tall stems with a knob near the bowl; the bowls were delicately curved in towards the rim and a line of Gothic characters ran round each.

"These glasses were given me by the students of a university where I once taught," said the professor. "It seems that in those days I had the bad habit of interlanding my discourses with hackneyed Latin tags. Vanity, my dear friends, sheer vanity, for in point of fact my Latin was never good. So these irreverent boys had some of my favorites engraved on these glasses. Believe me, it cured me of the horrid practice, I never do it now. Here is *'Principia, non homines,'* 'principles not individuals.' This one is *'Fiat justicia, ruat coelum,'* 'let justice be done though the heavens fall.' What have you got on yours, my boy?"

"Salus," said Dirk, stumbling over the Gothic lettering, which was al-

ways a difficulty to him. "*Salus—populi—suprema lex.*"

"The welfare of the people is the supreme law," said Amtenbrink. "Yes, but which people? Oh, this appalling war!"

"We shall win," said Hendrik Brandt, with conviction in his tones.

"God willing," said the professor with a sigh. "But, dear God, what a frightful waste of the best lives in the country! I see these fine young men going to the war, and I ask myself, my dear Brandt, why they should be sacrificed while the old and crippled and diseased and mentally deficient are carefully preserved. It is contrary to the law of nature, which says that only the strong shall survive. What sort of race shall we see after the war, if only the unfit are left to breed from?"

"It is a point which must have occurred to every thinking man," said Hendrik Brandt.

"But how could you send all the old crocks into the front line?" asked Dirk. "Unless the other fellow did the same, they'd be beaten in twenty-four hours."

"You could not. But you can take the front line back to the old crocks, as you call them. What else are we doing with our air raids on England? For, as you must know, they serve practically no military purpose apart from keeping a few men and guns at home for antiaircraft defense. We are carrying the firing-line back to the civilian population."

"In plain words, we are attacking their morale in the hope that their resistance will collapse from the rear," said the Dutchman.

"That the country behind the army will throw up the sponge. Yes. When we ceased to attack purely military objectives and turned our aim upon the civilians at home, we inaugurated a new era in warfare."

"Women and children," said Dirk. "Personally I'd rather fight in the front line."

"You speak with the generous chivalry natural at your age, my dear boy. You speak as I spoke myself until it was put to me—until I reconsidered, I mean, that logically that attitude was wasteful and unsound. Would you have me destroy my finest roses and keep the weaklings? No. If there must be this fearful pruning which men call war, let us at least destroy the rubbish and not cut off the flower of our land in its pride and beauty."

"You certainly make out a good case for aerial warfare," said Hendrik Brandt, with the air of a man already half convinced. "If we admit high-explosive and incendiary bombs, why not poison gas? Why not, to continue the thought to its logical conclusion, why not disease?"

"Logically," said Amtenbrink, "why not? Let me refill your glass. When for once I have the pleasure of the society of men of intellect and originality, I become so carried away that I forget my manners. I must admit, however, that the thought of using disease as a weapon is, at first, revolting to all one's ingrained ideas of what is decent and right. It shocks one, it does indeed."

"One should, however, distinguish between what really shocks one's conscience and what only shocks one's prejudices," argued Brandt. "Is it really any more cruel to infect a man with smallpox or cholera than to tear his limbs from his body with explosives and leave him half alive, perhaps, to lie for days in no-man's-land till merciful death releases him?"

"No," said Amtenbrink, "but it is a lot more cruel than shooting him dead. You mentioned cholera; have you ever seen a case? No? Well, I have." He made a grimace. "When I was a young man, I traveled, and in India I encountered a cholera epidemic in the Ganges Valley. I was so much impressed by what I saw—I will not sadden our young friend here by going into details—that I took up the study of cholera in the hope of finding an antidote. I may say, though it does not become me to boast, that Koch's discovery in 1884 of the so-called 'comma bacillus'—it is not a bacillus at all, it is actually a spirillum—only forestalled mine by a matter of a few weeks. Ah, well, when I was young I thought I was a great man and one of mankind's benefactors, and now I am old I know I am only a grain of dust in the sunshine, and I spend my days trying to find an antidote to the mildew on my rose trees. *Sic transit gloria mundi.* Dear me, there I go again, and with one of these glasses still in my hand. '*Sic transit*' is in the cupboard." He laughed gently. "Let me refill yours."

"Thank you, not again," said Brandt, getting up. "We must go. You never know, professor, there may be some great deed yet that you can do for the Fatherland."

"Are you sure you are quite recovered?" asked his old friend anxiously. "You looked quite white as you spoke."

"I am perfectly restored, thanks to your kindness, and now I must be about my business. I have enjoyed our talk immensely—it was most illuminating," said Hendrik Brandt.

"He's the bloke," said Hambledon, as they walked away from the house.

"You are quite sure," said Bill, "that he is not really growing mildew on his gelatin?"

"Don't be a fool," said Hambledon irritably. "Why should he grow it on gelatin when his whole garden is blue with it? As soon as he said that, I knew he was lying."

"You didn't believe it before, did you?"

"No, I didn't. Even now, you know, he doesn't really approve. He has been talked into it. Did you notice that he said once 'it has been put to me'? A damned clever specious argument, too. I did not point out the flaw in it: namely, that the children he proposes to murder would be in their turn the flower of the land. No. He's a nice old man really, but he's been got at."

"What are you going to do about it?"

"Tonight," said Hambledon grimly, "we shall deal with him. By the way, doubtless that laboratory of his is full of quart bottles brimming with sudden death—we shall have to deal with that too."

"Burn it?"

"Yes, burn it. That's easy; he uses oil lamps, did you notice?"

"Be a bit rough on those climbing roses," said Dirk.

"Yes, it'll be good-bye to the roses. There is a bridle road turning off here somewhere, which goes to Wermelskirchen. I want to make sure of it—there it is—we will go that way tonight."

They went a mile into the woods, waited for night to fall, and returned to the professor's garden.

"A quarter past ten," said Hambledon peering at his watch. "By the time we're ready the household will be abed, I hope. All except our professor, probably. I expect he sits up late; I never knew a professor who didn't. I wish I'd asked him where they kept the paraffin."

"In an outhouse, I expect," said Bill Saunders. "Is that the lab, that annex on the left? My hat, if we burn that, the whole house will go."

"Let it," said Hambledon. "Cheers, there's a light upstairs and the kitchen quarters are dark. Now, where's your outhouse?"

They found the paraffin and carried a four-gallon can of it round to the laboratory, which had a door to the garden. This Hambledon opened, and by the light of Bill's electric torch they poured oil over the floor and the tables, paying particular attention to a workbench which had rows of test-tubes in racks above it.

"Doesn't look much," said Bill. "Is that all he's got?"

"The main store will be in that cupboard, I expect. No, I wouldn't open it; pour some oil over it. Throw some up the walls. What a beastly mess! That will do; now let's go and pay our little call. Stop. Light that lamp first and turn it low."

They walked round the house, quietly, on the grass, and found a lighted room on the ground floor with french windows ajar to the warm night. Hambledon put his hand in his coat pocket, pushed the window open, and walked in, followed by Bill. Professor Amtenbrink started from his chair.

"Who—oh, it's you, Brandt," he said. "This is an unexpected pleasure."

"I am afraid," said Hambledon quietly, "that you will not find this visit a pleasure. We have come to see you about those cholera germs you are hatching out for British women and children."

"Cholera germs—I am not. I have some cultures of mildew—"

"Tell that to St. Peter," said Hambledon, with a mirthless grin.

"But, Brandt—"

"My name is not Brandt. It is Hambledon, and this man with me is William Saunders. We are British Intelligence agents."

Amtenbrink dropped back into his chair and merely stared. After a moment he recovered himself.

"I realize," he said, with notable dignity, "that you would not tell me this if I were going to continue to live."

"You are right. I am very sorry—I mean that, for I always liked you. But you realize that I have no choice between your life and that of hundreds, and perhaps thousands, of my own people."

"If I were to give you my word that I am not doing what you think?"

Hambledon hesitated—or appeared to. "I cannot risk it," he said. "I dare not. You might consider it your duty to lie for your country. God knows I have told enough lies for mine."

"I understand, my friend," said Amtenbrink gently.

Hambledon turned perfectly white, but spoke in a calm voice. "You would like a glass of wine and a cigarette before we go. Bill, you saw where the glasses were kept. Go and fetch three, and the wine."

When he came back the two men were sitting in armchairs talking quietly. Bill poured the wine and handed a glass to Amtenbrink.

"Which one have you given me, my boy? *Salus populi*—that's right."

"Sir—" said Bill, and stopped.

"What?"

"May I have the—it's awful cheek—would you mind if I kept your glass?"

"Certainly, take it. But why?"

"Next time I find myself afraid to die, I should like to look at it."

Amtenbrink smiled.

"We are becoming too dramatic," he said. "Death is not, after all, so very important. *Mors janua vitae*, it is the gate of life. There, I have offended for the last time." He rose to his feet and Hambledon did the same.

"Hoch dem Kaiser! Hoch!"

He emptied his glass and handed it to Bill.

"Well, shall we go?" he said.

They looked over their shoulders as they hurried away in the moonlight, for behind them tongues of flame were leaping between the trees.

"Come on," said Hambledon. "We'll sleep at Wermelskirchen tonight."

"I wonder," said Bill Saunders, "if he was really guilty."

"You are not really convinced, are you? Look at it like this. He answers the description we were given of the sort of man who was doing it. He had the means to do it. He had the knowledge and skill to do it. Finally, he buys from me the materials for it, and covers up his purchase by a cock-and-bull story about mildew. That should be enough. But, apart from that, you must preserve a sense of proportion. You liked him, and you are allowing personality to interfere with duty. Consider this, that it would be better that every retired professor in Germany should die tonight rather than that one of them should succeed in this. I tell you, I hated killing Amtenbrink. But I would kill him again tomorrow and again the next day and again every day for a fortnight before there is one little cholera outbreak in one little street in London."

"I expect you're right," said Bill.

"I know I am," said Tommy Hambledon. "But there are moments when I wish I'd joined the Household Cavalry, or Harry Tate's Navy, or the Church Lads' Brigade."

They crossed the river Esch, which runs through the valley between Remscheid and Wermelskirchen, and on the bridge Hambledon said: "Wait a moment, I want to get rid of this. Curse it, it's jammed tight."

He tugged at something and pulled a stout steel knitting-needle out of its handle. The knitting-needle had been ground till it was flattish towards one tip, and the point was extremely sharp; the handle was an ordinary rubber pedal block from a bicycle. Hambledon threw the pedal block into a clump of bushes and dropped the steel into the river below.

"Lie there and rot," he said.

CHAPTER TEN
REMEMBER HEILEMANN

EARLY in December 1917 Dirk Brandt strolled up the Höhestrasse in Cologne to meet Max von Bodenheim at the Germania and found him more than usually pleased with life.

"Somebody's done a good job," he said.

"Oh, good," said Dirk. "What is it?"

Von Bodenheim unfolded an English paper and handed it over. "You will find this easier to read than I," he said. "My English is rusty."

Dirk read, with suitable signs of delight, the account of a ship, loaded with high explosives, blown up at Halifax, Nova Scotia. How a Belgian steamer lying near by had caught fire, and how the explosion had raised a huge tidal wave that rushed up the beaches and tore down houses, wrecked trains and streetcars and tore up the roads. How an American warship fifty miles out at sea saw the flash and, long after, heard the roar, and rushed at top speed to the rescue, thinking it was a ship at sea that had gone down; and how the disaster was followed by a fearful blizzard which swept down on the unhappy city.

"This is good work," he said. "Who did that?"

"You must not ask that."

"Of course not," said Dirk, coloring. "I spoke without thinking."

"Between ourselves," said von Bodenheim, "that would not matter. But you must learn to guard your tongue at all times, so that it becomes instinctive."

"I was only wondering," stammered Dirk, "whether one could not help him—that is, if he came to England."

"If you can in any way help that brave and resourceful man, be sure you will be told."

"I am sorry," said Dirk, turning innocent blue eyes upon the German. "I did not mean to be presumptuous."

"I am sure you did not," said von Bodenheim, relenting a little. "But if you are to serve the Reich, you must learn to obey blindly and not ask questions."

"Yes, sir, of course," said Dirk, and went on sipping his wine. "This is good," he thought, "he thinks he's got me where he wants me. He's just showing me I'm not the only gun in the battery, but I bet I get put in touch with Heroic Horace one of these days."

"Butler, now, might be of use to him, if he came over."

"Oh, yes?" said Dirk, without lifting his eyes.

"My boy, there is no need for you to be jealous," said von Bodenheim kindly. "Butler is all very well to run errands, but you will be as good as Heilemann one of these days, if you are careful."

Dirk ventured to cheer up a little.

"In the words of the great Queen Victoria, 'I will be good,'," he remarked, and shot an obvious glance at von Bodenheim to see how he took it. The German smiled, and said: "You cannot be solemn for long. That is good, for you will not take things to heart so heavily as a more serious-minded man would; therefore you will not wear yourself out so quickly. Some of our best men have been *kaput* at the end of a couple of years; they cannot forget easily, then they will not sleep at night for fear they dream, then it is the bottle and finally the asylum, or, more mercifully, the little accident with the gun, and all because, perhaps, they cannot forget the look of astonishment in a man's eyes as you kill him when he did not know he was going to die."

"I have never seen anyone die, not even my father," said Dirk Brandt deliberately, and there rose in his mind a memory of Amtenbrink lying on the floor of the laboratory with his eyes wide open, a pool of blood spreading beneath his left shoulder, and a sudden roar of flame which curtained the picture. No, there was no surprise in that tranquil look.

He shivered slightly, and von Bodenheim's expression softened. "You are very young," he said. "Do not be afraid. One dead man is very like another, and they have this principally in common—that they no longer talk. You laugh at most things; remember Death is the final jest."

Dirk thought the subject a trifle somber, and said so. "Unless, of course, you want me to mop somebody up this evening?"

Max von Bodenheim leaned back in his chair, and his face settled again into its familiar lines of cynical amusement.

"There are several," he said decidedly. "One is that woman in the green hat near the window. She will never die."

"Are you sure?" said Dirk. "She looks mortal—shall I try her with a hock bottle?"

"No. You will only precipitate the catastrophe. When she passes through the change we call death, she will become a vampire; she cannot avoid it, she is one already. Do you know what vampires are?"

"Things that crawl out of graves?"

"Go and brain her with a bottle. I assure you her family will not bear you any malice—they may even club together and present you with a gold-plated fire-shovel—emblematic of where they think she's going. But I wander from the point. If you kill her that will mystically attach her to you—"

"I will forbear," murmured Dirk, studying the lady's incisive profile.

"… and one night you will dream you are being kissed. Wonderful kisses, that thrill your very soul. Next morning you wake up feeling a trifle tired."

"I shouldn't wonder."

"When you put your collar on you will find a tender spot—"

"Over my heart?" suggested Dirk.

"No. I said collar, not belt."

"Please continue."

"A tender spot on the right side of your neck, over your jugular vein. You take a hand-glass and after performing the idiotic contortions customary with people who can't work out angles of refraction in their heads, you find you have two little punctured wounds like the bite of a snake, only farther apart."

"Snakes cannot be too far apart, for me," Dirk said gravely.

"You have no pity for the love life of the reptilia. To return, it will be she."

"What will? The snakes' raptures?"

"The maker of the punctured wounds. She sucks your blood."

"At the same moment as she kisses me? Her mouth will have to stretch a bit, won't it? One of those elastic grins you read about, doubtless. Does she pop when she disconnects?"

"You are incorrigible," said von Bodenheim, with one of his rare laughs. "You even make me dislike her less. I shall smile when I see her in future and that will terrify her as nothing else can."

"Why?"

"She will think I am going to punish her for her sins. I had a little cousin once," said von Bodenheim, ceasing to be amused, "a nice child, if a little stupid. The sort of girl intended by nature to be perfectly happy, surrounded by an ever growing circle of babies, in a thoroughly respectable household on the outskirts of some provincial town. You know. She was suitably betrothed to the son of a Prussian officer of high rank."

"It sounds delightful."

"She thought it was, anyway. She was ridiculously happy. Unfortunately the woman in the green hat had a daughter."

"So she detached the fiancé?"

"Worse than that, she arranged a pretty little scandal. It is absurdly easy to arrange scandals in Prussian society, Dirk. Something to do with a handsome groom who was admitted to my cousin's bedroom to do something to the window. Then it appeared there was nothing wrong with the window. I don't know how she worked it."

"And the upshot?"

"There was one of those awful family scenes which have to be heard to be believed, and my cousin was thoroughly disgraced. Already half drowned in tears, she went and finished off the job in the baronial millstream, and my lady yonder is now the proud mother-in-law of the Herr Uberleutnant von So-and-so. I can't do anything, as really he's not a bad fellow, and terribly cut up over my cousin."

"Hellcat," said Dirk, referring to the lady.

"Yes. She kills people—not violently, I don't mean that. They just die. Her husband, her parents, her sister, and one of her brothers, they just faded off. She sucked their vitality, I think, that's why I said she was a vampire. Let's have another bottle."

"By all means," said Dirk, who was beginning to think that von Bodenheim had been celebrating the Halifax explosions to some purpose. Heilemann, mustn't forget Heilemann, must get away and find Tommy Hambledon somewhere and tell him. No violent hurry, of course he might as well come here as anywhere else, it might be advisable to wait a little longer, and in the meantime it was excellent wine on the second floor of the Germania, and he'd got the name, Heilemann.

"But I don't think I'll start my homicidal career with the green hat," added Dirk. "Not even to oblige you will I have that lady's spook attaching itself to me with expanding suckers. Show me something simpler."

"There is a large choice," said his sardonic friend. "There is the dashing girl with the come-hither look in ultra-fashionable clothes by the door."

"What's the matter with her? She looks what you might call really easy to talk to."

"That's it. She looks like that, and if you address her in the manner she seems to expect, she yells for mother. She is really very proper and rather dull; in short, she has what they call a thoroughly nice mind," said von Bodenheim viciously, "and if you know of anything more damning to say about a woman than that, tell me and I'll probably say it."

"Then why does she go about looking like that?"

"Heaven knows—presumably. See the lad in the tweed suit who has just come in? His father has a boot factory, so he's exempted from war service on work of national importance."

"Yes, he looks like that."

"He is, and he stinks of money. He thinks he's a lady-killer, he does. Look, is he going to sit with our Trudi? No, by Jove, he's sheered off. He is going to sit at the table of those two girls and pick acquaintance. He'll start with the weather and gradually lead up to a few doubtful jokes and see what happens. If they snub him, he'll sneer. If they giggle, they're lost."

"I shouldn't think they would," said Dirk. "They look like nice girls."

"They do," said von Bodenheim grimly. "In fact, they are, I know them slightly. But they may be hungry."

"Good God," said Dirk. "You don't mean—"

"I do," said von Bodenheim, pushing his chair back. "I shall go, I think. I am fairly hardened, but this sort of thing is more than my stomach will stand. Are you coming?"

"As far as the office, if you're going that way."

But when Bill Saunders got back to the importer's office, Tommy Hambledon had gone. This was not unexpected, but Bill had to get rid of von Bodenheim somehow and find Hambledon at the earliest possible moment to tell him about—what was the name? Heilemann. Mustn't forget Heilemann. Tommy might be at the Café Palant, so Bill strolled across there and had a drink or two with friends, but no Hambledon showed up. Bill wandered into the Automatische bar and noticed that they had again cut down the allowance of beer one got for one's twenty pfennigs. Heilemann, the man who caused the big bang and escaped with his life.

He walked purposefully out of the Automatische and made a round of sundry houses of refreshment in the neighboring streets, but drew blank at all of them—blank, that is, as regards Tommy Hambledon, but not blank in other respects. One cannot enter a pub, look round, and walk out again without making the usual contribution towards the prosperity of the house. By the time Bill arrived back in the Höhestrasse, the world was a rosy place full of charming friends and he was becoming really carefree, but still he did not forget Heilemann.

He inquired at the door of the Dom Hotel whether Herr Brandt was within, and got a negative reply, so he wandered off again and found himself near the railway station. Here was a streetcar, a nice clean comfortable-looking streetcar, and his legs were tired, they bent unexpectedly. Good idea, let's go in a streetcar.

So he got in and sat next to a soldier on leave, who had been celebrating his safe return.

"And now I'm going home to my old mother," said the soldier. "Nice old mother, she'll be so pleased. I'll knock at the door—no, not knock at the door. Just walk in and say: 'Nice old mother, I've come home.'"

"Where's your mother live?" asked Bill.

"Thielenbruck."

"Thielenbruck. Is that where this car goes to?"

"Course it does," said the soldier. "Look, it's got it up." He pointed to the sign. "If it doesn't go to Thielenbruck when it says Thielenbruck, there'll be trouble, won't there?"

"Yes," said Bill. He thought it over for a few minutes, and then said: "Unless it goes to another place with the same name."

The soldier disregarded this wild and beautiful picture of a new Germany covered with strange villages all named Thielenbruck, and said: "I've got a girl there."

"Nice for you," said Bill. "Is she nice?"

"Yes. She's got nice house, too. It's got four steps up to it, and a hat-stand. Very genteel, have hatstand."

"You've got Iron Cross," said Bill.

"Yes. Third Class. When I go to see my girl, she'll say: 'Brave Karl, get Iron Cross,' and then I'll—I'll hang it on hat stand."

"Thielenbruck," said the conductor.

"Come on," said Karl.

They alighted and, of course, found somewhere to have one or two more, after which they started off towards the soldier's home.

"Have you," said Bill, "ever been in big bang? Really big bang?"

They both stood still while Karl considered this. At last "All bangs are big," said he, "when you're in them."

"And a great big flash and it's good-bye to the roses."

"Why? Here's where my girl lives," said the soldier. "Nice house. But I'm not going there now. Going home first, see old mother."

Shortly after that Bill mislaid the soldier and strolled about by himself looking for the streetcar, because he had got to find Tommy Hambledon and tell him about Heilemann. Presently he found himself before a house he recognized, so he walked up four steps and rang the bell. A very large girl opened the door. Bill took his hat off and said: "Good evening."

"Good evening," said the girl in a tone of inquiry.

"Good evening. You have eyes like gazom-gazelles, only bluer. Your hair is just the color of ripe corn. Do you grow roses in your garden as well as in your cheeks?"

"No," said the girl, laughing.

"No? You have a mouth like—oh, there's hatstand. Good evening, hat-stand," and Bill took his hat off to it. "It's nice hatstand, isn't it?"

"What do you want?"

"Are you a good cook? Yes? Then tell me the way to the streetcar."

"Down the steps, for a start," said the girl, and pushed him.

He picked himself up at the bottom, replaced his hat, and strolled off. Later on he found himself in a garden leaning over to smell some flowers, when there came a pattering rush from behind and he was shot into a clump of azaleas. He smelt a strong and curious smell and opened his eyes to look straight into the face of an elderly goat. The goat had a chain trailing behind it, so Bill picked up the loose end and started off again with his new friend. But still he remembered Heilemann.

He discovered almost at once that it was better to lead the goat on a short chain because if it had a long one it retired to the limit and came back to butt him. Presently they came to a lamppost, the goat went one side and Bill the other, and both walked round it in opposite directions till they were brought up short face to face.

"There is a curious dreamlike quality about this evening out," said Bill, very distinctly, and he unwound the goat again. It was a long street, the lamps stretched in an endless vista for miles and miles, and Bill felt that if only he extended his arms and let himself go, he would just float, which would be less trouble than walking, but unfortunately every time he did this he fell down, slowly but inevitably.

Much farther down the road they met an elderly man carrying a bag and became entangled with him, so both men sat down on the edge of the pavement to sort themselves out while the goat stood off and blew bubbles.

"Who are you," said Bill, "and what do you do?"

"I am a cutler," said the man with dignity.

"Not a mason?"

"No."

"Pity. I've got a goat."

"Why?" said the cutler.

Bill felt this was rather beyond him, so he let it go at that, and the cutler felt about in his bag.

"Have a drink," said he.

For some reason the bottle had not broken when the owner fell down: it contained gin, and they shared it amicably.

"I want a streetcar," said Bill in a contented voice.

"Whaffor?" asked the cutler.

Bill considered this. Why did one want a streetcar? It was very pleasant here, although there was something a little wrong. Of course, it was the pavement, which was hard.

"To go sleep in," he said. "This pavement's hard."

The cutler prodded it with his fingers. "Perfectly right," he said, "it is. Very hard. Very unkind." He wept a little, but the goat came and breathed at him and he cheered up.

"I got a home," he said triumphantly.

"Where?"

"Down next street. Come on, let's go home."

So, helping themselves up with the goat, they proceeded in a southwesterly direction till they came to a small semidetached house and the cutler led the way to the back door. Outside the door he paused and produced the gin-bottle again.

"Finish this," he said. "My wife don't like drink. No bottle, she won't know, will she?"

"Give her goat," suggested Bill. "Nice present."

For some reason the cutler was loudly amused at this; then they emptied the bottle and he threw it away where it hit something that clanged.

"Hush," he said. "Mustn't wake wife."

He staggered slightly on the brick path, threw out his arm, and brought down a galvanized iron tub which was hanging on a nail. After which he opened the back door, switched on the light, and they entered—all three of them. Bill stood blinking painfully in the light and looked pathetic.

"Wha's marrer?" asked the cutler.

"Want to leggo goat," Bill said plaintively, and indicated the chain which was wound in a complicated manner round his left arm. His right arm was not, apparently, long enough to reach it, though he made several attempts, and the cutler kindly unwound him and between them they tied the goat to the kitchen table-leg.

"I like you," said the cutler frankly. "Sit down."

Bill looked round, but the only chair seemed too far away to be real, so he sat on the floor, and at that moment the inner door opened and a large fierce woman put her head in.

"You miserable idiotic drunken worm!" she said, addressing her husband, who took no notice whatever and sat down on the hearthrug to remove his boots.

"Who is that horrible repulsive-looking tramp you've brought home?" she asked, indicating Bill, who was so horrified that his eyes ceased to focus and the lady appeared to him to have two angry faces which slid apart and approached again but never quite coalesced.

Her husband took off one boot, poised it in his hand, and hurled it—not at his wife but at the electric light bulb, which exploded with a loud bang, and thereafter all was darkness and peace.

The last thing Bill thought of as he fell asleep was Heilemann—Heilemann and Halifax—

The next morning Bill Saunders was walking down the road to catch the car to Cologne, with a gnawing headache and a mouth so unpleasant that he could not bear to think of what it reminded him of, when he met a column of English prisoners of war being marched to work in the fields. He stepped off the pavement onto the muddy little path alongside, and stood to watch them go by, thinking mainly of what he would give for several cups of strong hot coffee, when a face in the line of marching men attracted his attention. He recognized it; though much changed, it was yet familiar; it was Dixon Ogilvie's.

Dixon Ogilvie was bent at the shoulders, his hair was more unkempt than ever and he was not recently shaved. Moreover, his walk, which, though athletic, was never soldierly, was now almost shambling.

Bill Saunders almost forgot about his headache and the foul taste in his mouth as he sat in the car for Cologne.

CHAPTER ELEVEN
TEMPORARY PRIVATE

"HEILEMANN," said Tommy Hambledon, "I think you'd better go to London and tell them about this; it's either a trap or very important. I smell a trap, I can't see von Bodenheim letting out a thing like that accidentally, and yet—and yet—to lecture somebody about being careless and immediately do something damn silly yourself is exactly the kind of thing that happens. If you'd ever been a schoolmaster you'd know. Besides, I thought the Hindenburg Line story was a trap and it wasn't; we missed that and it was my fault. If Reck had sent it out the night before it might have got through. However it's no good crying over unspilt beans."

"When shall I go," asked Bill, "tomorrow? I must see von Bodenheim before I start."

Hambledon took a turn or two up and down the office.

"No," he said at last, "not too precipitately, I think. I should think Heilemann would rest on his laurels for a bit after practically destroying the port of Halifax, and if you rush off at once, von Bodenheim may ask himself why, and himself may answer with a sudden recollection of having mentioned the name of Heilemann, after which he might lose his boyish faith in you, and that would be fatal—especially for you."

"I think he was fairly well stewed at the time," said Bill.

"But not so stewed as you became afterwards, eh? Take some aspirin."

"Thanks, my head is better now. By the way, I believe I saw Dixon Ogilvie in a batch of English prisoners this morning at Thielenbruck."

"Oh, really? Then he wasn't killed after all. I'm glad—very glad. How did he look?"

"Not very well. A lot older and very tired."

"Poor lad. Still, he's lucky to be alive."

"Couldn't we do anything for him?"

"Get him out, do you mean? Don't be a fool," said Hambledon energetically. "Will you realize that what we're doing is ten thousand times more important than the life of any man, including our own? You cannot risk your position here by meddling with a prisoner, not even if he were your twin brother. Get the idea right out of your head. It can't be done. I'm sorry."

"You're right, of course."

"Today is Friday. I think you might go on Tuesday, and, what is more, I think that I, Hendrik Brandt, will send you to England to arrange for some petrol to reach Holland. Tell von Bodenheim that. What is still more, you are due for leave, Private Saunders of the Hampshire Regiment, and don't forget you have been in the trenches all this time."

"Leave?" cried Bill. "Real leave? Ten days' leave all at once, and can I go home? Why, that will take me over Christmas. Do you know," he added wonderingly, "I had somehow forgotten about Christmas."

"This is a hell of a life," said Tommy Hambledon, and patted the boy's shoulder. "And when you're back in Weatherley Parva among the downs, where you know personally every single soul you meet, and people are packing up mysterious parcels, and the village children sing carols on your doorstep, and the Christmas bells are ringing for the Prince of Peace, remember that every little household in Germany will be keeping Christmas too. Blast you," said Hambledon, blowing his nose irritably, "why did you start that? Go and enter up the ledger, and if I find you adding up on your fingers, Heaven help you."

Bill put in a couple of hours at office work and then wrote two letters which would be taken to Holland that night and thence to France, to be posted in the British Expeditionary Force in the usual manner, as all his previous letters had been. One letter was to his uncle announcing his return on leave, and the other was to Diane Causton. He had been writing regularly to her ever since he came abroad, stilted boyish letters beginning: "Dear Diane," rendered all the more stilted because he always had to write about life in the trenches when he had almost forgotten what it was like, and describe events of which he had only heard. Now for once he could leave these lies and write from his heart.

2nd Batt. The Hampshire Rgt. Fri., Dec. 14, 1917
Somewhere in France
Darling,

Leave, leave at last, I'm coming home for ten whole days. Isn't it spiffing? And I'll be there for Christmas too.

We'll see *Maid of the Mountains* and *Dear Brutus* and— well, I've lots of other plans.

Can you get away from your Picks and Scots, sorry, shovels, and come down to W.P. for a week at least, if not for ten days? Do try. My papers will be through orderly room in two days, in another three I'll be home. Five days today and I'll be able to have a bath just when I want one.

Are you sure you won't mind being seen about with an infantry private? Because I believe there is an order out now that we must not wear civilian clothes, but we'll see.

Have been lucky and scored a green envelope, so this won't be censored by my C.O.

So I can say:

I love you, love you like hell, Diane. Will you marry me when I get to Blighty?

All my love, all my kisses,
All yours,
Bill

Bill Saunders arrived at Victoria Station on the evening of Wednesday, December 19, 1917, in the uniform of a private in the Hampshire Regiment, suitably muddy. As he walked up the platform he could see, beyond the barriers, a crowd of women waiting, with eager hungry eyes scanning the faces of the men as they streamed out, and one by one coming forward to greet her share of the Great War, but some there were who went home again alone. It was curious to notice, as he had learned to notice things, that many of them forgot completely how public a place this was, and there would be ecstatic cries of "Oh, darling," or little inarticulate murmurs, though some in the true English tradition shook hands formally, with: "Hullo, George! How well you're looking!" as though George had just returned from a week in the country. Not expecting to be met, he walked slowly along with the stream, when someone touched his arm with a breathless: "Oh, Bill—"

"Diane!" he said, and seized her hands. They stood looking incredulously at each other and impeding the passage of others while for Bill the dead face of Amtenbrink, von Bodenheim's eagle look, the roar and terror of a frontal attack, fell together into oblivion—for a time.

"C-come on," he said, stammering a little, "let's get a taxi," and they walked out into the icy air and gathering, drifting fog. But there were no taxis to be had—at least, not for a muddy infantry private—and Diane said: "Are you tired? No? Let's walk on, perhaps we'll pick one up."

So they went along Victoria Street, hand in hand, and looked in the windows of a furniture shop.

"I like that chair, don't you?" said Diane.

"No," said Bill, "it isn't big enough for two. How did you know which train I was coming by?"

"I didn't. I met them all until you came."

"Darling!" in a tone of voice which drew the sympathetic attention of two typists, an office charwoman, and an elderly postman, but Bill did not care. "Wasn't that pretty beastly for you?"

"No. It would have been if you hadn't come. Here's the Army and Navy, where are we going?"

"Does it matter?"

"No, unless you're hungry. When did you last have something to eat?"

"Oh, I don't know. Why?"

"Because there's the restaurant where I lunch every day just opposite; the girl who runs it is a friend of mine."

"In that basement? All right, let's go. Will there be many people there?" asked Bill.

This being their night, it was Kismet that the place should be empty, so they sank into a soft blue settee in a far corner, and the tall golden-haired proprietress nobly concealed the fact that she had been hoping to get away early, and made them welcome. Omelets, yes, and grilled kidneys, and something sweet, and cheese. Can do. Something to drink? Wine, possibly? She could send out for it. Can do, no, no trouble. She smiled and tactfully disappeared.

"She's a darling," said Diane.

"This is where I kiss you," said Bill, disregarding this childish irrelevance.

Presently Diane's friend returned, singing lightheartedly before yet she came in sight, and put out spoons and forks. So Diane said: "I've got ten days' leave, too."

"Splendid," said Bill. "How did you manage it?"

"Oh, urgent private affairs. Of course I forfeit my pay."

"Am I an urgent private affair?"

"Aren't you?"

They were alone for a moment, so Bill said: "I'm going to be your very public affair soon; do you realize that in three days—today's Wednesday, that's Saturday—we shall be married?"

The omelets arrived, but Diane was so busy gaping speechlessly at Bill that she did not even notice them.

"Come on," said the incredible young man, "this looks good," but Diane had a mind above omelets.

"But I can't marry you on Saturday," she began.

"Why not? I asked you to in my letter, didn't I?"

"But I didn't think you meant it."

"And then you met me at Victoria; that shows we're engaged. Only engaged people meet leave-trains, besides wives of course. Next time you'll be a wife."

"But—"

"Eat your omelet, then you'll feel stronger. There's a good girl, nothing like starting as you mean to go on. Love, honor, and obey—"

"But I've nothing to wear," said poor Diane, with her mouth full of obligatory omelet.

"That thing you've got on looks very nice," he said, critically regarding the fur cap and high collar which 1917 considered Russian.

"Oh, this old thing," said she who was wearing it for the second time.

"To return to this marriage business, I traveled over with a padre and got the dope from him. You can get a special license, which costs twenty-five pounds or so, but it isn't easy to get; apparently you have to apply to the Archbishop of Canterbury in person, entering the Presence on hands and knees—I may have got it wrong, but that's the impression received—and give your reasons for urgency in triplicate."

"But there aren't any."

"Yes, there are."

"What are they? We've got plenty of time."

"Oh, have we?" he said, and stared into her eyes till she shrank back into the corner.

"Please don't," she faltered. "Why do you look like that?"

"Like what?"

"I don't know. I saw something horrible behind your eyes."

"You poor little kid. I am so sorry—I have seen some rather awful things, but don't draw back like that, please. Please don't, it hurts me."

"Oh, Bill darling," she said, and laid her hands on his.

"Please don't be afraid of me, I can't bear it. There's nothing for you to be afraid of."

"I am not. I was startled for the moment, that's all. I'll never be afraid again."

"I hope not," he said doubtfully.

"Never again. Look, I'll prove it. When do you want to marry me? On Saturday? All right, I'll marry you on Saturday. It's mad, I know, but I'll do it," said Diane, and she laughed and kissed him.

" 'If I were the only girl in the world,' " sang the proprietress cheerfully, " 'and you were the only boy—' Grilled kidneys we said, didn't we?"

" 'And the morning stars sang together,' " said Bill wildly. "Good evening, morning star. What does that remind me of? I know, a hatstand. Have you a hatstand?"

"Yes," said the lady swiftly, "also the umbrella of the gardener's aunt; it has a white china knob on the end of each spoke."

"I know, angel," said Bill, "she sits and sucks them alternately during the sermon."

"Why 'alternately'?" asked Diane, holding her head.

"Alternately with the sexton's nephew, sweetheart," explained Bill kindly.

"Why so ecclesiastical, if it is not tactless to inquire?"

"Because we're going to be married on Saturday," said Bill and Diane, precisely together.

"Heaven bless you, may you always be so unanimous," said Diane's friend with enthusiasm.

"Have a pinch of salt," said Bill sardonically.

"Darling, have some wine," said Diane.

"I didn't know you were even engaged," said the lady of the restaurant.

"I wasn't," said Diane, dimpling.

"Then how are you going to manage it so quickly?"

"The lecture will now be resumed," said Bill. "I have already addressed the class on the subject of special licenses; let us now turn our attention to the ordinary license. This is obtainable from any surrogate upon payment of a fee of two pun' ten or thereabouts, and takes only three days to mature, as opposed to marriage by banns, which is cheaper still but takes three weeks and is therefore out of the question in our case. Tonight we are going to

Weatherley Parva, and tomorrow morning early I am going out to find the nearest surrogate."

"A very popular form of sport for men on leave, I understand," said the golden-haired lady, "hunting the surrogate."

"I dare say," said Bill. "How does one begin? Ask a policeman?"

"Or the local vicar, perhaps?"

"He's my uncle," said Diane. "Oh! I hadn't thought. What will my people say?"

"I'm very much afraid," said Bill, "that we shan't have time to listen just now. How old are you, Diane?"

"Nearly twenty-one."

"From the mere fact of being in the army, I am of age—at least, so I understand," said Bill, who was eighteen, "but just in case of trouble I think we had both better be quite twenty-one; do you mind, my bird of paradise?"

"No, my prize Pekingese," said Diane in a tone of affected submission.

"Do you mean to say," said Diane's friend with real concern, "that you are going to rush off and get married without either of you telling your people? If Diane's under age, I doubt if it will be legal."

"It will be legal all right unless her people make a fuss, and I don't believe they will," said Bill. "I mean, perhaps if they took it to all sorts of courts they might get the marriage annulled, but why should they? Are you a great heiress, Diane, or anything awful like that?"

"No," said Diane decidedly. "I come into about two hundred a year in March when I'm twenty-one; that's all I shall ever have."

"Splendid," said Bill heartily. "You'll be able to buy me presents without asking me for the money."

"But do Colonel and Mrs. Causton like you?"

"They haven't had a chance yet."

"Do you mean—?"

"They've never seen Bill yet, but they're sure to like him," said Diane confidently.

"It's your own affair, of course, but I do think you're a little mad," said the businesswoman of the party.

"If the rest of the world is sane," said Bill grimly, "I think we are better mad. If it's mad to want a little happiness between long stretches of hell, I am. If it's mad to want love instead of hatred—" he paused, and the bitterness died out of his face to be replaced by wistfulness—"I want someone I can come back to out of all the beastliness of life, as a man comes home; I want someone I can trust and who will trust me, someone who'll never lie to me and who'll believe me when no one else does, someone who'll show me how to live when I have only learned to die, Diane, my garden enclosed—"

"God helping me," said Diane solemnly, "I will not fail you."

Bill woke up early the next morning in his uncle's house at Weatherley Parva. He had that frightful stab of conscience that comes when a forgotten duty recalls itself suddenly to mind. Diane had met him at Victoria, and he had completely forgotten to go anywhere near the War Office. He must go at once, by the first available train; he would dress, shave, get some breakfast, borrow somebody's bicycle, and ride to Weatherley.

He woke up rather more thoroughly and calmed down somewhat. There was not this frenzied haste, he had no appointment at the War Office, probably they did not even know which day he was arriving, it would do perfectly well if he went up in the afternoon, or even the next day, for today he was going to find a surrogate. He turned over and tried to think of Diane and go to sleep again.

Heilemann, who blew up a ship loaded with munitions and, with it, much of the port of Halifax. The death roll must have been heavy. He must have been pleased with himself when he pulled that off, any man would be; probably he was well away somewhere in the hills behind the town, if there are hills behind Halifax, with a watch in his hand waiting. And presently there would be a flash in the sky, a series of flashes, and after that a loud bang and the roar of subsequent explosions. "Well, that went off all right," he would say to himself. "Now I'll just run over and see if I can't worry Montreal."

Bill sat up in bed, struck a match, and looked at his watch. It was half past six and a bitterly cold morning. He thumped his pillow and cuddled down again. Diane. Today was Thursday, tomorrow Friday, and on Saturday Diane would be his wife, dear lovely Diane, and he would never be all alone in the world any more with her to return to after his journeys. When a man lives the uneasy life of an Intelligence agent he must have some peace to retire to now and then, or his nerves would never stand it. Even if one were continually as successful as Heilemann, one would want peace. He wondered if there were a Mrs. Heilemann, and if so how much he told her. Nothing at all, probably. He would say: "I've just got to run over to Montreal, my dear, to see a man about a dog," and she would believe it—would she? She'd have to. He couldn't say: "I shall be away about a week, my dear; get your mother to stay with you. No, nothing interesting, I'm only going to blow up Montreal."

Bill sat up, drank some water, and huddled under the bedclothes again. Diane with the little curls on her white neck, and those awful solemn promises in the marriage service—the marriage service, he must read it up. Who was it said that it began with "Dearly beloved" and ended with "amazement"? Diane was dearly beloved all right, and they would leave the amazement to the people of Halifax, and perhaps Montreal too—Montreal, or possibly Quebec. It stood to reason a man wouldn't be content with one success like that; he would try to pull off another, naturally; somebody ought to stop him before he had time to do anything more. Probably he was planning something now, and it might take some time to trace him—already it might be too late.

Bill groaned dismally and rolled out of bed into the cold as the landing clock struck seven. He dressed and went downstairs to find the kitchen fire alight and the kettle already singing, so he persuaded the cook to give him tea and bread and butter, and wrote a note to Diane while he was waiting for it.

> Darling, frightfully sorry to leave you alone all day. Must run
> up to town. See you tonight, darling,
> > All my love,
> > Bill

He left a message for his aunt and called at the gardener's cottage to borrow a bicycle for the run to Weatherley Station, and to get the man to deliver the note at the vicarage. He would not take it there himself, though he passed the gate, for fear Diane would see him and want to argue or, still worse, come with him, since it was imperative that she should not know he was going to the War Office. Her father was a colonel; she must know that ordinary privates do not pay calls at the War Office even in wartime, and if she started asking questions there was no telling where it would end.

He saw the same man at the War Office whom he had always seen before, and poured out his tale about Heilemann. "It may be a trap," he concluded, "Hambledon thinks so, but he didn't hear the natural way it slipped out. Even if it is, we thought—"

"Even if it is," said his attentive listener, "we must prove that it is before we disregard it. I will have Mr. Heilemann looked up at once—today, in fact. It is now—" he looked at his watch—"about seven a.m. in Halifax;

they will have all day to look for him and I hope they find him. You are on leave, are you not? When do you return?"

"On the 29th; privates of infantry only get ten days," said Bill with a grin.

"Quite, quite; something might be done about that, but I shall want to see you before you go back. There may be some news from Halifax by then, and in any case there is a man named Denton whom I want you to meet. Where are you staying?"

Bill told him, but added: "I don't propose to stay there all the time. I was thinking of picking up a car somewhere and touring in the West Country with a friend, but I understand petrol is a difficulty."

"The laborer is worthy of his hire," said the man. "I will see that you have a petrol ration card for an adequate quantity, it shall reach you tomorrow, and I hope you'll have a pleasant trip. I suppose you are not staying at any one definite place? No? Then I should be glad if you would telephone the department at least every other evening between seven and nine. I trust there will be no occasion, but one is never sure and I want to make an appointment for you to meet Denton here. Is there anything else I can do for you?"

"Thank you, I don't think so," said Bill, turning down the idea of asking the way to the nearest surrogate. "They must be pleased with me," he thought as he walked along the now familiar passages. " 'Anything else I can do for you?' Wow!"

He found a surrogate by the simple process of asking advice at the first church he came to, and arranged for the marriage of Michael Kingston and Diane Mary Causton at ten thirty a.m. on Saturday.

Next morning at ten he waited for Diane in the Green Lane, which was a disused road of prehistoric antiquity, sunk ten feet below the level of the adjoining fields and completely overarched by trees. It was as private as anyone could wish since no one ever passed that way but laborers going to work.

Presently she came in a sudden gleam of winter sunshine, walking gracefully and smoothly even along the treacherous concealed ruts of the track, and he went to meet her. All was well while he poured out his story: "I just walked into St. Martin's and said: 'What about it?'," and the marriage at her parish church in London on Saturday morning, and the car and the driving license and the petrol ration book—"a man I know is going to wangle it for me, it'll probably come by the second post, so we'll pick up the car in town and just clear off somewhere, just us two alone, Diane."

She was loving and appreciative and her words were all that could be desired, but there was a faint chill in her manner which did not escape his notice.

"Anything the matter, sweetheart?"

"No," she said hesitantly.

"There is. Have I annoyed you in any way? Tell me."

She put her hands on his shoulders and said: "Why did you go off all by yourself yesterday and leave me here? I would have loved to go with you and see the parson and find the car; I was upset when I got your note."

"Sorry, darling. I'm afraid I'm rather like that; you see, I'm used to going about by myself."

"In the army, darling?"

"Well, not on duty, naturally, but when you're resting and you get any time off, you like to get away. You see, when the company is not very congenial, it's nice to be alone when you can. I always liked being alone a good deal," he added truthfully.

"It seemed such a waste of a whole day."

"Sorry, darling. You see, I woke up early and thought about things, and it seemed a much better idea to hare up to town and see the parson chap there than to start making inquiries locally. You know what villages are. So I hopped out of bed, got some tea from cook, and caught the eight fifteen."

"I see."

"Not quite satisfied yet, angel?"

"Yes, dear, of course. But—don't leave me any more than you can help, will you?"

Bill never remembered very much about the wedding, there was a sort of emotional haze over the whole proceedings from the time he kept Diane waiting while he changed into civilian clothes at Waterloo till the moment when, after sending brief but startling telegrams to their respective relations, he found himself driving down Hammersmith Broadway.

Towards evening, when it was getting dark, they neared Devizes. Bill said it was nearly time they made up their minds where they were going to stay the night, and Diane agreed.

Bill said he had never been to this place before and Diane said that that, too, was the case with her.

Bill said that though it seemed almost sacrilegious to refer to such a mundane matter upon a day so sublime as one's wedding day, he, personally, was hungry, and Diane admitted that in spite of an excellent lunch and a passable tea she also was human.

"We do agree nicely together, don't we?" said Bill.

"Just made for each other," she said.

They drew near the Bear at Devizes, pulled up the car, and looked at it.

"Passable pub," said Bill.

"It's a lovely old place," said Diane, and there was a pause till Bill said, "Well, what about it?"

"What, dear?" asked Diane innocently.

"Do you think it'll do?"

"It looks comfortable."

"Wonder if they've got any rooms vacant," he said in a detached manner.

"One might ask," suggested his wife.

"You go and ask them," urged Bill, with the paralytic shyness characteristic of a man on his honeymoon.

"No, you go."

"No, you go, then you can see if you like it."

"I'd rather you went."

"Woman, did I hear you promise to obey me this morning?"

"You didn't look as though you did."

"Oh, didn't I?" said Bill, very interested. "What did I look like?"

"You looked as though you were thinking of something else."

"Come to think of it, I was."

"What were you thinking of, my sweet?"

"Cold pickled pork," said her sweet with a burst of fearful frankness.

"Heavens! Why?"

"It takes your mind off," explained Bill, quoting Hambledon.

"Did it want taking off?"

"My girl," he said grimly, "if you knew what an awful ordeal marriage is—"

"But I do."

"I suppose you do," he said, regarding her with an air of surprise.

"Goose, darling."

"Gander, surely?"

"Both. Are we going to sit here all night?"

"I shouldn't mind," he said, laying an arm along the back of her seat. "I'm very comfortable."

"It might get a little chilly towards morning, don't you think?" she said. "Look at the icicles down that water-pipe."

"So annoying if the police kept moving us on, too. Right. You hop in and get a room while I take the bus round to the garage and get the luggage out."

"All right," she said, and went up the steps.

Bill drove into the yard and found there a retired ostler with legs of the characteristic curve, who opened for him the doors of a vast coach house at present occupied by a trap leaning on its shafts and a model-T Ford with brass fittings. Bill put the car away and got out their two suitcases, which had been the subject of much careful strategy at their respective homes that morning, and the ostler took them from him and preceded him across the yard; but at the sight of the entrance door waiting to receive him into a new life of theoretical bliss, Bill shied like a startled deer. Inside that door somewhere was Diane, his wife, so he would never be really alone any more, and he suddenly remembered that he liked being alone. Besides, people would look at them and say within themselves: "Ha! Newly married!" Barmen and waiters would smile covertly, housemaids would titter in passages, and it would all be too dreadful for words. He went suddenly sideways across the yard towards the gate and came to a dead stop when he realized that he was almost bolting. Got to go through with it now, all his own fault, would get married and now he was trapped—

"Forgotten something, sir?" said the ostler, pausing.

"Oh, ah, no—yes, that is, shouldn't we shut the garage doors?"

"I'll see to that, sir," said the man, and moved on.

Bill realized that there was nothing to be gained by continuing to stand on one embarrassed leg in the middle of a cobbled stable yard in the frosty air, so he put down the other foot, which did not appear to belong to him, clenched his hands, and stumbled after the ostler.

They entered the door, went down a passage, and entered the hall, where Diane was waiting for him. Nearer him was a lady sitting in a basket chair and reading a paper; on her lap was a Pekingese. Bill tripped over nothing in particular, probably his own feet, flung out his hand, and hit the gong, which responded, and the dog got up and barked.

"Quiet, Ferdinand," said the lady.

Diane turned gracefully to meet him and observed his flushed face and shortened breath. "Darling," she said kindly, "have you been running?"

After which things became a merciful blank to him till he found himself with Diane in a large bedroom, presumably upstairs, with the porter carrying in their luggage.

"Shall I draw the blinds, sir?"

"Please," said Bill, remaining near the door.

"See this, sir?"

"What's that?" asked Bill, without moving, but Diane went to the window to see what the man was showing them.

"It's something scratched on the glass," she said. "It's difficult to see by this light. I can read it, it says: 'John Blome merchant Carmarthen on his way from London to Bath and Bristol for execution February 23rd, 1766.' Come and look, Bill."

"I'll see it by daylight," he said. "Cheer up, he'd have been dead by now anyway. Draw the blinds, will you?" he added to the porter. "And send me up a double Haig and Haig, will you?"

"Certainly, sir," said the man, but Diane said: "Will you have it in here, dear?"

"Of course not," he said. "What am I thinking of? We'll go down. Come on."

Diane paused, looked at him uncertainly, and said: "I'll just tidy my hair."

"Right. I'll meet you in the lounge. Is there a lounge?"

"Certainly, sir, down the stairs and across the hall to the right."

"Good," said Bill, and turned to go, but Diane called him, and the porter went out, shutting the door after him.

"Don't you like this room, darling?"

"Of course I do," he said, looking round. "It's a very nice room."

"You seemed as though you didn't want to come into it."

"I don't like lighted windows without blinds."

"How funny of you! Why?"

"Oh, I don't know. I just don't."

Diane came across the room to him, still standing near the door, took his hand and said: "Shall we change the room, darling, if you don't like it?"

"No, it's all right. I don't like the wallpaper, but that's not really important."

"Oh, don't you? I think it's rather pretty, all roses. Why did you shiver?"

"Gray goose, old thing, that's all, and we can easily abolish the wallpaper—thus." He switched out the light, opened the door, and said, "The time has come."

"What for?"

"Sherry, my angel, come on downstairs." As they entered the lounge, he said: "By the way, did I buy you a wedding ring?"

"Of course you did, Bill darling, this morning."

"Odd, I can't remember doing so. Sherry for you," but she noticed that his was whisky.

"Happy days," he said, and smiled at her over the rim of the glass, his blue eyes on hers, and suddenly it did not matter any more if he drove recklessly and was moody one minute and laughing the next, and left her without warning or apology so long as he remained just Bill and went on wanting her.

"Bill—"

"What is it?"

"You do belong to me, don't you?"

"Do I?" His face changed and hardened and became suddenly years older. "I don't think anybody belongs to anybody else," he said slowly.

"Bill darling, don't look like that."

"Like what?"

"So like a stranger."

"Do I?"

Diane's eyes filled with tears and he noticed it. He sat beside her and took her hand.

"Listen, darling. You're such a kid, I don't know how to explain, but we're supposed to be about the same age, aren't we? Well, we're not. I've been at the war—what—fifteen months now; that means I'm fifteen years older than you. I've seen things and done things I'll never tell you about, and perhaps you'll come across things you don't understand about me which I shan't be able to explain, and to that extent I am a stranger. It isn't my fault. Try just to love me and trust me, Diane, won't you? I'll try my best to make you happy, but I can't belong to anybody or anything, Diane, except perhaps—" he stopped, and suddenly the memory came back of Dixon Ogilvie on the downs one moonlight night, talking of the things a man is bound to.

"What, darling?"

" 'O peaceful England,' " he quoted beneath his breath, and to that she found no answer.

CHAPTER TWELVE
"ABOUT THESE ZEPPELINS—"

They stayed on at the Bear, since, contrary to Bill's fears, the people were not unbearably sympathetic and, indeed, did not seem in the least interested in how long they had been married, which may have been either preoccupation or the height of tact. They walked, made excursions in the car, kept

Christmas together, made friends with people, and were absurdly happy considering it was wartime and Bill had ten days' leave—a fragile happiness like fine glass which might break at any moment and cut to the bone the hands which held it.

The days went on to Thursday, the 28th, and Bill did not say a word about returning, till in the evening Diane, very white about the nostrils but with chin well up, said: "Is this our last day, darling?"

"What?" asked Bill from the depths of an armchair.

Diane repeated her question.

"Oh, I shouldn't think so," he said, remembering certain telephone conversations with the War Office of which he had not told Diane. "I'll ring up the army and ask for a few days extra."

The daughter of Colonel Causton was horrified.

"But, darling, an escort will come and you'll be arrested."

Bill laughed.

"It's no laughing matter, Bill, overstaying your leave. Heaven knows I wish it could last for ever, but I know, perhaps better than you do, what happens."

"I know, 'when I was at Cawnpore in '88—' "

"Bill dear, really—"

At that moment a waiter came in and said: "You are wanted on the telephone, sir; the War Office."

"What?" gasped Diane, but Bill, uttering words that sounded curiously like "Blasted idiots" had already left the room. When he came back he said casually: "That's all right, precious. We have to go to town tomorrow if you don't mind, and I'll go and see a man and try to wangle a few days' extra leave."

"But why did the War Office ring you up?"

"To tell me to report tomorrow, old thing."

"But how did they know you were here?"

"Because I rang them up the evening we arrived. You see," said Bill, improvising brilliantly, "wartime isn't like peacetime, we never know from day to day what may happen. So every soldier who goes on leave has to let the authorities know where he can be found all the time, in case they want to recall him."

"I see," she said. "You didn't tell me that before."

"Would you have been happy if you'd known I might be called back at any moment?"

"No," she said. "It was sweet of you not to tell me."

"It is your husband's duty to protect you," he said solemnly.

He left Diane at a hotel in Kensington the following afternoon and went to the familiar room at the War Office.

"I did not wish to disturb your leave with business," said the officer in charge, "but in point of fact we gathered in Heilemann the same day that you told us about him."

"Good work."

"Oh, there was no difficulty about it; apparently he is a well-known and respected tradesman of Halifax whose family have lived there for three generations and who, although he has a German name, was never suspected of German sympathies."

"Are they sure he's the right man?"

"I think so. You see," he added significantly, "he was a gunsmith."

"With access to explosives!"

"Quite. There is no other proof of his having done it, so of course nothing much will happen to him; we shall only intern him with, perhaps, a little extra care and attention. There is another little matter which I wanted to discuss with you. You remember on a previous occasion asking me if I had heard anything about some new hydrogen pressure valves for the Zepps? I made inquiries, and you were right. The Zepp's climbing performance and ceiling is now something quite remarkable, and they have got four of the newest Zepps fitted with this device in the sheds at Ahlhorn. There is also a Schutte-Lanz there."

"It almost seems," said Bill thoughtfully, "as though something ought to be done about it."

"If something effective were done about it, it would be—not to beat about the bush—it would be one of the finest deeds of the war, and one of the most useful."

"Hydrogen is highly inflammable, if I remember my chem lessons correctly," said Bill, with a slow smile spreading over his face.

"Have you heard of the Pomeroy bullet?" asked the War Office man. "Phosphorus and fishhooks, roughly speaking. Perhaps you also recall the chemical properties of phosphorus?"

A messenger came in and laid a buff slip on the desk and the officer looked at it. "Bring him up, please." Bill got up from his chair and began to walk about the room.

"I should like to brood over this for a while," he said. "If Hambledon and I brood together, we might hatch out something."

"Carry on, I leave it to you. This fellow who is coming up now is the man

Denton of whom I spoke. He is going back to Germany shortly and I want you to meet him, as you might find it convenient to work with him some day. He is a queer bird, but has done one or two quite useful things; he may turn out to be quite good. He is going to Mainz."

The door opened and there entered a tall young man with an air of fatigue, a very smart uniform, wonderful boots, and a hat with a crown of the utmost floppiness such as was firmly discouraged in army orders. Nevertheless he wore it, even at the War Office, nor did anyone reproach him, for that was the sort of man he was. He greeted the man at the desk, sank into Bill's chair, and said: "Really, your passages get longer and harder every time I toil along them. If we win the war, will you have cork linoleum laid down?"

"I doubt it," said the War Office man. "Denton, this is Saunders from Cologne."

Denton uncoiled himself, greeted Bill, and said: "Have I pinched your chair?"

"No," said Bill with more politeness than truth. "I was walking about, thinking."

"When I think," said Denton, "I have to lie down and close my eyes."

"Well," said their senior, "how did you get on on your last trip? Don't go, Saunders."

Denton gave an account of various routine activities in the Lübeck district. "Very boring, all that office work," he added. "I wouldn't have believed how soon the thrill of being a dangerous enemy alien with death waiting for you behind every door, so to speak, wears off. The only excitement was tracking down the cholera fiend."

"Eh?" said Bill, who had only been half listening, with the other half of his mind engaged with the Zeppelin sheds at Ahlhorn. "What was that you said?"

"Feller who got the brainwave about dropping cholera germs into London's drinking water. It seems that if you just chuck the bugs in loose, as it were, they float on the surface, catch pneumonia, and die. They want to get away down to the bottom where there's no draft and a nice lot of green slime and whatnot. So this feller thought up a scheme for growing germs on small squares of linen, weighting 'em with a few split shot, and enclosing 'em in a soluble container. Drop container in reservoir, it dissolves, little linen square reaches bottom, and bugs resume active family life. So simple."

"Who was this?" asked Bill, who had gone very white.

"Funny old boy called Rüdesheim at Lübeck. So we disposed of him and burned his lab. Quite a number of eminent professors snuffed it about then—five, to be exact. He had a list of his coadjutors in crime, so they were mopped up. Here's the list, I souvenired it."

He threw it down on the table and Bill picked it up. One of the entries ran: "Amtenbrink, refuses."

"Amtenbrink, refuses," read Bill in a harsh voice. "My God, and we killed him."

The other two men looked at him.

"He said he was growing cultures of mildew to cure his roses, and Hambledon didn't believe him, so he died."

"If he'd been a few years younger," said Denton, "he'd probably have died much sooner and far less comfortably."

"There is this to be remembered," said the War Office man in quiet tones. "He knew all about it, he had been approached—"

"Yes," said Bill, "he said so himself."

"Quite. So when all the others died off, authority would have put the screw on him to take on the job whether he liked it or not, so it is even possible he is grateful to you, since there are some things a decent man will rather die than do."

There was a brief silence, after which Bill said: "Thank you. I will remember that."

"You would like a few days' extra leave, of course. You can have—"

"Thank you," interrupted Bill, "I would rather not, I think. I will go back tonight—no, tomorrow, if I may. About Hambledon's petrol?"

"That has been arranged. Just a moment." The officer rang a bell and gave a serial number to the clerk who answered it. The man went away and returned with a file in a stout paper cover with brass tags dangling from it. The officer extracted a couple of letters and gave them to Bill, who stowed them away in his wallet, and the clerk, who had waited for the file, took it away again. "We don't leave things lying about, you notice," said the officer. "Of all the government departments, we are the tidiest."

"Keep it up," said Denton with a yawn, "and we may all live to be grandfathers yet."

Bill arrived back in Cologne two and a half days later, and found Tommy Hambledon in his office, smoking a thin black cigar and talking on the telephone about petrol to someone whom he called *"Excellenz."* Bill realized the moment's need and handed him in silence the two letters he had brought from the War Office. Hambledon continued: "I was this moment telling Your Excellency that I expected news of the ship today. The news has this moment reached me. The tanker will arrive—" and so on. Bill strolled across to the window and looked idly out upon the people passing up and down the busy Höhestrasse. Frau and the elder Fräulein Bluehm, with shopping-bags, not very full. Jacob, the head waiter at the Café Palant, emerging from its doors on his way home for the afternoon's rest before the long evening began. Reck, the science master at Mülheim school, with his mackintosh pockets bulging with papers. Soldiers on leave, strolling along and staring in the shop windows. A boy on a bicycle who caught one of his front-wheel rimsprings in a badly fitting manhole cover and came a terrific purler accompanied by a bottle of milk and a small bag of potatoes, which shot all over the road; he had springs round the rim of his front wheel to take the place of the unobtainable tire. A little girl eating an apple.

Hambledon put the receiver down and said: "I'm glad to see you back. Have a good leave, and how's Weatherley Parva?"

"Quite good, thanks. Beastly cold, of course, but no worse than it is here. Weatherley Parva is much the same as usual. I had lunch at the vicarage, and all that. I went to the War Office the day before I came back. They have got Heilemann, he's a gunsmith in Halifax. The really important thing is about the Zepps." Bill repeated what had been said, and added: "It seems simple enough if only one could get in there. Phosphorus bursts into flame when it is exposed to the atmosphere, doesn't it? Reck will know."

"Yes, Reck will help us, but you must have some sort of official sanction to get to Ahlhorn."

"We shall have to think up a scheme for obtaining official sanction, then."

"If you could get some sort of job there," said Hambledon, "the thing's as good as done. But you can bet your last halfpenny that every man engaged there is as well-authenticated as Kaiser Bill. Have a drink, there's some rather good sherry in the cupboard."

"Thanks, I will," said Bill, and got it out. "But I am not any sort of an expert on any branch of Zepp construction, and this isn't a case where bluff would have a snowflake's chance in Hades."

"No. It will have to be something you can do. What could a little importer do to help the Graf von Zeppelin?"

"Sell him some winter underwear?"

"Less promising schemes have succeeded," said Hambledon. "Some brainwave may flood our minds presently. Anything else?"

"I met a long lad named Denton who is coming to Mainz. Authority thought it might be useful if we knew each other. He has been in Germany quite recently, at Lübeck, I believe."

"What's the matter?" asked Hambledon, watching Bill's face.

"Oh, nothing. Only he, or his little lot, found the real professor of the cholera scheme—if life were more like the books we should call it the C. Plan, shouldn't we?"

"Please go on," said Hambledon, and Bill told him. Hambledon listened without interruption, then "Amtenbrink, God rest his soul," he said, lifted his glass, made a little sign with it, and drank.

"Another mistake on my part," he went on. "It seems to be time I went home and took up breeding white mice."

Bill repeated the War Office man's words of consolation, and Hambledon said: "That may be true, I hope it is. But I still think that on the evidence—however, it's no good harping on it, let it go. Now, about these Zeppelins—"

Much later that evening Bill rang up von Bodenheim to announce his return with something to report, and was asked to go to the house in the Blumenthalstrasse forthwith, so he went there and was very cordially received.

"What I really wanted to tell you," said Dirk Brandt of the German Intelligence, after various items of news had been told, "was about an odd thing which happened on my last night in London. This English officer whom I made friends with at the Southampton hotel I was telling you about arranged to meet me for an evening together, and we had quite a good time, dinner, show—the Coliseum to be exact, there was a girl singing rather a good song called 'Not Yet'—drinks at the bar, and finally a club he belonged to, which had an odd name, the Clinging Codfish, of all things. It was a cheerful place."

"You seem to have enjoyed your trip," said von Bodenheim. "Though I can think of pleasanter things than codfish to have clinging to one. But I dare say the ultimate result would be much the same—you'd wish you hadn't."

"I dare say," said Dirk laughing. "Can't say I've got that far yet. Anyway, this fellow got pretty stewed as the evening went on, and he talked. Oh, how he talked! I had his life history as time went on, but that's not the point. There was another man in the club who rather impressed me; he was drinking hard and quite reckless. He had a girl with him, and just to impress her, I suppose, he ordered a half-dozen new-laid eggs and shied them into the electric fan. The results came back all over the adjacent diners, so, although they are fairly tolerant towards the amusements of soldiers in London now, he wasn't popular, and they persuaded him to go away. Striking man to look at, too, fine face, rather like a hawk. I said something to the effect that it was a pity to see a splendid-looking chap like that make such an exhibition of himself, and my friend said that perhaps I'd let myself go a bit if I had his job in prospect."

"Did you hear what it was?"

"Yes, he was going to burn the Zeppelins at Ahlhorn."

"What?" cried von Bodenheim, in a tone of voice that brought his soldier servant hurrying out of the back premises. "What was his name? (It is all right, Hans, I do not require anything.) What regiment did he belong to?"

"I did my best to find out his name and regiment, but my man was not so drunk as all that, so all I could do was to memorize his face; I should know him again anywhere. I didn't recognize his badges."

"Can you describe him?"

"I don't know that I'm much good at describing people," said Dirk, with a frown of concentration. "He had fair hair, a hooked nose, and a prominent chin. Rather a red face, but that may have been due to the evening. Tallish—no, not very tall, but considerably taller than I am, for example; five foot eight or ten. The most outstanding thing about his appearance was his air of being somebody, if you know what I mean. You couldn't help noticing him."

"Even if he wasn't throwing new-laid eggs into an electric fan, I suppose," said von Bodenheim sarcastically. "You mean he had personality, an attribute which he could shed in a moment. Otherwise he was tallish, with fair hair and prominent features. It is a description of about a quarter of the British and German armies."

"I'm sorry," said Dirk, quite crestfallen. "I can't think of anything—"

"It is I who should apologize. You come to me with a most remarkable piece of intelligence, and all I do is to snub you because you cannot give a detailed description of him. My dear boy, please forgive me, it was unpardonable. My only excuse is that the news is so desperately important— more so than you have any idea."

"Indeed, sir?"

"You have done extraordinarily well and rendered a great service to my—our—country."

"Thank you," said Dirk in a tone of some emotion.

"There is only one thing to be done and you are the only man to do it."

"And that is?"

"You must go to Ahlhorn and keep a lookout for the man yourself."

Hendrik Brandt demurred as strongly as he dared to having his nephew taken away from him when he had only just returned to the office, but was imperiously overridden by von Bodenheim in person. So young Dirk Brandt was provided with a special pass which enabled him to go anywhere and do almost anything, and orders had been sent in advance to the commanding officer of the troops guarding the airship sheds to supply Dirk with whatever comfort and assistance he might need; in fact, broadly speaking, to do what the boy told him. Bill was shown the orders.

"Oh, it's almost too good to be true," said Hambledon. "Either there's a catch in it somewhere or you're too lucky to be human, and if I were you I would sacrifice something to the gods. Throw the youngest Miss Bluehm into the Rhine."

"Why Marie Bluehm?"

"I thought you were rather fond of her."

"She's a nice girl, that's all; she plays the piano rather well. I'm not smitten."

"Glad to hear it; on our job we can't afford these distractions. By the way, wasn't there a girl at home?"

"There was," said Bill, who had such a rooted disinclination to bring Diane into even the remotest contact with the job that he would not mention her to Hambledon if he could help it; at least, not here in Cologne. "But why mustn't we talk to girls occasionally?"

"Oh, talk to 'em occasionally, by all means, but don't for pity's sake marry any of 'em."

"Why not?"

"Consider the life of an Intelligence man's wife. Either he tells her what his job is, or else he doesn't. If he does, she will never know another peaceful moment as long as she lives, because there's no end to our war—that is, if she cares for him. If she doesn't, she may talk, and then he'd have to shoot her. Suppose he doesn't tell her. He says instead that he is an insurance agent, or a traveler in pig food, or an inspector of nuisances, which last is nearer the truth than most of us get in this life. He tells her he's going to Bristol to see a man about a drain, but you can bet your boots that some dear school friend of hers will write and tell her that he was seen last Wednesday strolling along the promenade at Felixstowe with a dazzling blonde, after which he will spend the next twenty years of his life giving lucid and convincing explanations, and she won't believe any of 'em. No, we don't marry on our job, Bill. Pass the beer, lecturing is dry work. That's what's the matter with schoolmastering, too many lectures and not enough beer."

"Talking about schoolmasters, I've got to see Reck tonight."

"To collect the needful, of course. It's convenient having a chemist who'll get the stuff for you. When do you start?"

"At eight tomorrow morning."

Bill packed his shabby suitcase and departed for Ahlhorn in state and a staff car with a soldier driver, which had been placed at his disposal. It was only a hundred and fifty miles, but the tires were bad and the roads worse, and it was not till late in the evening that they arrived. The Landsturm officer commanding the small garrison was a portly Bavarian major of mature years, who was puzzled and pained at having to take orders from an insignificant civilian, and a Dutchman at that, and inclined to think it all too ridiculous for words.

"The country is going to the dogs," he said. "In my young days we'd have thrown a cordon of sentries round the place with instructions to shoot at sight anything approaching, from a rabbit upwards. All this stopping people and asking 'em questions, a lot of damned nonsense in my opinion, how d'you know they're speaking the truth? All this rubbish about English spies! In my opinion if the English spies are as clever as some people make out, they'll know better than to take on such a wild-goose chase. What? A total stranger to walk in here, set fire to the Zeppelins, and then quietly walk out again? Damned nonsense! I don't believe in your English spy, how do I know you aren't going to fire the balloons yourself? I don't know you, do I?"

This was nearly too much for even Bill's command of countenance, but he managed to assume an expression of pained surprise and to convey how unexpected it was to find an old and trusted officer in the army of His Imperial Majesty flouting the commands of authority.

"I don't flout them, sir; who says I flout 'em? I receive orders and those orders are obeyed, but that doesn't mean I'm going to sing a psalm about them. Well, it's your responsibility now, young man, not mine. If the Zeppelins are burned now, I wouldn't be in your shoes. Damned nonsense."

Dirk Brandt stayed at a hotel in Ahlhorn and drove the car the three or four miles to the airship station every day. At the times when the shifts went in, and at all times when anyone was admitted through the guarded gates, he was there to see that the sentries performed thoroughly their task of checking the passes carried by anyone, however unimportant, who sought to enter that sacred enclosure. He became intensely irksome to the management and the workmen because his inspection of passes and search for matches and other forbidden articles was so thorough as to delay considerably the entry of the shifts to their work. On three occasions he found splendid-looking men with fair hair and aquiline features and had them hauled into the guardroom for examination, but each time they proved to be perfectly honest Germans on their lawful occasions. As he explained to a sizzling works manager, it was not that he had forgotten what the man looked like—on the contrary, that ill-omened face was indelibly carved on the most retentive tablets of his memory—but that there would be a lot of difference in the appearance of a British company officer at a smart night club and a possibly grubby and inadequately shaved workman in blue overalls, and one must make sure. He, unworthy though he was of so great an honor, was personally responsible to the All-Highest in this matter, and he would fulfil his duties at whatever inconvenience to himself and others.

Von Bodenheim would have been pleased if he could have heard him, but even Dirk's magic pass barely saved him from personal violence upon one occasion when he detached a high-born and appropriately dignified Austrian officer from a party which was making a personally conducted tour of the sheds. Dirk kept him locked up all through the lunch hour and finally had him stripped to the skin to see if his pronounced figure was real, and examined his hair with a magnifying-glass to see if it had been bleached. The officer was, of course, released with profuse apologies, but Dirk hoped the Austrian would remember that curious and undignified things happened to haughty men who stuck monocles in their eyes, glared at unoffending strangers, and asked audibly: "Who is that funny snub-nosed little squirt?"

At times when there were no entrants to detain Dirk at the gates, he would wander about the vast echoing sheds, huge as cathedrals, where if a man dropped a spanner on the concrete floors the sound rang like the last trump. He formed the habit of making a final tour of the buildings the last thing every night, walking through every passage and every compartment in each of the airships and even climbing the ladders to the platforms at the top. He noticed with an interest he did not display that there was no protection provided against attacks from above and that even the guns could only be trained on a level and downwards; evidently the stories of the exceptional climbing capabilities and high ceiling of these new Zeppelins were true. They saw no reason to expect attack from above.

He moved about on these tours at a rapid pace, alert, purposeful, and determined, and the perspiring elderly Landsturm privates who were detailed by their distrustful commander to follow him everywhere soon became content to wait downstairs, as it were, till he returned from his too athletic excursions. And every day the Zeppelins were more nearly completed.

One day he took the commandant aside and told him that he had been officially informed that a man had been detected passing the Dutch frontier near Rhede. Though fired on by the frontier guards, he had evaded them, and was now somewhere in Arenburg, doubtless making his way towards Ahlhorn. He was described as a tall man with fair hair.

"God bless my soul," said the agitated commandant, "you don't mean to tell me this ridiculous story is true?"

"Of course it's true," said Dirk Brandt, justly indignant. "What do you suppose I walk miles every night climbing all over these infernal flying cathedrals of yours for? To keep my figure down?"

"I don't see what more we can do," said the major, disregarding in his distress this delicate but unkind allusion to his own form.

"We will have every single soul who is not absolutely indispensable out of these sheds as early as possible every night. The few who remain will be all men who are known to us and to each other personally. Your men will form a close cordon at a distance from the sheds so as to obviate the danger of someone dodging past them into cover, and they will shoot at sight."

"Good. That is sense at last."

"I myself will make an extra careful inspection every night, and after I leave, no one is to be admitted under any pretext whatever."

"It shall be done."

"We will foil him yet, Herr Commandant."

"Has he wings?" asked the commandant, becoming almost lyrical with excitement. "Can he change himself into a bird or a rabbit? No. He cannot enter."

"Splendid," said Dirk approvingly.

The Zeppelin crews had arrived and taken over, and only a few workmen remained making last-minute adjustments. The envelope compartments were fully inflated with hydrogen, which, in spite of all precautions, leaked out slowly but continuously and accumulated in the wide barrel roofs, so the enormous ventilators placed in the roofs for the purpose were frequently opened to allow the gas to escape, but it always accumulated again. Now the huge tanks were being filled with petrol and the racks with bombs; soon everything would be ready.

Dirk Brandt gave the commandant, whom he had encountered buying socks in Ahlhorn, a lift back to the airship station.

"It is not long to wait now," said the major. "Another two or three days and your spy will be too late; the airships will go out when this moon is full."

"I am glad," said young Brandt simply. "The responsibility is great and I am too young for it. I wish they would catch the man."

"It is true you are very young," said the German kindly, "but no one can say you are not conscientious. *Himmel*, you brood over those airships like an old hen."

"I want them to grow up big strong birds and lay nice eggs," said Dirk—a remark which amused the simple soul of the commandant.

"I have known eggs to burst with a loud report and scatter their contents abroad," he said, shaking with laughter like a well-molded jelly, "but I would not call them nice eggs. No, not nice at all."

They looked ahead of them across the treeless fields to where the great sheds stood up like slag-heaps against the sky.

"But what a blaze if they should go!" continued the German. "In this flat country the fire would be seen for fifty miles. Do be careful!"

"I am sorry," said Dirk, who was driving. "The tires are smooth and this pavement is greasy. That ditch seems to draw the car like a magnet."

"She is tired, poor thing, and wishes to rest perhaps," said the Herr Commandant with a yawn. "I shall sleep sounder myself when the airships have gone to wake up England."

Brandt went his rounds that night with particular thoroughness, leaving unobtrusive little packets here and there, since his Landsturm companion made no attempt to follow him along narrow passages and up steep spidery ladders inside the envelopes of the Zeppelins and right out on to the top. Dirk's orders had been obeyed; the great hangars were silent under the glare of the huge lamps which were kept burning all night, and only a faint whispering echo running up the walls now and then told of the movements of a belated workman busy on some final urgency.

He left the place, taking care that the commandant saw him go, and had returned to his hotel, eaten his supper, and was preparing for bed in the dark with his eyes on the uncurtained window when a brilliant tongue of flame shot into the sky, to be followed by another, and another. Dirk rushed downstairs, convincingly half-clad, to be met by the landlord.

"I should not go out, Herr Brandt," he said. "It is the accursed English aeroplanes, they have bombed the sheds. My son assures me that he saw them distinctly."

"I must go," said Dirk distractedly. "It is my duty."

"At least resume your trousers before you go out, gracious sir," urged the proprietor, and Brandt, with a look of horror at his own attire, uttered a strangled cry and rushed upstairs again. Here, strangely enough, he seemed in no particular hurry about clothing himself once more in the garments of decorum. He opened the window to listen to the roar of the fire just in time to see the first roof fall in and the flames shoot up hundreds of feet into the sky.

" 'Phosphorus and fishhooks,' " quoted Bill Saunders. "My giddy, sainted aunt, *what* a bonfire!"

He dressed himself and went out to get the car, expecting to find the streets full of staring people, but to his surprise there was no one about, though lighted windows and moving shadows on blinds showed that the town was wakeful and uneasy. He drove as fast as possible along the slippery road till at a point about a mile from the sheds he was stopped by a sentry, to whom Dirk showed his pass.

"I beg pardon, I did not recognize you," said the man. "Nevertheless, it will not be safe to take the car any nearer, for who knows that the whole countryside may not burn with such a start? Thank Heaven there is snow on the ground."

"Help me to back the car into this gateway," said Dirk, "and I will go on on foot. Heaven help us, it looks as though even the sky was in flames. I suppose there will be fire engines along soon, I must not block the roads."

"I expect there will," said the sentry, helping him to turn his front wheels, "though I think it would be just as useful if everyone gathered round and spat at it. Still, it is always a relief to one's feelings to feel one is at least trying to do something."

"How true!" said Dirk, and sprinted up the road.

The heat increased as he went on till before he reached the entrance gates it became unbearable, so he pulled up and joined one of many groups of men who, with arms flung up to shield their faces, were watching in grim silence the destruction of months of their devoted labor. The noise of the fire was so loud that no man could hear himself speak. Every few moments there was an additional roar as more of the great bombs exploded, and the circle of men backed away as the flame of the blazing hydrogen became more than their eyes could bear. The whole scene appeared to be dissolving in unquenchable fire, and even Bill Saunders's natural exultation of spirit was overawed by such an appalling success.

"Good God," he muttered, "this is really awful." He approached a Landsturm private who was standing near, touched his arm to attract his attention, and yelled in his ear: "Where's the commandant?"

The man pointed away to the left where a number of soldiers were running about like ants and apparently trying to make something work. Dirk Brandt went to the spot and found the commandant supervising the employment of a primitive kind of pump which might have been effective in putting out a burning cottage, but was mere waste of energy in the face of such a disaster. When Dirk came up to him he threw up his hands in a gesture of despair and signed to the men to abandon the attempt. Dirk took his arm and drew him away behind one of the numerous temporary buildings which surrounded the actual sheds, and which afforded some shelter from the intolerable heat and glare.

"It cannot be true," shouted the commandant. "He cannot have got through. It is impossible. Not a ghost can have passed through my line of sentries, and yet—"

"It is coincidence," yelled Dirk in an attempt to be consoling. "It is an accident; some spark caused by a dropped tool, some workman stupid enough to try and smoke."

"If one did, it was the last thing he ever did."

"Did any of the men who were inside escape?"

"Some from the farther sheds, yes, I saw them running like hares. Not from the end where the fire started."

Dirk shivered, and the old soldier, who had eventually come to like him, saw it and patted his arm.

"It is not your fault," he said, "you must not blame yourself. You could not have done more, could you?"

Dirk looked upwards where the incredible flames, high in the air, seemed to be licking the stars.

"No, I don't think I could," he said slowly.

CHAPTER THIRTEEN
"STRIKEN! STRIKEN!"

BILL SAUNDERS arrived in Cologne early in the evening and set out to see Hambledon, whom he expected to find at the office in the Höhestrasse. He noticed, however, that the old match-seller was crying his *"Striken! Striken!"* at the Cathedral side of the Dom Hof garden, so he crossed over the road and bought a box of matches, which contained also a small piece of paper with the words: "Metropol, haste," in Hambledon's writing. "Wonder what's up," he thought, and jumped on a streetcar which took him up the Breitestrasse.

He walked into the Metropol to find the place nearly empty and Hambledon sitting at a table entertaining two ladies, the Bavarian Nightingales, Hedwige and Elsa Schwiss. The entertainment did not seem to have been any too successful, for Hambledon looked uncomfortable and apologetic, Elsa was unashamedly crying, and Hedwige was patting her shoulder and uttering consoling phrases. Dirk went up and greeted the party, but Elsa, instead of languishing at him as usual, looked at him with tragic eyes and said: "Is it true he is dead?"

"Who?" asked Dirk. "I hadn't heard of anyone in particular."

"Flug-Leutnant Knirim," said Hambledon in a low tone. "He was killed in the trenches two days ago, and I happened to mention it to these ladies, not knowing—"

"We loved each other," said Elsa with unexpected dignity. "One night here—of course, you were here too, I forgot. He said something he shouldn't, and that devil von Bodenheim—" Her voice failed, and Hedwige put an arm round her and said: *"Liebchen, mein Liebchen."*

"Von Bodenheim had him arrested," said Dirk.

"And sent into the trenches like a common soldier," cried Elsa with flashing eyes, "and now he's dead dead, and it's his fault. Oh, Anton, Anton! I want him," she wailed.

Dirk bit his lip; the girl's genuine grief was very touching even to one who thought himself so hardened. "I—am very sorry, Fräulein," he stammered.

"I've got his pistol," said Elsa. "He was in my dressing room when they arrested him, you know. He had taken it off and dropped in on the table, and something had covered it up, I found it after he had gone. He used to come in every night," she said dreamily. "Of course he was drunk that night or he wouldn't have talked, but flying men always drink. He used to come in and throw his cap down anywhere. I'd come in and see it lying on one of my dresses—I liked that, it was the right place for it—I always saw that first, and then I knew I'd find him in the chair behind the door waiting for me. Sometimes he'd be asleep, that was when he'd been drinking, and he looked such a baby with his eyes shut—they are shut now—Anton—"

"Fräulein, for God's sake," said Dirk, and Hambledon said to her sister: "Can't you get her to go home?"

"Let her talk if it eases her," said Hedwige. "There's no one here, and if there were, tears are not such a strange sight these days."

"That's a good idea," said Elsa. "I've got his pistol, I'll shoot myself and then we'll be together again. We shall, shan't we? Nobody could be cruel enough to keep us apart then."

"Oh, you wouldn't leave me all alone," said Hedwige, weeping.

"You have your Kaspar, you will not be all alone," said Elsa wearily. "I must go to Anton, he will be so bored without me, and when he is bored he always does something stupid, he will vex *den lieben Gott*."

Hambledon looked significantly at Hedwige Schwiss, who nodded in reply. "Come home, darling," she said, rising from her chair, "dear little sister."

Elsa got up mechanically and the two men bowed over her hand and called her "*gnädige Fräulein*." She looked at them as though she did not see them, and said slowly: "But as for that devil von Bodenheim, a frightful thing will happen to him and he will burn in hell," and she turned and walked steadily out of the place, with Hedwige following after.

Tommy Hambledon stood until they were out of sight and then sank into his chair and mopped his forehead. "Heavens above, Bill, what a scene! Never, never, never again will I tell any woman that any man whatever has died in any manner at all so long as I continue to live. Order some brandy, will you? I need it. Incidentally, who exactly is Kaspar?"

"Bluehm, I believe," said Bill, and gave the order. "Do you think she will do as she says?"

"No, Hedwige will see to that. For one thing, if she did, it would break up the act."

"It is always as well to be practical."

"There is no need to be sarcastic. When you are older you'll realize that lovers come and go, but the necessity for bread and butter remains with us till death—that is, if you ever live to become older, which at the moment seems to me improbable."

"Why this pessimism?"

"Because von Bodenheim has sent for me. Think that over. Sent for me, not you. He rang up on the telephone and asked if I was in, and following my usual custom—thank goodness—I impersonated our nonexistent officeboy and replied that I was down at the wharves and could I give me a message? He did not ask when you were expected back though all Germany is ringing with the story of Ahlhorn—congratulations—he said he would be glad if I could call at his house any time after seven tonight on urgent business. I said I was not sure whether I had any engagements tonight and he said that I was to tell me that it would be most unfortunate if

I had, and I didn't like his tone at all. He-who-must-be-obeyed in person. I have a horrid feeling that if I don't go I shall be fetched, and the idea simply revolts me. So I fled the office, left old Striken a note for you, and floated up here for a little peace and quiet. And did I get it? Oh dear, oh. Köbes! The same again."

"But what has happened?"

"I don't know, but the gaff has been stridently blown somehow. Does a gaff produce a strident note? Describe a gaff, with notes on at least three different methods of blowing it, and to think I used to get bored with life at Chappell's. You see the point, don't you? Why send for me, whom he has only met once and in whom he shouldn't have the faintest interest? The only possible answer is that he has discovered what we are and didn't expect you to return from Ahlhorn; he thought you'd skip over the nearest frontier. So as David was out of his reach, he proposed to concentrate on Jonathan. He must know that if you're in it, I am too. It is more than possible that every policeman, Intelligence agent, and other arresting body in Germany is hunting for us while we sit here and drink brandy. I don't know where the balloon has gone up, but it certainly has. Talking of balloons, I congratulate you, I do indeed, I take my hat right off and lay it reverently upon the floor. It must have been an imposing sight."

"Exactly like hell," said Bill absently. "You know, I am not convinced that you are right, it is quite possible he only wanted you to get him something urgently, and if you'd been yourself on the phone you'd have been told what it was. Haig and Haig, for a guess. Probably the faithful Hans said: 'Last bottle, master,' and if you'd seen him at it as I have you'd know one bottle is merely an annoying reminder of lost delight."

"You didn't hear that incisive voice."

"He is always incisive, and particularly on the phone. I think I'll just go along and see him."

"I think you are quite mad," said Tommy Hambledon. "Have you still got the staff car at your disposal, and that almighty pass of yours? I think we'd better leave at once."

"Think how silly we shall look running like blazes with nobody running after us. 'The wicked flee when no man pursueth, but the righteous is as bold as a lion.' Besides, wouldn't it be as well to make sure whether he suspects us or not? I propose to find out."

"I will agree on two conditions: one, that we arrange our getaway first, and the other, that I come with you to see von Bodenheim. After all, he asked to see me; it will look natural enough."

"No. If you're right, there's no sense in both of us walking into the trap," said Bill. "Would you come in support, instead? The front door opens by merely turning a handle, and I will draw you a plan of the ground floor. Then you can enter with the appropriate stealth, bewaring of Hans, and back me up with an automatic. Yes, I still have the pass and the car is in the garage of the Dom Hotel."

"Good. It is obviously no use our attempting to get out by the Dutch frontier, because that is the way they will expect us to go. I have been thinking it out. There's always some place where whoever wants you will never think of looking for you—if you ever commit a real civilian murder, get yourself six months for robbery on the way home and stop in jail till the hue-and-cry dies down. Where will they not look for us? Driving down towards the front line of course. I have the uniforms of a German major in a Westphalian infantry regiment complete with cloak—I kept it for a rainy day—and private's uniform to match. I am Major Dirk Brandt on very important business, hence my special pass, and you are my orderly. We will drive the Staff car through Aachen, Maestricht, Malines, Ghent, and Bruges to Ostend, because I'm certain no one would think us fools enough to drive straight into the lion's mouth—praying for a prolonged yawn."

"What happens at Ostend?"

"We shall find a boat waiting for us, a rowboat, my pippin. Are you an oarsman? Neither am I, but we shall find we are when the time comes, believe me. We shall row out into the cold North Sea for two or three miles and rendezvous with the M.L. boat sent there by a not ungrateful country. It's been done before."

"Has it?" said Bill, entirely without enthusiasm. "Not by the same man twice, I'll bet. However, if we must row out into the North Sea in a small boat which probably won't be there when we want it, to pick up without lights or compass a rendezvous with an M.L. which won't be able to see us if we do meet, by all means let's. But I shall have to be very heartily on the run before I find any real fun in it."

"You'll be on the run all right after you've seen von Bodenheim," said Tommy Hambledon grimly. "That is, if you are still capable of movement."

"I love your moods of unquenchable optimism. How do we get in touch with the Royal Navy?"

"Reck and his wireless. We must warn him before we do anything else."

"Unless Heaven sends another electric storm such as we had over the Hindenburg Line message."

"You getting scared now?" asked Hambledon. "I hope so, there's no loneliness like that of the only man in a party who's panicky. I am. I think you're cracked to go and see von B., but if you insist I suppose you must."

"We must make sure. It would be too absurd to throw up the game, drive three hundred miles through most of the German army, and inconvenience the British navy on its lawful occasions all because one crippled German wants half a dozen cases of whisky."

"You're doing it too," said Hambledon shrewdly.

"Doing what?"

"Sitting here talking because you don't like to go out into the street. I'm going to ring up the school and find out where Reck is. I hope he's some-where in Cologne—I can telephone from here."

"Do you know what?" said Bill.

"What?"

"We are perfectly safe so long as we look like keeping your appointment in the Blumenthalstrasse. Von Bodenheim wants us all to himself—if you're right. If we tried to bolt first, they'd drop on us."

Hambledon cheered up noticeably.

"You are probably right," he said. "I am going to telephone Reck. What's today, Thursday? Four days to drive to Ostend. Remember we can't drive after dark in the battle areas, and the days are short; that brings us to Monday. M.L. off Ostend on Monday night."

He returned and said: "Thank Heaven, Reck's at the Germania; he gen-erally is when he comes to Cologne. If I go there and meet him, will you fill the car up with oil and petrol and wait for me at the Dom Hotel? Pack two small suitcases; who ever heard of a major without luggage?"

All these things having been accomplished, Tommy Hambledon in their sitting room at the hotel said: "One last drink? I think so; it's a pity to leave this whisky to the waiter; it might give him ideas above his station. Well—cheerio!"

"Prosit!" said Bill.

"We will take the car along and leave it in the Reichenperger Platz. After which I think you had better precede me and I will follow just behind like the celebrated lamb I so much resemble. Well, are you ready? Forward, and St. George for merry England!"

Dirk Brandt rang the bell at von Bodenheim's house and was admitted as usual by Hans and shown into the sitting room at the back, where a fire was blazing in the fireplace opposite the door, and the long french windows were curtained against the January night.

"Come in," said von Bodenheim in his usual friendly manner. "I am very glad to see you again. Hans, put the whisky on the table, and then you can go. Hans has a disabled ex-service-man's club he likes to attend on Thursdays," he went on when the man had left the room. "I usually try to arrange for him to go if possible; it is not much of a life for him, waiting on me."

"It is considerate of you," said Dirk Brandt, picking up his glass and walking over to the fire. "I hope you will be equally kind to me, for I have come home with my tail between my legs. Though upon my honor I do not believe the Englishman got through; I think the fire was an accident. There were quite a number of men working there all night, but not enough to make it easy to oversee them all; one of them might have thought it safe to have a smoke. They will do it, especially now when most of them are continually hungry—the food is very bad up there, and short, too."

Outside the room a door banged somewhere. "Hans going out," thought Bill, and a pulse began perceptibly to beat in the base of his throat; now for it, one way or the other. "They had one practice which is not officially allowed," he went on in a perfectly calm voice while von Bodenheim sat completely motionless and watched him intently. "They turned one of the empty hangars into a workshop. They are supposed to keep the workshops a certain specified distance away from the sheds for fear that a spark from an emery-wheel or from some such cause might set off the escaped hydrogen; it always leaks out, you know. But there wasn't a convenient shed, and there was the hangar empty." He turned away from his host for a second to toss his cigarette-end into the fire. "In my opinion it is—"

He turned round again and looked straight down the barrel of von Bodenheim's automatic.

"What is this—?" he began, but the German cut him short.

"That will do. You are very clever, you English agent, I congratulate you, you even fooled me, von Bodenheim, with your boyish look and simple manner. So I send you off to Ahlhorn, I myself, and you thank me so very much, don't you, and off you go and burn the four Zeppelins that might have won the war for us, and at least thirty-seven honest men died in the flames with them. So now it is your turn to die."

"Listen," began Bill, but it was of no avail.

"I will not," said von Bodenheim. "I have listened to you too much. You are a wizard when you talk, it seems impossible that you can be lying, but now I know, I tell you, I *know*. Sit down," he went on in a less acid tone, "finish your drink, and have a last cigarette with me. No, hands up! Do not put them near your pockets. If you will just hold them up while I light a cigarette for you, you may put them down again afterwards. There are several things I want to say to you, and one is that I always liked you and now I respect you as well. Here is the lighter you gave me, we will use that, and I shall keep it as a memento. Is that all right?"

"Yes, thank you," said Bill. (Hambledon, why doesn't Hambledon come?)

"You may put your hands down, but keep them on your knees. Tell me, did you kill Amtenbrink?"

"Yes. I understood that he was arranging a little cholera outbreak in London."

"He was not."

"So I heard later," said Bill, with a little grimace.

"You did not enjoy doing that, eh? No—some of the things we have to do are utterly vile, are they not? Or they would be in any other cause. Tell me, Butler, he was not real, of course?"

"Of course he was," said Bill with a laugh. "If you had inquired at Euston you would have found a porter named Butler—we don't leave anything to chance." (Where the devil is Hambledon, can he have mistaken the house? It will be too late soon.) "I'd like to say, before it's too late, that—well, when I showed pleasure in your company, there was no sham in that. That was real enough."

"Thank you. I am sorry this had to happen, though I know perfectly well that if our places were reversed you would put a bullet through my head with as little hesitation as I shall have in putting one through yours in a few minutes. Finish your glass and have another, will you? I don't want to prolong the agony, if you find it so, but I should like to talk with you a little longer if you do not mind."

"The longer the better," said Bill, and laughed to think how particularly true that was.

"I expect so," said von Bodenheim, also amused: "Tell me—"

"No," broke in Bill. "Tell me something instead. Tell me where I slipped up."

"Heilemann," answered the German without hesitation. "You see, it was like this. Just before the war I went on a shooting trip in Canada, and I stayed first with some friends in Halifax. Heilemann was a gunsmith of some repute. I got some of my tackle from him. When I heard of the Halifax explosion, I began thinking about the place and remembered this. Then you asked who had done it, do you remember? I did not really distrust you, but some little spurt of caution made me throw out the name of Heilemann, just to see if anything happened, and today I hear that he has been arrested. He has nothing whatever to do with us, believe me, and only you could have told. So I knew then what you were, and when immediately upon that came the news of the Ahlhorn disaster—well—"

The door behind von Bodenheim opened without a sound. Tommy Hambledon slid into the room, took in the situation at a glance, and leveled his automatic at the German's head. Bill hastily averted his eyes; von Bodenheim must not notice that he had something interesting to look at. What was he saying?

"—very good idea of yours not to send the news through, as when it became obvious that the English were completely taken by surprise, of course I thought you were all right—"

What's all this about and why doesn't Hambledon fire? Bill risked another glance and saw he had lowered the automatic again. (What the devil's the matter?—my God, I'm right in the line of fire.)

"—though of course it would have been awkward if we had been attacked just then—"

The Hindenburg Line of retreat, of course. Bill pulled himself together.

"The fact is," he said, "I didn't believe it. I thought it was a trap, and it seemed a pity to spoil a good career at the outset by falling into it." He picked up his glass from the floor and drank.

"Which reminds me," said von Bodenheim, "I shall have to deal with that alleged uncle of yours. I think there is no doubt that he is in it."

"Up to the neck," said Bill cheerfully. "Believe it or not, he was one of the masters at my school."

He emptied the glass and reached out to put it back on the table. He was a little too far off, so he slid his chair back and stretched out his arm.

"He must be a good man," said von Bodenheim, "he has been here for—"
Crack!

As von Bodenheim slumped forward in his chair, the automatic in his hand discharged, fired by the nervous jerk of his finger, but the bullet passed over Bill's head and buried itself in the wall, and he sprang up and caught the German as he was falling.

"Lay him back in his chair," said Hambledon. "Nice tidy affair. It's only the back of his head, he looks quite normal in front. That will do. I had another idea while I was following you down the street just now, I am going to leave a little note."

He pulled a letter out of his pocket, tore off the blank half-sheet, and scribbled:

"I saw the man but missed him again, so be careful, he was heading your

way. Have warned Brandt." He folded it up and put it in one of von
Bodenheim's pockets.

"Person or persons unknown," he said. "That ought to confuse the issue
a bit. What's the matter?"

"Put the lights out, I can't stand his eyes. He was a friend of mine."

"Better not."

"I'll put the reading lamp on," said Bill, and arranged it so that a shadow
fell across the German's head. "Turn out the others now. That's better, he
might almost be only asleep. *Auf wiedersehen*, von Bodenheim." He picked
up von Bodenheim's automatic and pocketed it.

"Another *memento mori*? Come on, for Heaven's sake, or we shall meet
the servant and have to deal with him too."

"It's all right," said Bill; "he's got the evening off, luckily for him."

"Yes," said Hambledon, "otherwise we'd have had to send him to attend
his master among the shades."

They walked without hurry up the Blumenthalstrasse towards the turning into the Reichenperger Platz, where they had left the car. "I didn't quite
get the idea of the note," said Bill. "What did you put in it?"

"Merely an informer's note telling him there was somebody after him. I
wanted to suggest a subsequent caller because Hans knew you were there
when he left. I think there's just a chance von Bodenheim did not tell anybody about us, you see; he really blundered frightfully over you, and he may
have wanted to clear up the mess himself before reporting it to the authorities."

"Yes," said Bill thoughtfully, "that's a sound idea. It would be like him to
want to deal with the matter himself, without assistance from anybody,
even Hans. So it's quite possible we are now perfectly safe."

"Possible, but not likely. We should have gone through his safe, but there
wasn't time—where was it, do you know?"

"No idea," said Bill.

"He may have written out an account of the whole affair, for all we
know. In any case, I think a brief spell of absence won't do us any harm—
whenever I think of the Ahlhorn affair I get an unpleasant feeling as though
people I can't see are staring at me from behind, and on top of that we go
and abolish one of their star performers on his own hearthrug. No, we go, I
think, without undue delay. Every trade has its hallmark, you know." He
went on talking to steady Bill's nerves. "The potter's thumb, the seaman's
balanced walk, do you know the Intelligence man's?"

"No, what is it?"

"A tendency to sit with his back to walls and even, in advanced cases, in corners, and never in front of windows or doors. This sensation from which I suffer tonight is practically an industrial disease. There is usually coupled with it a morbid dislike of being asked questions even by your best girl, let alone your seniors."

"I know," said Bill. "I've got that already."

"Yes, I expect so. Here's the car, will you drive? We will go first to the high-level freight station. I can telephone Reck from there, and, what is more, we can change into uniform in one of the freight sheds and nobody be any the wiser at this hour in the evening."

A major of Westphalian infantry, driven by his orderly, passed in a car along the Hohenzollern Ring and turned right at the Opera House into the long road to Aachen and the Belgian coast.

CHAPTER FOURTEEN
OUR 'ORACE SAYS

She opened the front door and walked straight in with a step as assured as though the house were her own, passed down the hall and into the sitting room at the back. She knew the way, because the owner of the house used to give parties sometimes, and she had sung there. The owner of the house was sitting in his usual chair by the table and did not look up when she came in, so she paused by the door and began to talk to him.

"You should at least look up when a lady enters," she said in a low but steady voice, "even if it is only someone like me; a great gentleman like you should have better manners, I think. Are you asleep?"

The only light in the room was a reading lamp with a dark green shade, standing on the table. The man's head was in shadow, but the light fell full upon his long slender hands, which were folded on his knees and curiously still. From where she stood she could only see him in profile, so she walked round towards the fire in order to see him full-face, and as she did so the logs in the fireplace, which had only been glowing, fell together and burst into flames, which threw a flickering light over his quiet face and bitter, sensitive mouth. His eyes were half-open and shone in the firelight, and she thought he was not asleep but only disdainful.

"I see," she said. "You do not think I am worth speaking to, you know all about me, of course, you who know everything, while I am only a cabaret singer and the mistress of a common soldier who died the other day. You thought him a drunken fool and probably you did not think of me at all, just two nobodies, and you killed him. But I'll tell you something, Herr von Boden-heim, you who think yourself so clever and so great, we knew something you'll never know, and that was love."

She paused, and the wavering shadows on his face cast by the leaping firelight made it appear as though his expression changed.

"You need not sneer," she said, "for Anton is out of your reach now, you can't hurt him any more, and soon I shall be with him and beyond your power too, and our love will go on and on without end where you can never break it again. I have brought you a present," she said, pulling something out of her coat pocket, "a present for each of us, four for you and one for me. Look grateful, you sneering devil, even if you aren't; a gentleman always says 'Thank you' for presents, four for you and one for me."

The outer door opened. She heard the sound and knew she must be quick. "Say a prayer, hurry," she said, lifting her hand, "four for you and one for me—"

Hans, locking the front door, heard four shots, which he recognized as coming from an automatic, and after a momentary pause, a fifth. He stumped along on his artificial leg and burst into the room to find his master with his head shot to pieces, and a dying woman on the floor with an automatic in her hand.

"Anton!" she called. "Where are you? I am coming."

Hans heard nothing of this except a murmur instantly stilled, but it is possible that Anton answered.

The Westphalian major and his orderly made good time to Ostend, in spite of occasional difficulty in obtaining petrol and still more difficulty in getting lubricating oil, since of all the shortages from which Germany suf-fered, the lack of oils and fats of all kinds was perhaps the most serious. On the run between Malines and Ghent the oil level in the sump became so low that they had to stop repeatedly to let the engine cool, and it was with great relief that they came at last upon a dump at the roadside from which it might be possible to obtain some oil. The dump was in the charge of a harassed-looking noncommissioned officer wearing the gilded badge stamped with a steel helmet and crossed swords which was the German equivalent of the British wound stripes; with him were two or three other German soldiers, obviously convalescents, and a squad of British prisoners of war stacking cases and carrying oil-drums and petrol cans about.

Tommy Hambledon got out of the car with the air of command appropriate to a German field-officer, and his depressed-looking driver also alighted and opened the hood.

"Five gallons of petrol and a gallon of oil," said the Westphalian major, and the British prisoners left off working at once and leaned on things.

"I am sorry, sir," said the sergeant. "I can let you have two gallons of petrol, but I am regrettably forbidden to issue any oil."

"I like the way our 'Orace says 'is little piece," said one of the prisoners to another in English. " 'Umble but unyieldin'."

"There must be oil," said Hambledon peremptorily.

"Hear the tone o' command," said another prisoner. "Wad ye ever think the likes o' a wee fat man like that un cud be sae lorrdly?"

"I am sorry, sir," said the sergeant again, "but there is very little oil here and I am ordered to keep it for a convoy which is coming through tonight."

"I'll bet he's a corker to work for," said a prisoner with a scar down his cheek. "Look at his driver, poor downtrodden little worm; looks as though he hardly dared to breathe."

Which was true, for Bill was afraid of laughing.

"Damn the convoy," said Hambledon. "I said five gallons of petrol and one of oil."

"Look 'ow 'is ears stick out," said the cockney of the party. "Coo, an' ain't they red?"

"Ye wad almost think the creature cud understand us. See him blushin'."

"Garn, the pore old Fritzy can't *sprechen Anglais*. Not 'less 'e was a waiter before the war."

The sergeant turned on them. "You—work!" he shouted, in two of this twelve words of English. "Baumer, get three gallons of gas."

"I said five!" roared Hambledon. "And the oil I ordered!"

" 'Children, you should never let,' " quoted the scarred prisoner, " 'your angry passions rise. Your little hands were never made—' "

"*Sprechen verboten!* Work!" shouted the sergeant, and the prisoners went through the motions of men beginning to lift things and desisted the moment he turned his head. "*Herr Gott*, these prisoners will be the death of me. Sir, I will issue five gallons of gas, if you insist, but the oil—"

"Look at this, you insubordinate hound," said Hambledon, and showed him the pass.

"Sir," said the man with natural dignity, "if you had shown me this before,

I would have served you at once, but it is my duty to obey orders. Baumer, get a gallon of oil."

"Lumme, 'e's goin' to get it," said the cockney. "Must be a cousin o' Kaiser Bill's."

"Bit of a nut, ain't 'e? Look at 'is cap, all o' one side to give the girls a treat."

"B'lieve you're right," said the scarred prisoner thoughtfully, "the driver can understand English. He's turning purple."

Happily at that moment Baumer returned with the oil and Bill was able to busy himself.

"Do those fellows give you much trouble?" he asked in a low tone.

"Yes, but they're not bad fellows, really," answered Baumer. "One wouldn't mind if one wasn't always so tired."

The car drove on again and Hambledon said: "I don't want to use this pass more than I can help. I have a nasty feeling they may be looking for two men carrying it."

"It's worked all right so far," said Bill.

They drove into Ostend as dusk was falling, left the car in a side turning and walked down the Avenue de la Reine towards the sea.

"Somewhere down here," said Hambledon, "there is a crossroad with a well-known tobacconist's shop at the corner, called *Die Bronzen Paard*."

"The Bronze Leopard?"

"No, 'Horse.' Our friend who will tell us the rendezvous and obtain us a boat lives at the opposite corner to the tobacconist. It should be just here somewhere, he keeps a—Good Lord!"

The house for which they were looking was represented by some tottering roofless walls, a large hole in the ground, and heaps of rubble with broken glass sticking out of it.

"He doesn't seem to have kept it very well," remarked Bill. "I trust he is not still at home?"

"You are completely heartless," said Hambledon indignantly. "You have no sympathy for poor folk in misfortune. Do you realize that if he is, we may not be able to get a boat?"

The tobacco shop was scarred from the effects of the explosion, and the shattered windows were boarded up, but the door was open and business evidently proceeding. The travelers entered and inquired about the welfare of M. Jules Braem, who had until recently lived opposite.

The tobacconist said that M. Braem still lived, but not, as the travelers would observe, opposite; he had gone to stay with his married sister down near the harbor. The elder traveler said that he had indeed noticed the results of some disturbance, such as would cause a peace-loving man to change his residence, and could the owner of the Bronze Horse provide him with the new address?

The tobacconist shook his head, but his wife, who was also in the shop, said that they did not themselves know, but that possibly the wife of the greengrocer yonder might be able to supply it, and as for disturbance, it was a mystery to her how even those so fortunate as to escape bodily injury succeeded in remaining mentally intact. The elder traveler then bought some cigarettes, and they passed on to the greengrocer's.

Here once again they found husband and wife in the shop, which was unfortunate, because at the mention of M. Braem the lady glanced nervously at her husband and retired modestly behind strings of onions, while the greengrocer said that Providence in its mysterious wisdom had seen fit to preserve the life of M. Braem owing to his having been elsewhere at the time the bomb fell.

The major said that it had occurred to him that something of the sort must have happened, but the point of immediate interest was where M. Braem was now. The greengrocer only regretted his inability to be of more practical assistance and suggested, sourly, the gendarmerie. The major thanked him for his very helpful suggestion, which they would at once proceed to put into action, and went on talking about the said bomb outrage in a sympathetic manner, interjecting instructions to his orderly to buy some apples. Now, no one breaks off a conversation with a major to serve a private, so Bill drifted across the shop to speak with Madame, received his bag of apples, and they left.

"Where is he?" asked Tommy Hambledon.

"At the Café of the African Lion, down by the harbor."

They took the turning opposite the Bronze Horse and walked through streets becoming progressively narrower and older towards the harbor. "This town," said Bill, "seems to be mainly populated by elderly artillery men."

"Yes. There's German gun about every seventy-five yards all down this coast, and these men are the guns' crews. They are here in case the British try to land, but as the British are not, so far as I have noted, afflicted with mass dementia, they're not likely to attempt it. So these worthy gentlemen lead useful but not exciting lives, for after all if they weren't here the British probably would be, but in the meantime I imagine most of 'em have never fired off their fieldpiece."

"They must be bored stiff."

"Yes. I hope we don't afford 'em any comic relief tonight. Where's your African Lion?"

"Somewhere along the quays here."

They walked along in the dark, stumbling at times over unseen obstacles, for there were, of course, no lights showing, till in a ray of light from a door momentarily opened they saw a man and a girl emerge and two men enter.

"Wonder if that's it," said Hambledon, and when they reached the house he shone for a moment the light of a pocket electric torch upon a signboard dimly seen above the door. It bore a spirited but blistered painting of a lion with an alarming black mane and a singularly sweet smile. Hambledon pushed the door open and stalked in, respectfully followed by Bill.

There were quite a lot of soldiers there, a few seamen of the German submarine fleet, and one or two women, and the air was thick with the smell of tobacco, drinks, and onions. The clients lifted their heads and stared coldly at the Westphalian major, who looked them over with distaste and strode slowly down the center gangway and through a door at the back, and the private went too. They were followed by some unappreciative comment, because the staff officer was never popular with the frontline soldier in any army, and by the beginning of 1918 the German troops were becoming mutinous. Madame, however, rising swiftly from her desk near the door, hushed these remarks with a few well-chosen words, hitched her gray cloth shawl up round her shoulders, and pattered after the invaders who were waiting for her just inside the kitchen.

"Bo' soir, messieurs," she began.

"Is Monsieur Jules Braem here?"

"Upstairs, messieurs."

"I should like to speak to him, please."

The woman looked scared, but asked no questions and led them upstairs to a stuffy little sitting room too full of furniture, where they waited till Jules Braem came in, a thin man with a long nose and sharp black eyes.

"Good evening," said Hambledon. "You were expecting us, I think."

The man's face brightened. "Yes, messieurs—you will excuse me—my sister did not know you and one always wonders who one's visitors may be."

"You have a message for us, I think."

"Yes," said Braem, hauling up his jersey to get at the waistcoat pockets underneath and producing a scrap of paper, "Yes, here it is." He handed it over. Hambledon took it and read it aloud.

" '51 degrees 16 minutes 20 seconds north, 2 degrees 51 minutes 30 seconds east from 11 p.m. till 4 a.m.' Yes, well, I hope we find it. I wish these navy people weren't so infernally technical; if only they'd say two miles out in a straight line from the third automatic machine counting from the pier, it would be so much simpler."

Braem laughed. "If the gentlemen will row northwest for two hours when they are clear of the harbor, they will be about there," he said. "It is only the difficulty of keeping a straight course in the dark—it is overcast tonight, there are no stars to steer by. Have you a compass?"

"No," said Tommy Hambledon, and Bill shook his head. "You had better have this," said the Belgian, and gave them a brass pocket compass about an inch in diameter. "It is not much good, but it will keep you from rowing in circles, provided you keep it away from the rowlocks, that is, and you will find the waves are a help; once you get your course, you will keep them at much the same angle. It is past nine o'clock; it will take you an hour to get clear of the harbor since you will have to be much more quiet than the little mouse, eh? Just paddle with the oars, you know? Like the ladies rowing on the fine summer day, very soft and gentle."

"I wish I were sure the sea was going to be perfectly ladylike, too."

"Oh, it is not too bad tonight, just the little lop, you know. And it is fine exercise, rowing—no standing about getting cold, eh?"

"I wonder if you'd be so enthusiastic if you were going," said Hambledon.

"I would not mind if I were going to England, where nobody arrests you so long as you are good," said Braem wistfully. "It is not so pleasant, always, to stay here with all the neighbors knowing you too well—mon Dieu, those neighbors!"

"We met some of them," said Bill with a laugh.

"So? You may laugh, m'sieur, you have not to live with them. Well, will you have something to eat before you go, or a litre of wine perhaps?"

"Thanks," said Hambledon, "but I'll wait till I get aboard, I think. You, Bill?"

"I agree with you," said Bill. "Business first."

"Will you follow me, then, gentlemen? We will go out the back way, I think."

They went out by the back door of the café and stumbled among empty boxes and full dustbins down an alley and out on the quayside again. The place was curiously deserted. Bill would have expected more sentries and said so, but Braem explained that there was no particular object in placing guards about the outer harbor where they were; in the inner harbor, where the submarines were moored, it was a different matter, there were always men about there, inquisitive men who wanted to know one's business. They went on in the darkness, splashing into shallow puddles and shivering in the bitter wind which swept in from the North Sea and left a taste of salt upon their lips. Braem led them to a place where an iron ladder descended the face of the harbor wall to the water below.

"I have the dinghy tied here," he said, "I will go first and pull her up to the foot of the ladder. Will you follow?"

He swung himself over the edge, a black shadow against a background only less black, and disappeared jerkily downwards, and the two men left behind waited a few moments before following him.

"Only the most deep-rooted instincts of self-preservation," said Tommy Hambledon, "would induce me to carry on with this singularly unattractive expedition." He, too, vanished from sight and Bill followed. They found Braem in the dinghy holding her up to the foot of the ladder.

"I have bound the oars with cloth," he said, "to muffle the bump against the rowlocks. If you could manage it, it would be better not to row till you are clear of the quay wall. There is a sentry just at the end there, and he may make a fuss if he hears anything. We do not want any fusses, eh?"

"Absolutely no fuss," agreed Hambledon, "but how do we propel the boat if we don't row? Put our heads under water astern and blow?"

Muffled sounds of amusement came from Braem, who said: "You pull yourselves along by the face of the wall, m'sieurs; the tide is going out, that will help you."

"Oh, splendid. When clear of the harbor we find northwest on the compass and row like blazes for two hours. Is that all?"

"Also be careful not to run upon a mine."

"Mine?"

"The sea is heavily mined off the harbor mouth, m'sieur. There is a channel left for the submarines; it would be as well if you could find it."

"If we don't?"

"You should be able to avoid the mines in a dinghy. You will hear the little slaps the waves give them even if you cannot see, and it will be lighter outside."

"At the slightest sign of any slap-and-tickle we will modestly retire," said Tommy. "Au 'voir, Monsieur Braem. Heaven will certainly reward you, and I trust the British government will follow suit."

"So do I," said Braem, and wrung their hands in his horny palm. "Heaven defend and guide you, m'sieurs. Bon voyage!"

He stepped upon the ladder again, untied the painter, and threw it in the bows of the dinghy, which immediately sidled away. "Bon voyage," he whispered again, climbed up the ladder, and at once disappeared from sight.

"*Allons, mon brave*," said Hambledon. "We approach ourselves to the harbor wall and propel ourselves along it, but our boat doesn't seem to want to approach it. One moment while I ship an oar and shove up a little. You've been very quiet lately; what's the matter?"

"Nothing," said Bill. "Should one talk here? I say, this is all very well, but there's nothing whatever to take hold of and this wall is deuced slippery, it's coated with slime. I can't get on at all."

"I think if I could ship this oar aft and just waggle it we should get on better. Can I—yes, I can. That's quiet enough, I can't hear anything myself. You are right, we'd better not speak. I wonder where exactly the sentry is."

They proceeded, slowly indeed but in complete silence, keeping close to the wall, till suddenly the quiet was broken by a step on the quayside above their heads and a clink on the stonework as a rifle was grounded. At once Hambledon froze into immobility and the dinghy just floated along on the tide. "Keep your head down," he whispered, "he might see your face."

The sentry high above their heads picked up a pebble and dropped it into the water merely for the pleasure of hearing the splash, then another and another. "If one of those hits the boat," thought Bill, "there won't be a splash, there'll be a thud, and he'll look over to see why."

But luck was with them and they passed in safety, cleared the harbor walls at last, and headed for the open sea. They shipped a pair of oars each and pulled steadily if unskillfully for a quarter of an hour, till Hambledon said: "Stop now, and let's look at the compass." He laid it on the floorboards of the boat and, sheltering the beam of the torch with his hand, directed a glimmer of light on the compass face.

"Due west, apparently, is where we're going at the moment," said Bill, "I should think that would be about right for Dover. We want to turn half-right, don't we?"

"Swing her half-right," said Tommy Hambledon. "I don't really want to row to Dover tonight. That's it, hold her. I'll leave the compass there and take a look at it now and then. Carry on."

Some time passed in strenuous exercise, till Bill said: "Could we stop? I want to take this coat off."

They shed their uniform greatcoats and went on again. After a time Hambledon said: "Isn't this sea awkward? Either it isn't there when you dig for it or else it's all there at once. Let's try with one oar each."

They were unshipping the spare oars when Bill suddenly said: "Listen!" and, twisting round on the thwart, stared over the bows, and Hambledon heard it too. Slap-whoosh. Wheesh.

"Back off, for God's sake! Can you see it?"

"Yes," said Bill, backing furiously. "Right under the bows. Come up, you cow!"

They got away from the mine at last and skirted carefully round it at a respectful distance till they were clear.

Bill said: "I've got a flask in my pocket."

"Even at school," said Tommy Hambledon, "you showed rudimentary symptoms of intelligence. Pass it over."

Things went better with them after that, one oar was much more manageable than two in the irregular lop of the sea on that shelving shore for men whose little experience had been gained on peaceful rivers, and though they stopped frequently to listen and look, they encountered no more mines.

"We are keeping our course fairly well," said Hambledon, taking one of his frequent peeps at the compass and another at his wristwatch. "Two hours now since we left the African Lion, another hour should see us through. I should think we've passed the mine-field now. Any more in that flask?"

Midnight came and passed, the overcast sky cleared and showed a few stars, and the sea became dimly visible for quite a distance round them. "We might be able to see her now if she does turn up," said Bill.

"Who? Oh, the navy, not Aphrodite? Yes. When we see her we show my pocket torch, and a lot of good that'll be I expect, but it seems the right thing to do, and yell like hyenas. She should be hereabouts soon."

One o'clock, and Bill said: "Do you think we've gone too far?"

"I think this joke has. Let's ease off and listen," but they heard and saw nothing. "Have a cigarette?"

Bill shivered suddenly, but said: "Good idea. I think we've done enough work for the moment." They smoked in silence for a few minutes, and Bill remarked: "Wonder what they thought when they found von Bodenheim."

"I expect they thought he was dead," said Tommy practically, "and then they had another look and found they were right. You know, you should have left his gun; then they might have thought he'd committed suicide."

"What, by shooting himself in the back of the head?"

" 'Strange,' they would say, 'but then he always was an original chap. That bullet in the wall was a first attempt, he aimed too high and missed himself.' "

"With only one bullet discharged?"

"Your criticisms are captious. By the way, why is nothing ever captious except a criticism? He reloaded, of course."

"Those prisoners at that dump near Ghent were nearly too much for me," said Bill, after another interval for intensive listening. "It's got a lot darker again, hasn't it?"

"Yes, getting overcast, the stars have gone. Yes, those fellows seemed fairly happy, considering; that noncom was a good man. By the way, did you notice anything on the run?"

"What was that?"

"The Sunlight Soap advertisements, those enameled iron things nailed up to walls? I saw them here and there all the way down. You'd think they'd—"

"Listen!" broke in Bill, and "Look out!" he yelled at the top of his voice, "She's on us! *Hi!*"

There was a yell from Hambledon and a grinding crash as the M.L.'s bows emerged from the darkness and ran them down. The next instant they were both struggling in the water. There followed shouts from the M.L.'s deck. "Thank God they've seen us," thought Bill, and the next moment one of the ex-yachtsman crew, remembering his "man-overboard" drill, rushed aft and pressed a button, and a calcium float flopped into the water and burst at once into dazzling flame.

The result of this surpassed imagination, and it seemed to Bill, swimming round and trying to avoid the propeller, that the German gunners of the coastal defense must have been sitting with their hands on their levers or whatever it was that gunners held, and pulled, for in twenty seconds there was a succession of mighty bangs from the shore as every German gun for miles trained on the calcium flare and fired.

Bill rose as high as he could in the water and continued to shout "Hi!" wondering as he did so whether that was why hyenas were so called; he could hear Hambledon not far off producing a healthy selection of zoo-like noises, and the M.L. swung round and came back slowly. As she passed, a man flung a rope and Bill plunged at it, caught it and wound his arms and legs round it as immediately the launch increased speed, for significant splashes were occurring unpleasantly near. He was dragged through the water revolving like a patent log, gasping with cold, spluttering and choking, and eventually hauled on board more dead than alive, but still clinging to the rope, and arrived on the encumbered deck dripping, shaking in every limb, and barely conscious. The boat appeared to be traveling faster every moment judging by the vibration and the fact that the calcium flare seemed to be miles behind, and everything else was in total darkness.

"Drink this," said someone invisible but tangible, and offered him what felt like a tin mug. He drank obediently, but found it was gin, which he detested.

"My soul, look at that," said another voice, obviously referring to the Belgian coast, sparkling with flashes from gunfire as far either way as they could see, and roaring like a volcanic eruption.

"Please," said Bill with chattering teeth, "I'd rather have a whisky, may I?"

"Sorry," someone answered. "Only got gin."

"Do you know you were miles away from where you should have been?" asked a stern voice.

"No," said Bill mutinously, "and we damn near didn't even get there."

"Take him below where it's warm, for pity's sake," said the voice which had offered him gin.

"Where's Hambledon?" asked Bill.

"Who's Hambledon?"

"The man who was with me."

There was a momentary pause before the stern voice answered him.

"Was there a man with you?"

CHAPTER FIFTEEN
SECOND HONEYMOON

BILL SAUNDERS reached London the following afternoon, had a bath and a shave, changed into civilian clothes out of the naval uniform which had been lent to him, and went to the War Office to report.

He found, however, that there was little he could tell which was news to those in authority except the innocence of Heilemann and the death of von Bodenheim, and, as has been seen, there was a sequel to that story which was not known to Bill himself at the time. He explained that there was just a chance due to Hambledon's note that he might not be connected with it, or, if von Bodenheim had not reported, with the fire at Ahlhorn either, but it was rather a remote chance, so they had thought it best to clear out. He reported also that they had noticed signs of activity behind the German lines. "It looks as though they are getting ready for a big push somewhere."

The big man behind the desk sat still and said "Yes" and "Yes" and "I understand," and noticed the dark rings under Bill's eyes and a certain difficulty he had in keeping his hands quiet.

"You did perfectly right to come home," said the War Office man. "Heilemann, of course, will have to be released with profuse apologies. I am having this business of a new German push looked into, yours is not the only report I have received; it looks like being something big. I will try to find out if you are accused of the death of von Bodenheim and whether he did report or not. It would be in accordance with his reputation to deal with you first and report afterwards, and as for writing an account of it, there wasn't much time, was there? He said himself that he only heard of Heilemann's arrest on the day you returned from Ahlhorn. Do you know how soon the news of the fire reached Cologne?"

"Some time in the morning," said Bill.

"One wonders whether he sent word to Ahlhorn to have you arrested."

"I shouldn't think so. He must have known that, whether guilty or not, I shouldn't hang about there. There was nothing to stay for."

"Exactly. What I was getting at was this: that even after he had got his facts, it would take him some little time to convince himself that there was no flaw in the reasoning, and that, incredible though it seemed, you were a British agent. I should imagine he might still be wondering if it could possibly be true when you arrived at his house. No, I don't see him writing a long detailed account to his department that evening. If you are not accused of his murder, I should think it quite likely you have got away with the Ahlhorn affair, in which case there's no reason why you shouldn't return to Cologne later, if you will."

"I shouldn't mind."

"I am glad; the importer's office is too good a cover to be wasted. You fled, of course, because Hambledon's unknown informer warned you, Hambledon himself presumably just went off on business to Holland and met with some accidental death there."

"Yes," said Bill, and his fingers twitched.

"I am very sorry about Hambledon, I need not tell you that, I'm sure, very sorry."

"I didn't know he wasn't on board," said Bill loudly and rapidly, with a suddenly flushed face. "You see, it was pitch-dark, you couldn't even see the men who spoke to you, they were all just voices, and I was pretty well done in when they hauled me up, I couldn't think properly, it never occurred to me they hadn't got him too, and we were miles away by the time I said:

'Where's Hambledon?' and somebody said: 'Who's Hambledon?' and I said—"

"Yes, yes, I know," said the quiet voice of the man who had heard so many stories of sudden death. "It was frightfully unfortunate, but it was nobody's fault, least of all yours." He went across to a cupboard by the fireplace and took out a whisky bottle and two glasses. "Here, drink this. You have had a difficult time and a hideous shock on top of it. It's all right, it will pass. What do you think of this stuff?" he went on in a lighter tone. "Denton does me the honor to say that one must come here to get the best whisky in London."

"He's right," said Bill, speaking with effort. "It is—quite excellent."

"Splendid. Drink that and have another."

Bill obeyed, the lines of strain in his face eased, and he leaned back in the chair. "Thank you, sir," he said. "I'm sorry—making a scene like that." He laughed unsteadily. "Wonderful stuff, this."

"You had better have some leave, I think. Take fifteen days and then come and see me again. Don't report in the meantime, take it easy and don't worry about things. I may say that you have done extraordinarily well," and he went on to add words of praise which would have sent out the Bill of two months earlier walking on air down Whitehall, but which seemed to this one rather distant and beside the point. Hambledon—

He became aware that he was being kindly but firmly told to go away and play, so he drifted out, looking at his watch and finding it a little after seven. Dinner somewhere, presumably, and later on a train to Weatherley Parva—he stopped in the middle of Whitehall so suddenly that a taxi missed him by inches and a woman screamed, but Bill took no notice. Diane, of course. Incredible, impossible, idiotic but true, he had completely forgotten Diane. He stood still outside the Admiralty and tried to remember when he had last thought of Diane, somewhere ages ago—yes, at Ahlhorn. He had noticed the moon one night as he walked back from the sheds to the car, Diane the moon-goddess, so far away, and so is my Diane; that was the night before the great fire six days ago, and ever since then time had passed in one rush of excitement, danger, terror, grief—Hambledon. He had never told Hambledon about her and now he never would.

Well, it was a pity but couldn't be helped, and it was all over now anyway and there was nothing to be gained by fretting over it, so he thrust the thought to the back of his mind, signalled a taxi, and gave the Kensington address. Diane, dear Diane.

He arrived just as the family were going in to a truncated wartime dinner, to be greeted with a rush of emotion by Diane, a rather stately courtesy by her mother, and the most surprising and unexpected warmth of cordiality by her father. Bill and Diane were both so taken aback by this that they left off clinging to each other and merely stood hand in hand and gaped at him.

"Come in, come in, my dear fellow. What about a glass of sherry before dinner, eh? My dear boy, I am thankful to see you back. You look tired, though, very tired. Diane, don't stand there staring as though you'd seen a ghost. Go and tell the maids to lay another place at table. There aren't any maids, only one and she's out? Well, go and lay it yourself, then. Come in my study, Bill; not much in the cellar now I'm afraid, but there's still a bottle or two of Amontillado left, I'll go and get it."

Mrs. Causton murmured something about the soup getting cold, but was merely swept away.

"I suppose it'll warm up again, won't it? Don't stand there making difficulties, Eliza."

Bill conquered with a heroic effort an attack of giggles which came suddenly upon him, and said: "I'm giving you the most frightful trouble, sir."

"Not at all, not at all. Unless you'd as soon have whisky?"

"I'd rather, sir, if it's not a frightful admission."

"Of course not, all the better, I've got some in here. Dammit, the fire's nearly out."

"I'll get some firewood," said Diane, awaking as from a trance, and ran to fetch it.

"Here's a peg for you," said the colonel, pouring out one that would have startled Noah.

"Oh, steady, sir," said Bill. "I've had one or two already."

"Nonsense, do you good. Water or soda?"

"Just show it the siphon, sir, will you? Here," to Diane, who was dropping sticks into the grate, "let me do that."

He took them from her and stood them up on their ends, building up an erection like the skeleton of a wigwam with some paper underneath and a few small pieces of coal on the top.

"Do you know, you can light a fire with green sticks if you prop them up like this, especially if you notch them with a knife and have the notches pointing downwards," said the demonstrator, applying a match. The flame took hold and almost at once the wood began to crackle.

"You are an expert fire-lighter, aren't you?" said Diane admiringly.

There came a sound between a cough and a roar from the colonel, whose whisky had taken the wrong turning. He choked and spluttered, and Bill banged him between the shoulders.

"Thank you, my boy, thank you," said the colonel as soon as he could speak.

"What ever made you do that, Father?"

"Oh, nothing. Have you laid the table?"

"Not yet."

"Well, for goodness' sake, go and do it. Expert fire-lighter," he went on, as Diane left the room, "oh dear!" Their eyes met, and both men burst out laughing.

"Who told you, sir?"

"Oh—I have ways of acquiring information. I will admit frankly that when I realized I had an unknown son-in-law, I made inquiries about him."

"Naturally, sir, don't blame you at all."

"But make no mistake," said Colonel Causton, becoming serious, "I shall never ask you anything, I shall never expect to be told anything. It is not my business, I know as much as I wish to, and I am satisfied."

"You are very good."

"But you should have seen the face of that feller at the War Office! I went in as innocent as a baby and asked if they knew anything about a Private William Saunders of the 2nd Hampshires—Lord bless my soul! Come into dinner."

Bill and Diane sat in the study before the resuscitated fire, both in one armchair and rejoicing to be together again, he feeling that for once the thing he had hoped for was really coming true. Here was someone apart from the agonies and stress of life, with whom he could be at peace; peace, and not to be continually on his guard, not always mistrustful and anxious. Diane seemed to guess that he did not want to think about the war; she talked instead of what they would do when it was all over. He said he thought it would be great fun to run a garage in a country village.

"I shall go back to my own name again and you will be Mrs. Michael Kingston."

"But, Bill darling, why do you want to drop the name of Saunders when you've done so well in it?"

"Who said I had done well?"

"Nobody, darling, but haven't you got a decoration or something?"

"Not to my knowledge. What put that idea into your head?"

"Only the way Father has come round, darling. You know, he hasn't been a bit nice about you all the time till—when was it? Last Saturday. He came in looking awfully pleased with himself and asked me if I'd heard from you lately, and if you'd said anything about leave."

"Oh, yes?"

"I said I didn't suppose you'd get leave yet, privates didn't get leave very often, and he said: 'Oh, really?' and I thought it was silly of him because, being a colonel, he must know that. Darling, how did you manage it? Father was funny about you."

"When?"

"After you'd gone back. He kept on staring at me and muttering: 'But I don't *know* anything about the fellow. I don't know anything *about* the fellow,' till Mother and I got fed up with it. Then when I told him I'd met you at Weatherley Parva, he said: 'Oh, ah,' and wrote to Uncle James."

"The vicar, yes."

"I don't think he got much out of him, because he didn't seem any better, so he wrote to your uncle."

"He did, did he?" said Bill, considerably amused. "Did he get any satisfaction out of that?"

"I don't think so, except that they are annoyed with us, too. So then he wrote to your school."

"He's a persevering old bean, isn't he?"

"And that wasn't any good either, and I don't know what he did after that except that he came home all pleased about it on Saturday. Darling, are you sure you haven't done something wonderful?"

"Quite," said Bill shortly.

About the middle of March, Bill was in France again, but not with his regiment although in the same sector; in point of fact, he was once more Private Hans Hommellhoff from Duisberg, German down to the skin, in one of the "cages" together with a number of German noncommissioned officers and men. He sat usually in a corner near the gate, a depressed little private shivering in a threadbare uniform, to whom everybody talked, but who was chiefly interested in swopping buttons, badges, and German picture-postcards for cigarettes with the sentry. The sentries, who had no idea that he was other than what he appeared to be, called him "that funny little Jerry in the corner" and were carelessly kind, and the German soldiers considered that his only claim to distinction was that he had managed to retain his watch when he was captured.

He was there to try to find out as much as possible about the Big Push. A good deal was already known about it at headquarters, and it was generally believed to have been fixed for the end of March, the 27th or thereabouts, but further information was eagerly desired. So he mooned about, or sat rereading old letters from home and showed to everyone who would look at them photographs of his mother, sisters—one married, with baby— and best girl, and talked. The German soldiers would have been surprised if they had realized quite how much they told him in return, and all went well till the morning of March the 21st, which began with a terrific German barrage.

No news, of course, filtered into the cage, but Bill was at first curious, and then painfully interested, to see long columns of men, transport, guns, field-kitchens, staff cars, officers on horseback and on foot, and all the various details that went to make an army in 1918, streaming back towards the rear on a road that ran within view of the camp. The other prisoners were equally interested, but less painfully.

"It looks like a retreat," said one.

"It is a retreat," said a sergeant authoritatively. "The English are being driven back."

"Has it come?" they asked in effect, "has it come, and are we seeing the onset of Victory?" But still the sentries marched up and down and the Germans did not dare to cheer.

About ten o'clock came an officer who knew Bill for what he was, and said to the sentry: "Get me out that miserable little blighter in the corner, I want to talk to him," and accordingly Bill was pulled out without ceremony and marched off. When they got out of sight the officer said: "You'd better run like blazes. Jerry has broken through on practically the whole battle-front from what I hear, and God knows we've got nothing to stop him. I must go. Best of luck," and he went about his business.

Bill thought this such excellent advice that he broke into a trot at once. Here was he, not only in the uniform of the German army, but German in every detail to the recesses of his raiment and the bottoms of his pockets, and if he was captured by the Germans he would be given "escaper's leave" and sent back to the bosom of the Hommellhoff family at Duisberg. There they would gather to greet him, that alarmingly adequate mother, the pretty married sister complete with baby, the two plain sisters, one with a long nose and the other with a snub-nose, and the chubby fiancée with a turned-up nose, and they would all stand round and look at him, and with one accord they would say: "This ain't our Hans," and then— Bill broke into a cold perspiration, the trot became a run, and he went through a couple of hedges without really noticing them.

He toiled up a long slope and came upon a large body of infantry which was also retiring in a more orderly but scarcely less rapid manner than his own, for the German shell-fire was becoming increasingly intense. Bill thought that the height of irony would be reached if they shot him for being German, whereas the Germans would certainly shoot him for being English, but he need not have worried; the retiring troops had their own troubles to contend with and were much too full of them to bother about him. One panting cockney did just indicate Bill to his neighbor. "Look at Jerry—'oppin' it our wiy—don't seem ter 'anker for 'is—Fatherland, does 'e?" but that was all, for the neighbor was too busy trying to cover the ground like a cross-country runner, while in full battle order, to answer.

Just over the crest of the ridge they came upon a line of guns, with their crews staring in amazement, but cries of "Nothin' in front of yer!" woke them to a frenzied activity of shouted orders, men running about and working feverishly, and plunging, startled horses, as the gunners limbered up and got away while there was yet time.

Much later Bill found himself plodding down a road where he passed a body of men resting. One of them looked across and called to him: "Run, Jerry, run!" and the others laughed. A painful moment.

As the retreat reached what had been peaceful areas behind the lines, the existing confusion was aggravated by a general exodus of the entire civilian population, who, with astonishing singleness of purpose, simply fled. They came out of their houses with children and bundles and grandparents and birds in cages and babies and clocks and dogs and goats and squawking fowls tied by the legs and unspecified impedimenta of all kinds, and left in a southerly direction with quite incredible speed—that is, except those wealthy enough to have a cart to drive, for these had to keep to the roads and crawl with the rest of the crawling traffic, and the German gunfire followed them up.

Some time during the retreat Bill passed through a village from which the civilian population had already departed, but which was full of troops waiting to be sent somewhere, or possibly merely waiting for Jerry to reach them. Anyway, they were waiting, and one man had taken a phonograph out of a deserted shop, and a pile of records, and was sitting at the roadside with them. As soon as he had played a record, he took it off the turntable and smashed it in the gutter, for why should Jerry have it?

Bill found some food in a shop where there was no one to take the money, and walked on, munching. It seemed necessary to go on and on, for the German advance continued night and day, and if weary men lay down to sleep, soon there would be a cry of "Jerry up!" and they would stagger to their feet and march on again. Bill got seriously annoyed about all this, for in another day he would have been out of the cage and in British uniform again instead of scouring the country in a dress which made both sides equally dangerous, and all because the wretched Germans had attacked six days before they were expected.

The whole battlefront was in a state of indescribable confusion, units parted from their companies, companies which had become separated from their battalions and mixed up with details from other regiments with whom they had no business to associate, and battalions which had lost their brigades. Headquarters staffs were being captured, and hospital trains and field kitchens; and little bunches of men, led by a corporal or merely by the private with the longest service, fought savage little rear-guard actions, and retreated and fought again. The German advance eddied forward like the flowing tide in unexpected little salients, so that you would go back from an area of comparative peace and run into a battle, and the front line was no longer a line at all except as the cotton from a spool may still be called a line when the kitten has finished playing with it; and always the guns thundered, the great shells burst, and the little gas-shells went phh—plop! and you jammed that beastly gas-mask on again.

They fell back upon Hazebrouck and turned at bay, and there the German advance went no farther, though in some parts of the line it continued for fifteen days. When the army was at last sorted out, Bill managed to get into touch with someone who knew what his job really was, and was sent back to London with instructions to report at the War Office and keep out of the way of anybody who knew him, because it was barely eight weeks since he had been on leave before, and the most unsuspicious relative would know that a real private should not be back again so soon. So he was not to see Diane and he ought to have been grieved, but was surprised to find within himself a sense of relief of which he was horribly ashamed. Dear, sweet Diane, loving and beautiful, but if she asked even three questions one after another, he knew he would throw something at her, and she was quite capable of asking a dozen straight off the reel.

So he spent one night at a hotel in Bloomsbury at which he had stayed the first time he came home from Cologne, and in the morning took a bus for the War Office, and even as he stepped off it in Trafalgar Square, for this bus went down the Strand, he came face to face with Diane, who was attempting to board it.

"Bill!" she cried, and came to him with hands outstretched. "How lovely! How did you manage it? Whatever are you doing here?"

At that any hesitation he might have had vanished. More questions. He stood still, removed his hat—for he was wearing civilian clothes bought in Paris—held it in his hand, looked at her with precisely the may-I-come-on look the average man gives to the pretty stranger, and said with a slight but perceptible American accent that though the pleasure sure was his, he guessed the advantage was hers; and he looked her up and down with plain appreciation.

Diane hesitated. The face was the face of darling Bill, but the speech and manner and look and clothes were all different, and one had heard that everyone has his double.

"Are you not—" she stammered, "you are so like my—Bill Saunders, I mean. I'm sorry, I can't believe—"

"I'm sorry too, lady, believe me. I wish I was this lucky fellow, what's his name?"

"Bill Saunders," said Diane, still staring.

"Won't I do instead of Bill Saunders, lady? I've nothin' much on this forenoon."

"Oh no, no, thank you," said Diane, backing away. "You are very kind, but I must go—" and she fled, stopping to glance back once or twice, and Bill stared after her till she was out of sight. Then he mopped his brow, replaced the somewhat broad-brimmed hat, and went on his way.

At the War Office he heard, to his intense surprise, that Max von Bodenheim had been murdered by some woman who had thereupon shot herself. Denton did not know who she was, but there was no doubt about the story.

"Impossible," said Bill. "They are cooking the story up to make me think I'm safe. Then, when I return, they will have a reception committee waiting for me."

"No," said the War Office man, "I don't agree, I think something extraordinary has happened, for these people aren't fools. If you shot him, you must know you've shot him and wouldn't be taken in; they wouldn't put up a feeble story like that. Besides, Denton talked to Hans, who found them. I sent Denton up from Mainz to make inquiries."

"Hans wouldn't lie, he wouldn't be able to think of one, though of course somebody might have told him to say that."

"Denton met him drowning his sorrows at the local pub. He told the story with a wealth of gruesome detail."

"Then it must be true. Hans might repeat a statement, but not a wealth of detail. I give it up."

"Furthermore, no inquiries are being made for you by the German authorities, which shows not only that von Bodenheim did not report, but also that they swallowed Hambledon's note. They are not surprised you have disappeared, so it looks as though it would be safe for you to go back."

"I will go back and carry on with the importer's office. I shall have to get a clerk of some kind, there is really quite a lot of genuine business, if only in telling people their butter's marge this week."

"I am giving you Denton. You will be senior to him, of course. He is a German-Swiss officially, anything to keep him from being called to the colors. He is a good chap, it's amazing the amount of energy that weary manner conceals."

Bill returned to Cologne in May of 1918 and found a Germany going from bad to worse. The food was of poor quality and hopelessly insufficient, there was very little money, and prices were rising. The tone of public opinion was changing; now that the great advance had been held and turned, defeatism took the place of defiance; the last great effort had been made and failed, and the army was becoming mutinous. The navy was in worse case still; the great battleships rusted in harbor, fast cruisers and destroyers went out on raids and were chased home again, the submarine service was becoming a suicide club, and the personnel was openly Communistic. Bill found that there was not really much of outstanding importance to do but observe and report. Denton helped him not to feel the loss of Hambledon too keenly, but there was nobody on the German side to take the place of von Bodenheim, and Bill missed him intensely. Von Bodenheim's death appeared to have been more or less hushed up; there was no doubt that a woman had been concerned in it, but nobody wanted to talk about it and Bill was hardly in a position to inquire. As a friend of the house, he did try to find Hans, but the servant seemed to have disappeared. Probably he had gone back to the village where he belonged, and Bill had never heard where that was.

He received instructions from German Intelligence for forwarding the ghostly Butler's reports, but as the months passed and the situation in Germany grew steadily more desperate, the connection became pointless, and at last Bill was empowered to report that British Intelligence had dropped on Butler and gathered him in. Formal regret was officially expressed, but nobody seemed to mind very much, for, after all, what was a Butler in the general cataclysm?

Dirk Brandt, heir to his uncle Hendrik Brandt, who was accidentally drowned in Holland while paying a business visit there at the end of January, and his new assistant, the German-Swiss Ludwig Wolff, found themselves extraordinarily welcome in Cologne society, for if young Brandt had been worth cultivating a year earlier for the good things his uncle was able to procure, how much more was it the case now that conditions were so much worse and the young man was his own master! Ludwig Wolff, besides his connection with the horn of plenty, was welcome for his own sake, as he was friendly, cheerful, and always good-tempered, and his sleepy manner was in welcome contrast to the feverish harassed ways of most of the Cologne people in those hard times. Dirk Brandt took him everywhere and introduced him, and one night in August at the Café Palant they met Kaspar Bluehm, home on leave.

"Bluehm, I'm awfully glad to see you," said Dirk sincerely. "I see your people occasionally and hear news of you, but it's an age since we met."

Bluehm glanced up wearily. He looked years older and the life seemed to have been drained out of him. "Brandt, well met," he said. "Yes, I've been lucky so far. How are you?"

Dirk introduced Wolff, "my new partner," and Bluehm said: "I was sorry to hear about your uncle, though I never knew him. He will be missed in Cologne. Did you say you saw my people sometimes?"

"Yes," said Dirk. "I saw Frau Bluehm the other day, she wanted something for your sister Greta, who has not been very well."

"She is nearly starved, that's what's the matter with her," said Bluehm bluntly. "I know, you got them flour and butter, it was good of you. But my sister Marie, have you seen Marie?"

"I have seen her out with people once or twice," said Dirk guardedly; "she has not been at home when I have called."

"No," said Bluehm. "No, I dare say not. Are you a stranger to Cologne, Herr Wolff?"

"Not now," said Ludwig Wolff, "I've been here about four months, weighing out beans and helping Brandt to count the shekels, you know."

"I hope it amuses you."

"Frightfully thrilling at first, never seen so much money before. We aren't rich in my country, you know, especially since the tourists have all gone shooting instead of skiing."

"I thought you had rather a lot of visitors in Switzerland just now," said Bluehm, rather entertained by the tall young man's nonchalant manner.

"Oh yes, lots and lots of visitors, but not the kind who spend money. Fact is, we're always afraid about eighty per cent of 'em will become chargeable to the parish, and then up go the taxes, eh? Wonderful place to learn languages just now, my country. Reminds me of Noah's Ark."

"The Tower of Babel, possibly?"

"No, no, Noah's Ark," insisted Wolff, "all the different kinds of animals, you know. And they go in two by two as a general rule," he added, with his lazy smile.

Bluehm laughed rather perfunctorily, and there was a short pause during which he glanced at Dirk Brandt once or twice, and Wolff, realizing that he was not wanted, said: "Excuse me, please, some people over there I ought to say a kind word to," and went. Even then Bluehm did not seem to have much to say, and Dirk, to make conversation, remarked that the prevailing depression did not seem to have much effect on the spirits of the Café Palant's clientele, and he looked round the room at several noisy parties of young officers and rather too decorative ladies. Bluehm's glance followed his with an expression of distaste.

"Rotten, all rotten," said Bluehm. "Here's the country on the edge of starvation, defeat, disintegration, and damnation, and all they think of is getting drunk and having a good time."

"Perhaps that's all they dare think of," suggested Dirk, and Bluehm looked at him keenly.

"Yes, you've got older, too, since last we met, haven't you?" he said, and Dirk shrugged his shoulders. "I should like to ask you something," Bluehm went on hesitantly, "but I hardly know how—a favor—it is not fair to—"

"Please go on," said Dirk, looking straight into the German's honest, puzzled blue eyes. "You should know I will do anything I can—we have known each other for some time now."

"It is this," said Bluehm and paused. "By the way, have you seen or heard of anything of Hedwige Schwiss lately?"

"One of the Bavarian Nightingales. No, not for ages, not since—let me see. It was the day after the Ahlhorn disaster. I remember we were talking about it, my uncle was there too, it was at the Metropol."

"The day after the Ahlhorn disaster," repeated Bluehm slowly. "I see— yes, well, that was not what I was going to ask. Tell me—forgive me, I do not wish to be intrusive—I thought at one time that you liked my sister Marie, did you not?"

"I like her very much," said Dirk with complete truth. "She used to play the piano for me. She was always kind and she plays beautifully, but it is a long time since I have seen her to talk to. I see her about with people sometimes; it is a change for her, she used to be so quiet."

"That is so, she is changed. Brandt, my mother and I are terribly worried about her. I came out this evening thinking I might meet her, she would not stay at home, she had engagements, she said—Brandt, what can I do? I have only four days' leave. My mother is tied at home with my sister Greta, who becomes weaker every day—she is in a decline, I think—and Marie goes about alone; it is not done by young girls in our class as you know. She says she goes with friends, but they are not our friends," went on Bluehm, who, once the ice had been broken, poured out his story as though he would never stop; "we do not hear good accounts of these people, rich profiteers and suchlike, patronizing Marie Bluehm. I don't want you to think I am hard on her, believe me, I understand. It is miserable at home now—no maids, no money, not enough to eat, Greta always ill, and my mother, dear kind soul as she is, always lamenting the good old days—it is not cheerful. I think it is breaking Marie's heart and she runs about to distract her mind."

"Nobody could possibly blame her or be hard on her," said Dirk gravely, thinking of Marie's clear blue eyes and smooth fair hair shining in a beam of sunlight as she sat at an old-fashioned upright piano in the Bluehm apartment playing Chopin for him, "she looks so young."

"She is young—barely eighteen. She was the baby sister always, for Greta is older than I am. Brandt! She will come to harm as sure as I sit here, and what can I do? Brandt, for God's sake, have you any influence over her?"

"I don't know, Bluehm, on my word I have no idea. Why should I have?"

"Brandt! You know how things are. You are the only man in Cologne whom I would call a friend who is always in Cologne, my own school-friends and brother officers are either dead or crippled or always away like myself. You know the sort of degenerate money-making swine who have somehow managed to evade service and remain at home, you've seen for yourself the set she has got into. Brandt," hammering the table with his fist, "you are the only one who can do anything. It is a frightful lot to ask, but we look on you as one of us now—will you do what you can?"

Dirk hesitated, as well he might, but it was impossible to refuse this good fellow, and besides, there was Marie. He shivered slightly.

"I will do whatever I can," he said solemnly, and they shook hands. "Of course," he went on in a lighter tone, "she may tell me to run away and chase myself."

CHAPTER SIXTEEN
"I HAD A COMRADE"

A few days later Dirk Brandt saw Marie Bluehm at the Rosenhof dancing with a young man of unprepossessing appearance and too much jewelry.

His manner was patronizing and her merriment was a little too obvious to be quite genuine, so Dirk leaned one shoulder against the wall and watched them. Moreover, it seemed to him that he had seen the man before somewhere, and presently there returned to him a recollection of an evening at the Germania with Max von Bodenheim in an expansive mood pointing out his various bête-noires, and among them the flashy young man going to sit at a table where were two girls unaccompanied. "This," said Max acidly, "is more than my stomach will stand, let's go," and Max von Bodenheim was gone indeed while slimy little beasts such as this remained to take out girls like Marie Bluehm. When at the end of the dance he left her without too much ceremony, Dirk went up and greeted her.

"It is an age since we met, Fräulein. I hope you are well."

"Very well, thank you. No, we haven't met for a long time," she said, and looked at him doubtfully like a child who expects to be scolded.

"I had hoped you might play to me again some day, Fräulein."

"I'm out of practice with Chopin and Schubert and all that stuff, I'm afraid. I like this dance music now, don't you? It's so gay, and I like to be gay."

"It is natural, Fräulein Marie. It is a change to see you going about dancing at parties, you, who used to be so quiet."

"Have you been talking to Kaspar?" she asked at once, with a look between defiance and appeal. "Are you trying to lecture me, too?"

"I was trying to summon enough courage to ask if you would dine with me, Fräulein, if your friends would permit."

"Oh, they won't mind," she said carelessly. "I'd love to—shall we stay here?"

"What about the Metropol?" he said, for he wanted to get her away from the party. "The food isn't too bad there sometimes."

"I'd love that. Just a moment while I speak to Lottchen and get my cloak."

At the Metropol he noticed her thin hands and almost transparent skin, and ordered a meal which should be as nourishing as possible, and after the Rhine trout cooked in white wine and Wiener schnitzel had disappeared, he had the pleasure of seeing a more natural color come into her face, and her eyes grow less unnaturally large and bright. She leaned her elbows on the table, cupped her chin in her hands, and regarded him with the old friendliness instead of the veiled distrust with which she had greeted him.

"You know," she said, "my friends are awfully kind and generous and there's always plenty of drink going, but it never seems to occur to them that a poor girl wants a square meal occasionally."

"I remember when I was your age," said Dirk who was a whole year older, "that I seemed to want square meals all day long. After all," he added to himself, feeling quite fatherly, "I expect the kid's still growing."

"Have you got such a thing as a cigarette?"

"Yes," he said with a very slight hesitation, "will you have it now?"

"Why not?" she flashed, up in arms instantly. "Are you trying to say it is not proper for a *hochgeboren Mädchen* to smoke in public? You are as bad as Greta!"

"I wasn't thinking of that," said Dirk with his most disarming smile, "though perhaps I ought to have done so. No, I only thought it would spoil your appetite to smoke between courses."

"Of course it does, that's why we do it, so that we shan't want any more to eat."

"But why not have some more to eat?"

She stared incredulously and said slowly: "What—more steak?"

"If you wish. Or what about *Krostcher wärm*?"

She laughed and clapped her hands. "Ooh! Lovely and vulgar! Do you know, it's"—she counted on her fingers—"seven and a half weeks since I had meat? Real meat I mean, not sausage stuff."

"You poor kid," muttered Dirk, "it's a damned shame," and he beckoned the waiter and gave the order, but the man demurred.

"Second meat course? Naturally it's a second meat course," said Herr Brandt, importer. "Not allowed to serve? Send me the manager."

But the manager only looked to see from whom the order came, and the second meat course arrived instead.

"I say," said Marie, gaping, "how do you do it? Why, even Jakob doesn't have managers jumping to it like that."

"Doesn't he?" said Dirk, leaning back and sipping his wine while Marie attacked the stew, "and who's Jakob?"

"Goertz. The man I was dancing with. His father makes boots or something."

"Oh, ah, yes. Do you like him?"

"What a queer tone! You don't, evidently."

"I asked if you did."

"Not like him, no. I find him useful."

"Useful! What for?"

"Oh, he always has plenty of money and gives lovely parties. He's giving one at his house one night soon," babbled Marie between mouthfuls, "and he's sure to ask me."

"Will you accept?"

"Of course. All the girls in Cologne are wild to be asked to his place, he gives such lovely presents."

"What for?"

"What do you mean?" asked Marie, lifting limpid blue eyes to the darker blue ones watching her intently.

"Never mind—if you don't know," he said, and Marie bit her lip. "Don't go, Marie," he said, dropping his voice nearly to a whisper, "don't go there. Little Mariechen, to please me, don't go, will you?"

"I—" she began, but a shadow fell across the table and she looked up. "'Lo, Marie," said Goertz.

"Good evening again, Jakob. Herr Jakob Goertz—Herr Brandt."

Dirk rose slowly to his feet and the man said: "Good evening. Just going?"

"No," said Dirk, and continued to stand, looking him up and down while Goertz stared back for a long moment and then turned and bent over Marie.

"I am giving a little party at my house on Thursday," he said. "You'll come, won't you? Eight thirty."

"Er—" began Marie, and quite involuntarily her eyes met Dirk's, which annoyed her because she had no intention of taking orders from him however imploring he might look, "thank you—"

Dirk broke in. "The gracious Fräulein regrets," he said in a hard voice, "but she has an engagement with me that evening."

Goertz straightened up and looked at him. "Surely the gracious Fräulein can speak for herself, can't she?"

Marie glanced up, caught sight of Goertz, and looked hastily away again; it was as though she saw him for the first time. "I am sorry—I have an engagement—"

"You hear," said Dirk, "the lady confirms it."

"Oh, la la! Then I find someone else, eh?"

Dirk leaned forward over the back of his chair to speak more clearly. "Find the devil and his wife, but if I ever catch you pestering the Fräulein Marie Bluehm again I'll break your rotten neck, put you through the mincing-machine, and feed you to pigs!"

By some miracle, possibly prearranged, Ludwig Wolff's lanky form materialized at Goertz's elbow. "Better buzz off," he murmured, "he did that once. And the pigs died. Dreadful feller."

"There is no need to be uncivil," said Goertz rather too hastily. "If the gracious lady does not desire my company—"

He backed away, followed by Dirk's cold glance and Wolff's amused grin, but Marie was too busy staring in a puzzled manner at Dirk to notice Goertz's departure.

"Why did I let you do that? I didn't mean to."

Dirk's expression softened at once. He sat down again and said: "It was sweet of you to let me, I must make up to you for that. I'll see you don't regret it."

"This is a great life," said Ludwig Wolff to himself as he strolled away. "I pop up, say my little piece, and tactfully fade out. I shall go and rescue somebody for myself who will spend the rest of her life saying: 'Darling, *please* don't go.' Oh Christmas, what a frightful prospect!"

Negotiations for an armistice began on November 6th, on the 9th the Kaiser abdicated, two days later the Armistice was signed, and in London and Paris the bells rang and the people laughed and cried and danced in the streets because the war was over, but many a German town saw fighting for the first time when the rest of the world was at peace. In the first days of November mutiny broke out in the German navy at Kiel and spread to Hamburg and Bremen, revolution flared up in Berlin when the government fell, and sporadic fighting broke out in the streets of all these places and spread by degrees to other towns all over Germany, getting worse as the angry dispirited soldiers drifted home, bringing their arms and ammunition with them.

Dirk and Marie stood by the roadside close to the Hohenzollern Bridge and watched the Kaiser's armies come home, long, intermittent lines of weary men in all stages of shabbiness and disrepair, hardly one with his equipment complete and some without even their rifles, tramping along three or four abreast and not even keeping step, the very picture of defeat.

Dirk stood with his shoulders slightly hunched and his hands deep in his pockets, Marie, as had become her custom, a little behind his shoulder with an arm through his and an occasional glance at his profile to guess from his expression what his thoughts were. This time he was even more inscrutable than usual, with his lower lip pushed out in a way his uncle would have recognized and a suppressed gleam in his eyes, the fact being that half of him was crying: "Victory! We've done it at last!" and the other half saying: "So this is defeat. My God, how awful!" Presently Marie shook his arm slightly to attract his attention and said: *"Liebchen?"*

"What is it?"

"Where are all the officers?"

"Oh, gone home by train, I expect. Come on, let's go back to the office, shall we? This is a dismal sight. Besides, I want to see Ludwig."

They found Ludwig Wolff waiting for them, sitting on the corner of a table and singing to himself in a melancholy voice:

> *"Ich hatt' einen Kamaraden*
> *Einen bessern findst du nicht,*
> *Der Drommel schlug zum Streite*
> *Er ging an meiner seite,*
> *In gleichem Schritt und Tritt—"*

" 'I had a comrade,' " repeated Dirk. "Why the funeral dirge?"

"Because I feel I have been attending a funeral on the grand scale," said Wolff. "Didn't you see the army coming back?"

"But, dear Ludwig," said Marie, "must you sing it quite so dreadfully flat?"

"I do it on purpose," he explained, "it sounds more doleful like that. There is going to be trouble here before we're much older."

"Why?"

"Because the sailors from the Grand Fleet are coming down to convert us all to Bolshevism. Marie, little treasure, I've got a button loose on this coat."

"Give it to me now," she said, hunting in a drawer for needles and thread, while Dirk said: "The army won't stand for that; there'll be a row, to say nothing of what the townsfolk will think."

"If you get several thousand starving angry people all armed to the teeth and holding diverse opinions, what happens?"

"Most uncivil disturbance, I expect," said Dirk. "Marie, my dear, at the first sign of any trouble when you're out, you will dive into the nearest building and hurl yourself flat on the floor, do you hear? What are you putting in that drawer?"

"*Ja, lieb'* Dirk," she answered to his good advice, and "Only sewing things," to his question. "There's your coat, Ludwig."

"Thank you very much," said Ludwig. "I am an awful bother to you, am I not?"

"Not half such a bother as this one," she said, stroking Dirk's sleeve with her finger till he took her hand and kissed it. "He is always coming undone somewhere, aren't you, my rabbit? Let my hand go, sir, I want to dust the office, it's simply disgraceful."

"We are getting terribly tidy, aren't we?" said Dirk. "I don't see that there's much wrong with it."

"I must have some outlet for my domestic instincts somewhere, grubby one," she said. "You wait till we find our flat we're looking for, I'll show you how a place should be kept."

"I did hear of a small flat to let up near the Neumarkt," said Ludwig, resuming his coat. "Where's the clothes brush, Marie? The widow Kraus is going back home to Bingen."

"We might go and look at it," said Marie, "though I don't believe it's big enough. We must have a room for Ludwig, mustn't we, my angel?"

"Yes, dear," said Dirk absently. "Where are those consignment details from Rotterdam, Ludwig, do you know? Half an hour, Marie, and we'll go to lunch. I don't trust you to eat enough when you're by yourself."

For Dirk had discovered in the last few months that in doing what he could for Kaspar's sister he had acquired a responsibility, a delight, and a slave, who would not trouble to be warmly clad unless he insisted, who would rather see him eat than be fed herself, and to whom he alone was sunlight and air and life itself, and in the early days he hardly knew whether to laugh or weep at the situation into which kindness and a sort of indulgent affection had carried him. As the weeks went by and he became more deeply absorbed into the agonizing daily life of a stricken Germany, his separate identities drifted farther apart till it seemed only a dream that Dirk Brandt should be also an Englishman named Michael Kingston, who married a colonel's daughter whom he scarcely knew. The dream was just real enough to keep him from marrying Marie, and she never mentioned the subject though she did occasionally look at him as though there were something she expected him to say and was puzzled because he did not. Puzzled, but not hurt, for whatever *lieb'* Dirk did was right, and as time went by, her flaxen hair took on a smoother gloss, her blue eyes deepened with a happy peace, and her flowerlike face blossomed into greater beauty.

Later on, the trouble Ludwig had foretold began in earnest when the seamen arrived from Hamburg to preach Communism and came into collision with the army, preaching Socialism, and the town authorities preaching law and order. The soldiers, as they reached home, just demobilized themselves without waiting for formalities, by the simple process of cutting off their various badges and replacing their uniform buttons with plain ones; but they retained their arms, particularly a pet machine-gun or so, and when the rioting began they brought them out and used them in the streets.

Early in December Marie came to the office in the Höhestrasse and said that there was some cretonne in a shop window higher up the street, which was quite attractive and very reasonable in price, it was a pattern of pink carnations with gray-green foliage on a cream background, and if the *lieb'* Dirk liked the idea it would make very nice curtains for the flat. Dirk smiled at her eager face, told her it sounded delightful, and gave her some money to go and buy it.

"I think twelve yards will do the three windows quite well," said Marie earnestly, "though of course fifteen yards will make more imposing curtains."

"Let the curtains be as imposing as possible, my dear. Will fifteen yards be enough?"

"Quite enough, more would be a waste. Thank you, darling. Will you be in to lunch?"

"Not today, angel, and Ludwig won't be back till evening."

"In that case I think I'll take the cretonne home. Are you sure you like carnations? There's another one with roses on it, but I don't like it so well."

"I'm sure I shouldn't, either; let's have the carnations. Unless you can find one with lettuces on it, and then we can chew them if we really get hungry."

"*Du bist ein Esel, liebling.* Then I might go home and see mother and Greta; there may be news of Kaspar."

"Yes, dear, do. Oh, look here, would it be out of your way to pass here when you go home?"

"Hardly at all. Is there anything you want?"

"I left a notebook on the piano—a small red one. Would you mind—"

"Of course not, I'll bring it. Is there anything else?"

"No, nothing, thanks. Oh, Marie—"

"What is it?"

"Be quick and careful, won't you? I don't quite like the look of things. Too many men lounging about."

"I'll run so fast nobody will be able to see me."

Dirk settled down to work after she had gone, and an hour or so had passed when he heard some stray shots farther along the street, followed by a shout outside, the sound of running feet, and a burst of machine-gun fire so close that Dirk threw himself on the floor just as a windowpane shattered near the chair in which he had been sitting. The gunner in the street outside fired off a few more shots and was silent, while the noise of battle died away in the distance. Dirk got up and shook off some stray bits of broken glass which had fallen upon him.

"Curse these street riots," he muttered. "Another pane gone. Hope they haven't frightened Marie."

He went to the window and looked out, but could see nothing but some town police removing the body of the gunner, who had had the best of reasons for suddenly falling silent. The next moment Wolff passed the window hurriedly and burst into the room.

"Ludwig! You're back early. Did they get you on the run?"

But Ludwig merely stared at him and did not answer.

"What the devil's the matter?"

His partner swallowed with an effort, and said, in English: "You'd better come outside, old man, there's something there that—belongs to you."

Outside, Dirk stopped to pick up something from the pavement where it lay beside the quiet body of Marie Bluehm.

"I told her," he said stupidly, "I told her to bring me a red notebook."

CHAPTER SEVENTEEN
LET THE BRIGHT SERAPHIM

Dirk Brandt and his partner, Ludwig Wolff, stood on the steps of the west door of Cologne Cathedral to see the British Army of Occupation march in on the 13th of December 1918. By three in the afternoon there were thirty-two thousand British troops billeted in Cologne.

Brandt and Wolff, suffering from that curious unsettled feeling which persists throughout the day for those who have seen something exciting in the morning, closed the office and wandered about the town, watching British sentries being posted and the military police putting up notices which applied to the troops and the civilian population too, since Cologne was under martial law. Some time in the afternoon they strolled into the railway station to see if anything was happening there, and noticed a group of British prisoners of war waiting for a train. They looked underfed and ill-clad, but happy, and one of their number stood a little apart by a pile of packing-cases and solemnly performed five-finger exercises, first with each hand separately and then with both together.

"Look at that poor chap," said Ludwig. "Do you think he's gone a little cracked?"

"No," said Dirk, "he's only a musician in the act of realizing that life is beginning again. I know, because I was at school with him—his name is Dixon Ogilvie."

During the evening the streets filled with cheerful soldiers walking about, staring in the shop windows, and mildly surprised to find the town so brightly lit. They went into the shops for cigarettes and picture-postcards, and into the cafés for beer, which did not meet with their approval, and were friendly and unembarrassed, and immediately the ice between victors and losers showed signs of cracking, as both sides were equally ready to fraternize.

The firm of Brandt and Wolff went into a restaurant for supper and found a table next to two English officers, major and captain, who were being waited upon by a German ex-service-man. At least, he started by waiting upon them but presently forgot he was a waiter as he and his clients laid out a sector of the front line with forks and spoons on the tablecloth. "You were here, and here," said the German waiter, "and we were attacking from this angle."

"The war is over indeed," said Ludwig, observing this.

"Yes," said Dirk, "and the world isn't such a bad place after all. Have some more *schnapps*."

The days passed into weeks, the novelty of seeing British uniforms and hearing English speech in the streets gradually wore off, and the English agents found to their pained disgust that the blockade still continued, so that they had to go on giving themselves indigestion with the soggy, almost uneatable bread, to starve for lack of oils and fats, and to drink coffee brewed from burnt wheat with no Marie there to make it so like the real thing as to be almost delicious.

It must be remembered that Dirk Brandt, importer, had a very considerable position among the Germans in Cologne prior to the occupation, but, for obvious reasons, he received no consideration whatever from the British authorities. He became just one of the German population and simply hated it. In fact, there was only one advantage to him in the British occupation: one could obtain, and be seen smoking, English cigarettes.

One evening he and Wolff encountered Reck at the Germania sitting at the same table where on a memorable day Dirk had sat with Max von Bodenheim more than a year before. Reck, always insignificant, now looked older and shabbier, and it is to be regretted that he had been drinking.

"Hullo, Reck," said Brandt, "how's things?"

"Rotten."

"And how are the silkworms?" inquired Wolff. "All nice and warm and maternal, what?"

"No," said Reck.

"Oh, I say! I thought they laid thousands of eggs continually."

"Not in January," said the expert, and ordered another bottle.

"What do they do, then, spin?" Wolff got no answer to this, so he went on: "What do you feed 'em on? Flannel trousers?"

"No," said Reck, and shot him a malevolent glance.

"Shut up, you ass," said Dirk in an undertone.

"Oh, please don't stop him," said Reck bitterly, "I like it. I live on it. I get it all day long."

"Get what?"

"An unending succession of blithering idiots asking inane questions. My God, the British Tommy!"

"Oh yes," said Dirk, "I heard you had some billeted on you."

" 'Let the bright seraphim,' " said Reck unexpectedly.

"Eh? By all means, but what?"

"I don't know. Probably I shall never know."

Dirk and Ludwig exchanged glances, and Reck saw it.

"You think I'm drunk, don't you? Well, I am, but I can't get drunk enough to forget the bright seraphim."

"They sound nice things to remember," said Ludwig helpfully. "A steadying and purifying influence, what?"

"There is a lance-corporal—" began Reck, shuddered visibly, and poured himself out another glass.

"Yes?"

"He comes into my laboratory and asks me to show him something funny."

"Did you tell him to look in the glass?" suggested Dirk.

"Yes. Then I wished I hadn't."

"Why? What did he do?"

"They. There were several of them, all smelling things in bottles."

"What did they do?"

"They partially undressed me," said Reck modestly.

Dirk spluttered over his Braunberger, but Ludwig let out a howl of laughter that made most of the other clients look round.

"But what has that to do with the bright seraphim?"

"He comes in and asks me if there are any amusing experiments he can make. I gave him two bottles one day and told him to mix them, as probably the result might amuse him, I personally was going for a walk, but he looked at the labels and decided against it."

"What were they?"

"Nitric acid and glycerine, but he seemed to have heard of that one," said Reck mournfully. "They catch cockroaches and race them. It's curious to see how really fast a cockroach can run with a drop of alcohol on his tail."

"Cheer up," said Ludwig encouragingly, "perhaps the war will break out again," but Reck only made growling noises, so Wolff continued: "In the meantime there are the silkworms, aren't there?"

"There are a number of cocoons containing insects in a state of suspended animation, if you regard them as intelligent companions for an educated man."

"There are the British troops."

"Who look on me as a comic German professor. Thank you, I prefer the silkworms. They at least do not play practical jokes."

"Well, there are the bright seraphim, wherever they come in."

"He sings it."

"Who sings what?" asked Dirk.

"The lance-corporal. 'Let the bright seraphim,'," sang Reck in a cracked tenor.

"But what comes next?"

"I don't know. Presumably he doesn't know. That's all."

"But do you mean to say," said Wolff, "that he merely sings those four words over and over again?"

"Exactly."

"And then stops?"

"He does not stop. He goes on."

"Isn't it a Handel oratorio, or something?" suggested Dirk.

"It is very probable, I am no musician."

"Evidently the poor chap's got it on the brain," said Ludwig.

"That," said Reck acidly, "is quite impossible."

Dirk glanced round the room, which was nearly empty. "Tell me," he said, to change the subject, "what was that odd story about von Bodenheim being shot by a woman?"

"I never inquired into it," answered Reck. "That was the official explanation and that's enough for me. I am only a stupid old fool of a schoolmaster, but I'm not idiot enough to poke my nose into a wasp's nest. If they said he was shot by the Emperor of Japan in mistake for the Prince of Wales I shouldn't argue. I might say 'Dear me,' but no more."

"You are very wise," said Dirk.

"Wise enough to go home before curfew hour," said Reck, emptying his glass and getting to his feet. "I have no intention of subscribing towards the cost of the British occupation by getting myself fined for being out late. Curse the curfew. Good night."

He struggled into his coat with the help of a waiter and tacked between the tables to the door, while Dirk and Ludwig watched him.

"Poor old bean," said Ludwig.

"He is going to pieces," said Dirk, "and really one can't wonder; it isn't much of a life. I wish he wouldn't drink. One of these days he might begin to talk."

"He wouldn't dare, surely?"

"Not about himself, probably. About others."

" 'Thou art in the midst of foes, ,'" hummed Wolff. " 'Watch and pray.' "

"That's just it, he doesn't feel he's in the midst of foes, he's at home here. I've never heard him speaking English, but I'll bet it's infernally rusty, and England's a foreign country to him now. If anything happens to make his life here impossible, he'll break up, poor old geezer."

Greta Bluehm died in January 1919 and Frau Bluehm gave up her apartment and went to live with a widowed sister near Munich. Dirk never saw them again after the day of Marie's funeral. Kaspar Bluehm remained in what was left of the army and had only two days' leave before his mother left Cologne. He came to the office to see Dirk, who had unfortunately gone to Holland on perfectly genuine business, so the two friends missed each other for that time. He was reported to have been asking for news of Hedwige Schwiss.

In March, Bill Saunders returned to England, accompanied by Denton, and the importer's office in the Höhestrasse at Cologne was closed for good. They went through Holland from habit rather than necessity, and when the cross-Channel steamer drew away from the quayside at the Hook they leaned on the rail to watch the shores of Holland sink into the sea astern.

"You know," said Denton wearily, "I suppose we ought to be saying: 'Hooray, hooray, the war's over, we're going home,' but somehow it isn't noticeably like the last day of term, is it? Well, the sun is over the yardarm, what about it? We'll drink to tomorrow, shall we?"

"Better drink to yesterday, I think. There were some good spots in that, anyway."

"You've got the blue devils all right! Come on."

Bill Saunders went to the War Office and was there received in a manner calculated to exorcise most blue devils, but which only made his worse,

because it displayed his uninviting future in even sharper contrast, and from
there he went straight home to Weatherley Parva, to be kindly received by
his uncle and aunt, who were unfeignedly glad to "have the boy back again."
What they did not realize and never quite understood was that the boy who
went had *not* come back. That boy had died, died by degrees with the
guiltless Amtenbrink, with his friend Hambledon and his adversary von
Bodenheim, and finally and conclusively with the gentle Marie, but his people
knew nothing of that and he could not tell them. In the boy's place was a
stranger in his image, tired, nervous, irritable, and unhappy, with a mind too
full of memories to find peace, and a heart too full of yesterday to care
about tomorrow. On the night of his homecoming he wrote to his wife:

> DIANE:
>
> I'm in England again. I was going to say, home in England
> again, but I can't, somehow. Things are so difficult, the whole
> world has gone wrong. What are we going to do? It looks as
> though I must finish my apprenticeship, and you know what
> that means, don't you? Anyhow, I'll talk to Uncle and see the
> firm, and let you know, and God help us both.
>
> Yours,
>
> BILL

The first evening at home passed pleasantly enough. It was rather nice
to sit in his usual chair and look at the same old furniture standing in the
same places and hear the familiar voices talking of village matters—how
well the vicar had spoken in his sermon at the thanksgiving service for
peace, about forgiving your enemies and letting bygones be bygones, so
typically British one hoped it would not be mistaken in Germany for weak-
ness, and how we must all turn to and build a new world out of the ruins of
the old.

Bill sat and drowsed by the fire and listened, thought of something else
for a while and listened again, and said, "Yes," and "No," and "Very nice,"
in the right places, till gradually the voices died away in the distance and the
next moment his uncle was shaking him by the shoulder and saying that bed
was the right place for tired soldiers. "But I'm not a soldier now," he protested, and stumbled wearily upstairs to lie awake and listen for the chimes
of Cologne Cathedral and want Marie. Marie, where are you?

At breakfast his aunt asked him if he had seen Diane the day before.

"No," said Bill, "she was out of town," for he did not choose to start an argument by admitting he had not attempted to see her. "I wrote to her last night and told her I was at home."

"She will wish to come here, no doubt," said his uncle kindly.

"Thank you, but that won't be any good, as I must go to Southampton and see if the shipyard will have me back. I haven't finished my apprenticeship, you know."

At the end of a few months the firm, who were extremely good to him, gave him his indentures a whole year before he was entitled to receive them, and found him work in the drawing office.

Diane came from London on Sundays to see him sometimes, and they would take a bus to the Forest and walk, or if the motorcycle was in a good mood he would take her for rides on the pillion seat. One such Sunday they found an inn where the beer and cheese were good, so they lunched there and afterwards sat on a rickety seat in the inn garden.

"Have a cigarette?" he asked.

"Thank you. Listen, darling. I've got a message from Daddy, he does so want to help us."

"He is very kind," said Bill woodenly.

"Oh, he is really, dear. He makes awful fusses, but they don't mean anything."

"Oh, no. Are you sure you aren't getting cold out here?"

"No, darling, of course not. He does so want us all to live together."

"Does he? Where?"

"In town, of course. You don't sound very interested, darling."

"I can't have your father keeping me, Diane. You must see that."

"He wasn't going to, dear. He says he is sure he could get you a nicer job than this."

"That's nice of him, but engineering is my job."

"But there are other things you could do, dear. You see, Daddy is chairman of lots of companies, or director, or whatever it is, and he says he is sure he could fit you in where it would be much more suitable for you than working like this. He says we could have the top floor of the house all to ourselves, with a little kitchen and bathroom all fitted up, and not see them at all unless we liked. Wouldn't that be fun, darling?"

"But I'm an engineer, not an office clerk."

"Daddy said he thought you'd be quite useful in an office, darling; and then he laughed. What did he mean, Bill?"

"No idea," said Bill shortly. ("Damn the man, why can't he hold his tongue?" he added to himself.)

"Besides, it would be so useful your being an engineer when little things went wrong with our flat."

Bill's thoughts flew back to a flat in Cologne, with a defective tap over the kitchen sink which Marie said simply devoured washers, because it was worn inside and there were no new taps obtainable. Marie used to put in new washers herself till she discovered that Bill liked doing things for her, after which she seemed to lose the knack of it. He caught his breath suddenly.

"What's the matter, darling?"

"Nothing. What you want is a plumber, not an engineer."

"But I didn't marry a plumber, darling."

"You didn't, did you? Shall we push off now?"

"But about Daddy's offer?"

"It is very kind of him, but I think we're better off as we are."

"I'm very disappointed. Bill darling. I don't think you're being a bit nice."

"I'm afraid I'm a disappointing person, Diane."

"Oh, Bill darling, couldn't you be just a little bit different? We might be so happy if only you were."

"I'm sorry, Diane. I am, really. I never ought to have married you. But then, you see—"

"What?"

"I never expected to live through the war. To tell you the brutal truth, I didn't want to, and I was sure I shouldn't. So one might as well do whatever one wanted to, as there weren't going to be any consequences. Do you understand? I'm sorry now, because it's unfair to you."

"Have you always done whatever you wanted to, darling?"

"Except for one thing, yes."

"What was that?"

"I didn't die."

"I understand one thing," said Diane with tears in her eyes. "You never really loved me."

"I'm sorry, Diane. I thought I did, till—"

"Till you met someone else, I suppose?"

He did not answer, and she stamped her foot. "I hate her, I hate her! I wish she was dead, I suppose you're keeping her somewhere."

"She is already dead, Diane."

"I'm glad to hear it!"

"If you don't come along now we shall lose your train."

It was a very long time before Diane came to see him again, but Bill felt that he had escaped out of a net that was being tangled round him.

The short postwar boom came to an end and the slump set in, paralyzing the shipyard in which Bill worked as it did every other industry all over the country. Men were discharged to draw the dole and stand in miserable little groups at the street corners while the busy workshops grew silent and dust settled on the lathes and benches. Bill, who had been promoted to having a little room of his own, sat there for eight hours a day with nothing much to do, and read novels and kicked his heels and designed gadgets which would probably never be made.

"I can't stand this much longer," he said to the works manager, who wandered in one morning to sit on the table, smoke, and pass away an insufferably idle hour. "It's giving me the jim-jams, sitting here doing nothing all day."

"It's worse for me than it is for you," said the manager. "You can at least sit here out of sight, while I have to walk about and show myself looking cheerful."

"I tell you frankly," said Bill, putting his feet on the edge of his table and tilting his chair back, "if I could find anything else to do I'd do it."

"Hang on, lad. This slump must end some time, and when it does you won't be sorry you stayed here, believe me."

He went out, leaving Bill grateful but slightly mystified. Lest anyone should think that to be treated in this manner by works managers is the ordinary lot of industrious apprentices, let it be said that it isn't. Bill was an excellent draftsman and as a designer had bright ideas, but the fact was that the manager knew more about his career than Bill himself had any notion, and his unusually rapid rise in his profession was, though well earned, the work of a grateful country.

But month after month the stagnation continued, and the monotony became more than Bill could bear. He began to think again over the idea which he and Diane had once discussed, of starting a garage in some country village and settling down among quiet neighbors who knew nothing of Bill Saunders or Michael Kingston either, to repair cars and reapers and plows and milking machines, and sell petrol and mend punctures, but not with Diane, no, never with Diane, who meant well but never understood. Marie, now— However, starting a garage needed capital, and he had none so long as his uncle and aunt lived, dear old Uncle John, who did not understand much more than anyone else how the war had left a man—how should he, not knowing what one had been doing?—but he always took one on trust ("Let the boy alone, Dora!")—bless his heart. Perhaps he would lend Bill the capital. Five hundred pounds would be heaps—a lot less would do. No harm in asking, anyway. …

Michael Kingston, garage proprietor, had only been settled in the village of Lime in Hampshire for a few months when his uncle died, and as though life without John were too wearisome to be worth living, his aunt died also a short time later and left Michael some three hundred a year which he promptly made over to Diane. For the first time since his childhood, life seemed to be ordered and secure and very much as he had described it to Diane. People came in with jobs for him to do and waited while he did them, and other men with an idle half-hour drifted in and leaned against doorposts or sat on up-turned boxes, smoked cigarettes, and talked. By degrees, as the village learned to trust him because he did not repeat what he was told, he heard various things which the squire and the parson and even the police would have been most interested to hear, such as who set the gypsy encampment afire and why, the reason for young Mrs. Marlow's marriage to old Mr. Marlow, what the retired Commander R.N. said to the vicar about foreign missions, why the vicar's wife disapproved of the governess that the doctor's wife imported to teach her four daughters, the real reason why the bellringers went on strike, and a host of other matters of equal importance.

For the first year or so Michael was rather amused by all this. He was working long hours and gaining experience, his nerves improved and he was sleeping better, when trouble began in Germany, the French occupied the Ruhr, and Bill Saunders reawoke. All this going on, and he out of it, buried alive in this funny little village among these funny little people whose insignificant affairs were so much more important than the state of Europe. He felt he must get out of the place sometimes, so he took to going to Portsmouth in the evenings, roaming about there making friends with a variety of people, and driving home at a high rate of speed in the small hours.

CHAPTER EIGHTEEN
FOR ALL YOUR SINS

MORPETH, who was probably the most important farmer in Lime, brought his car in one evening saying that the carburetor wanted adjustment and he would call back for it about midday tomorrow. He then leaned wearily against the side of the car, lit a cigarette, and said he had been haymaking ever since six that morning, that Heaven forbid he should grumble when dry weather was such a blessing, but that really the heat in the open fields at midday had to be felt to be believed. Michael said that he had spent the afternoon, or most of it, changing a tire on one of the new split-rim wheels from an American car, that in his opinion split rims were invented by Satan in person, and that even in the shade of the open workshop the heat had been enough to make you sick. Morpeth looked about him at the garage yard, with three or four lockup sheds, the workshop with benches along one wall, and tools in racks above them, and the little bungalow behind, and said: "Nice place you've got here."

"Not too bad," said Michael.

"Bit lonely here of an evening?"

"Not enough to worry about."

"You want a dog," said Morpeth decidedly.

"Would be company," admitted Kingston.

"Tell you what. I've got a litter of bull-terrier pups comin' along any day now. You shall 'ave one for ten bob."

"Bull-terrier," repeated Michael thoughtfully.

"Thoroughbred, too. Well, as near as no matter."

"I'll see them when they come along."

"Do that," said Morpeth heartily. "Ten bob I said—well, we won't quarrel about the price."

He went off and Michael put the car away and went indoors to get his supper. Bull-terrier, good idea. Sleep on the foot of the bed. A man could sleep sounder with a bull-terrier about the place. Heaven help anybody who crept in with a beast like that loose in the house. It would be nice not to have to do all one's listening in the night for oneself.

He went into his tiny kitchen and lit the oil stove to fry some bacon rashers which Mrs. Lomas had left ready for him, and put a kettle on to boil because he was thirsty and tea seemed a good idea. He carried the tray into his sitting room and read, while he was eating, a book the doctor had lent him called *Bulldog Drummond*. How delightfully easy the career of an Intelligence agent would be if only life were a little more like that! One went about upon entirely unlawful occasions armed with automatics and never, never met a policeman at the wrong moment.

He took the tray out again and stacked up the plates, thinking as he did so of the bull-terrier pup Morpeth had promised him. It would be company to have a dog pattering about the place and waiting for him when he came home late. Michael sometimes wondered when he was driving home from Portsmouth whether there would be someone waiting to receive him, someone whom he did not wish to meet. Perhaps it would be as well to try out the automatic, it was some time since he had given it any attention.

He took the pistol into the garage, and fired one shot at the wall. The gun failed to eject the empty case and jammed. Michael said: "Dear me," mildly, and took the gun into his bedroom, where he got out the tin box in which he kept spare ammunition, cleaning-rod and brush, an oilcan, and some bits of soft rag. He laid out these necessaries on a small table near the window and turned his attention to the automatic. At the second attempt the sliding breech threw out the case, which dropped on the floor, and the next cartridge rose into its place ready to be fired.

Someone hooted outside. Michael looked through the window, for it was not yet ten o'clock and still daylight, and recognized a traveling salesman in motor oils and grease desiring to see him, so he put the gun down and went out, shutting the bedroom door behind him.

"Hullo, Ellis," he said. "I was thinking only yesterday that it was about time you came round."

"I must apologize," began Ellis, "for coming so late. May I have four gallons of Shell, please? I ought to have been here hours ago, but I've had a string of calamities."

"I expect you deserved them, if one only knew," said Michael unkindly. "In the tank, or in cans?"

"In the tank, please. I particularly wanted to get round to you tonight, as, if I hadn't, I shouldn't have been this way again for four months. How are you off for our distinguished products?"

"I want some, I think. Let's dip the tanks and see."

Kingston gave Ellis an order, and then said: "Come in and have a drink, will you? I want one and I hate drinking alone."

"I could bear it," said Ellis. "I've had a trying day."

"Come into the house. Have you got much more to do tonight?"

"No, only drive home. I'm going to rejoice my loving family with the sight of me for the first time for a fortnight. Yes, lots of soda, please, I'm thirsty. Tomorrow morning I go off again for three weeks or so. Thanks awfully. Well, here's luck. I don't get much money but I do see life."

"Must be rather amusing," said Michael.

"Yes, but you get tired of never being two nights running in the same place; you lose touch with things somehow. Why, some days I hardly see the paper. You do meet some odd people, though," and he entered upon anecdote.

When he had gone, Michael remembered that he had several orders to make out for his wholesalers and settled down to them, running through catalogues for prices and reference numbers. Spare burners for carbide lamps, cat. no. 25/1.1721a/402 in boxes of 1 doz., 6s. Carriers for bicycles. Bicycle bells, tires for bicycles, tires for cars, inner tubes.

The time slipped on to midnight as he pushed the papers back with the task completed, and a cool wind blew in at the open windows, moving the curtains and bringing a scent of stocks into the room. He leaned back and was wearily stretching his arms over his head when there was the sound of a step outside. Even as the thought: "I forgot to lock it," flashed through his mind, the door was flung open and a man appeared in the doorway holding a leveled automatic in his hand.

"Good evening," he said. "Will you keep your hands up, please?"

Michael obeyed, staring in amazement. "Good God!" he said slowly. "It's Kaspar Bluehm."

"Yes, it's Kaspar Bluehm. I have had a long hunt for you, but at last I find you."

"But—but why on earth should you be looking for me with a gun?"

"Have you not done enough for any German to search for you, and me in particular?"

Michael's brain began to race. "What a fool I have been!" he thought. "Kaspar Bluehm was in German Intelligence and I never guessed it."

Bluehm came forward. "Will you push your chair back till you are clear of the table? Thank you."

He pulled up with his left hand a chair for himself and sat in it. "On your honor, are you armed?"

"I am not."

"You may put your hands down, but do not move. I want to talk to you—to ask you something."

"May I have the usual glass of wine?"

"The usual glass?" repeated Bluehm in a tone of surprise. "Where is it—and the wine?"

"In that cabinet," said Kingston with a jerk of his head towards it. "There's a decanter in there, too."

"If you will move quite slowly, you may pour yourself a glass, but I warn you that at the first sign of a hasty movement I will shoot."

Michael rose to his feet, walked slowly across to the cabinet, took out a decanter of port and a glass, and deliberately filled it to the brim. The glass had a tall stem with a knob near the bowl, which was delicately curved in towards the rim and had a line of Gothic characters engraved round it. He lifted the glass with a steady hand, carried it back to his chair and sat down again.

"You wanted to ask me something, I believe?"

"Yes. It was about my sister—my sister Marie."

Michael looked at him steadily but did not speak, and Bluehm went on:

"I asked you to look after her and keep her from harm. I must have been a fool! But, you see, I trusted you."

Michael turned perfectly white, but still made no answer.

"I asked you to look after her, but I didn't expect you to—to—my God, man, why could you not marry her? Wasn't she good enough for you? Of course, you are one of the stars of British Intelligence, and she was only one of the conquered enemy; it would have been too condescending—"

"Stop!" shouted Michael. "Listen," he went on in a quieter tone, "and please believe me. I would have given all I have and all my hopes of heaven to have made Marie my wife. If she had lived we should never have parted again. I—I cared for her very much." His voice shook and he stopped abruptly.

"Then why on earth—"

"Because I was already married."

Bluehm drew a long breath, and the bitter anger in his face eased a little. "I see," he said. "Perhaps it would have been possible for you to have married her some day."

"I intended to."

"I believe you."

"I wanted to tell you this," said Michael, "after Marie—when you came back; but I missed you, and one cannot write these things."

"No," said Bluehm. "I came to the office, but you were away."

Michael nodded and relapsed into thought. ("If that's all he's got against me, he's satisfied. No, he knows I'm British Intelligence, so he probably knows about Reck and certainly about Denton. He may have connected us up with the fellows in Berlin and Essen and Wilhelmshaven and Hamburg, the gaff is blown on the whole lot of us, stridently blown, as Hambledon said, describe gaffs and at least three ways of blowing them, with musical illustrations. Stop that driveling at once and think. If he knows all this he has got to die, not me, I must find some way out.")

"There's another thing," said Bluehm. "If you must murder von Boden-heim, why did you leave that poor girl to take the blame?"

"Von Bodenheim? Am I to hear the truth about von Bodenheim at last? I killed him—or, rather, Hambledon killed him, because he was trying to kill me and damn nearly succeeded. He had got me at the wrong end of an automatic when Hambledon came in and shot him."

"Since this seems to be the time appointed for explanations," said Bluehm, "who was Hambledon?"

"Onkel Hendrik Brandt, don't you remember? Oh no, of course, you said you'd never met him. He is dead also, he really was drowned. But who was the 'poor girl' and what did she do?"

"Do you mean to tell me you don't know?"

"No idea. I heard that a woman was supposed to have shot him and committed suicide, but as we'd shot him ourselves, I naturally didn't believe a word of it. In fact, I thought it was a trap of some kind."

Bluehm's grim face relaxed again. "Of course, it must have seemed absurd; in fact, I don't understand it now. Elsa Schwiss entered his house some time—it must have been after you left—shot his head to pieces with an automatic, and killed herself with the last shot."

"Oh, did she? On account of Knirim, I suppose. She heard the news that day, I remember; in fact, Hambledon told her, not knowing she was particu-larly interested. She might have saved herself the trouble, he was quite dead already. I propped him up in his chair myself."

"Propped him up—so he may not have looked dead?"

"No, he only looked asleep, he was not—disfigured. I suppose she just walked in, said: 'Take that,' and carried on." Michael laughed, but Bluehm was not amused.

"That seems comic to you, does it not? You do not know what happened afterwards. Hedwige Schwiss—you remember Hedwige Schwiss?"

"She was the other sister, wasn't she? What did they call themselves, now—I have it, the Bavarian Nightingales."

"Yes. You remember with difficulty, but I remember very well, every day and all day and all night too," said Bluehm, his voice rising and his face a mask of pain and disgust. "You see, we cared for each other, too, and when Elsa died, it broke up the act and Hedwige did not get on well. I received one letter from her saying she had written repeatedly, and as I evidently did not care any more she would not write again. She was singing in cheap music halls then. I made inquiries for her whenever I was on leave, but after the war, when I was eventually demobilized, I did look for her thoroughly. I did not find her, however, till last year. I met her in the street in St. Pauli."

"St. Pauli?"

"Hamburg. You wouldn't know it, it is the lowdown part of the town where the sailors go. She belongs there now."

"Good heavens, Bluehm!"

"I had a little talk with her and then we parted and I haven't seen her since. I was third steward on a liner then. I'm getting on now, second steward in the lounge. Lots of tips, I'm getting quite well off, but I don't go ashore at Hamburg."

"Bluehm, I wish I'd known, I might have done something—"

"I think you have done enough. Don't you? You disgraced my sister Marie. She is dead and that is your fault too, I think; if she hadn't been running about after you she probably wouldn't have been killed. You deserve to die for that alone, but that is not all. If it hadn't been for you and your damned free drinks, Knirim would not have talked, of course. That's what you did it for, to make us talk. Well, you succeeded and he was disgraced and killed, so Elsa died also, and Hedwige—it's a pity she isn't dead, too. I expect she will be, soon, and that's your fault also. You would deserve to die for that anyway, wouldn't you?"

Bluehm tipped some whisky into one of the glasses on the table, put a splash of soda into it, and drank it, and a little color came back into his white face.

"I don't suppose you meant any of it," he said, a little more kindly. "But wherever you go, evil things happen. You are a messenger of death, so I will give you death yourself."

"May I have a cigarette?" asked Michael calmly. He felt quite sure now that Bluehm was a little mad. If only he could get the man off his guard for a moment something might be done. Something had got to be done to safeguard Denton and Reck and the others.

"I suppose you may," said Bluehm rather grudgingly. "Here's one of mine, and the matches. Move slowly."

"Thanks," said Michael mechanically. "It's the custom, isn't it?"

"Is it? Whose custom?"

"Of course it's the custom, you know that. The usual glass of wine and cigarette, we always do it. Von Bodenheim gave me one, I remember."

"Do you mean among people in Intelligence? But I've nothing to do with that."

"What?" said Michael, sitting up so suddenly that Bluehm leveled again the automatic which he had rested on his knee while they were talking. "How the devil did you come to know that I was, then?"

"Reck," said Bluehm. "He talked. He drank, you know, till his brain went silly and he had to be put away. He got a little better after that because they cut off his supplies. I went to see him."

"Why?"

"Because after I'd found Hedwige I used to think things over, and it became clear to me that you were to blame for the ruin of my life—Marie first and then Hedwige. I've explained that. So I made up my mind to kill you. I went back to Cologne and talked to everybody I could find who had known you, and waiters at the Palant and other places, and a waitress at the Germania remembered you talking to Reck and told me what had become of him. So I went to see him—with a bottle of schnapps—and he talked. Oh, he talked all right."

"I see," said Kingston thoughtfully. "Yes, I remember saying to—to somebody once that he was the sort who might talk. He was beginning to drink then."

"You ought to have shot him," said Bluehm acidly. "He was more dangerous than Amtenbrink, wasn't he?"

Michael shivered, as he always did at the mention of Amtenbrink, and it seemed that in that moment the old man stood there in the room and looked kindly at him.

"This was his glass," he said. "He was greater than either of us. Bluehm."

"That is true," said Bluehm shortly.

Michael thought of the loaded automatic on the table behind the closed door of his bedroom. He must get at it somehow; this fellow had got to die for the sake of Denton and the others, though for himself he had almost ceased to care. If Bluehm had carried his story to German Intelligence it was already too late, but if he had not, there was still a chance, one must find out.

"Your own Intelligence told you about Amtenbrink, of course," said Michael. "Reck didn't know."

"Oh yes, he did. He told me all about that, and the Ahlhorn affair, and hinted darkly at other much more important things even than that which you had done, but I could not find out what they were. I had a feeling he did not really know much about them himself, he was just boasting, in my opinion. He said you had altered the course of history."

"I doubt if you found your Intelligence much more helpful," said Michael, with a laugh which sounded almost natural.

"Do you suppose I would run howling to German Intelligence with news of you? You don't know me, Brandt. They would have thanked me kindly and I should never have heard any more about it; no doubt they would have dealt with you themselves, but I pay my own bills, Brandt. How could I tell them about my sister, and Hedwige? I should be ashamed. When you are dead I will go back and tell them, and they can clear up the rest of your foul spider's webs of espionage and hunt down your associates. But you—I deal with you myself."

"That's it, then," thought Michael, "he is alone in this and if I can manage him I've won again. I must clear my brain and think deliberately and a plan will present itself. O God, send me a plan, just one little idea, I don't want You to do a miracle, I'll do all the work if only You'll give me an idea."

Kingston awoke from what seemed like an endless reverie to find the cigarette burning his fingers and Bluehm still talking, so he threw the stub away and listened.

"… failed, and that was your doing, and there was all the foul propaganda that broke the civilian morale, and that was your doing, too. Oh, not you personally, perhaps, but your lot. Then the army mutinied—mutinied! The German army! And they tore my badges off and we all trailed home with the damned Belgians jeering at us and the children throwing mud and stones. Your fault, all your doing. Our army was never defeated."

Michael said: "Don't you think we have had enough of this? I am a little tired of being scolded at the point of an automatic for doing what I regarded as my duty."

Bluehm looked at him intently for a moment, and said: "I beg your pardon, I forgot myself. I have suffered so much that I forgot my manners. You are a better man than I, Brandt, for all your sins."

"Oh, rubbish. There's no need to be so dramatic, is there? You've won this time, anyway. I have one favor to ask, if you choose to grant it."

"What is it?"

"Shall we—er—perform the ceremony in my bedroom instead of in here? It is only through that door, and I always had a fancy to die in bed. It sounds more respectable, but I never thought I should manage it. It's only an idle fancy, and you can refuse if you like, but it can't make any odds to you. There's another point, too. I have a good motherly old soul who comes in to look after me. I'd hate her to walk in, all bright and breezy, at eight o'clock tomorrow and the first thing she sees is me making a mess of the carpet, whereas if she can't get an answer when she knocks, she may get an idea there's something wrong. I don't expect you to care what an old English charwoman feels, but I do, and I should take it as a personal—"

"Stop, stop for Heaven's sake," said Bluehm, almost laughing. "One sees that you are the same Brandt as of old, always talking. We will go in the other room if you wish."

"Thanks awfully," said Michael casually, as though it were of no particular importance. He rose to his feet, held his glass up for a moment and then drained and hurled it crashing into the fireplace. "Well, shall we go?" he said.

He turned his back on Bluehm and walked steadily to the bedroom door with the German following. As Michael laid his hand on the doorhandle he felt the automatic cold against the back of his neck. "No trouble, now," warned Bluehm.

"Of course not," said Michael with dignity. "What chance have I?"

He opened the door and switched the light on, took two slow steps into the room, and then leaped for the table, snatched up the automatic and was in the act of turning—

The coroner's inquest was opened at the Dragon Inn, Lime, in Hampshire, at two thirty p.m. on Saturday, July the 19th, 1924, the first witness being Mrs. Lomas. She said that the deceased man employed her daily for domestic work. ...

THE END

About the Rue Morgue Press

"Rue Morgue Press is the old-mystery lover's best friend,
reprinting high quality books from the 1930s and '40s."
—*Ellery Queen's Mystery Magazine*

Since 1997, the Rue Morgue Press has reprinted scores of traditional mysteries, the kind of books that were the hallmark of the Golden Age of detective fiction. Authors reprinted or to be reprinted by the Rue Morgue include Catherine Aird, Delano Ames, H. C. Bailey, Morris Bishop, Dorothy Bowers, Pamela Branch, Joanna Cannan, John Dickson Carr, Glyn Carr, Torrey Chanslor, Clyde B. Clason, Joan Coggin, Manning Coles, Lucy Cores, Frances Crane, Norbert Davis, Elizabeth Dean, Carter Dickson, Michael Gilbert, Constance & Gwenyth Little, Marlys Millhiser, Gladys Mitchell, James Norman, Stuart Palmer, Craig Rice, Kelley Roos, Charlotte Murray Russell, Maureen Sarsfield, Margaret Scherf, Juanita Sheridan and Colin Watson..

To suggest titles or to receive a catalog of Rue Morgue Press books write P.O. Box 4119, Boulder, CO 80306, telephone 800-699-6214, or check out our website, www.ruemorguepress.com, which lists complete descriptions of all of our titles, along with lengthy biographies of our writer